Dearest Enemy

Also by Joan Druett

A PROMISE OF GOLD
Judas Island
Calafia's Kingdom
Dearest Enemy
Finale

THE MONEY SHIP
The Launching of the Huntress
The Privateer Brig
The Dragon Stone
The Midwife's Apprentice

IN THE WIKI COFFIN SERIES
A Watery Grave
Shark Island
Run Afoul
Deadly Shoals
The Beckoning Ice

OTHER FICTION
A Love of Adventure (Abigail)

NON FICTION
The Notorious Captain Hayes
Eleanor's Odyssey
Lady Castaways
The Elephant Voyage
Tupaia, Captain Cook's Polynesian Navigator
Island of the Lost
In the Wake of Madness
Rough Medicine
She Captains
Hen Frigates
The Sailing Circle (with Mary Anne Wallace)
Captain's Daughter, Coasterman's Wife
She Was a Sister Sailor
Petticoat Whalers
Fulbright in New Zealand
Exotic Intruders

Dearest Enemy

JOAN DRUETT

Old Salt Press

Dearest Enemy

THIRD IN THE OLD SALT PRESS TRILOGY published by Old Salt Press, a Limited Liability Company registered in New Jersey, USA.

For more information about our titles go to www.oldsaltpress.com

ISBN 978-0-9941246-9-2

First published in this format 2018.

A Promise of Gold

Book Three

DEAREST ENEMY

ONE

FRANK Sefton's ancient hacienda had burned down more thoroughly than Harriet would have believed possible.

Even the most massive adobe walls had collapsed with the heat, and now they looked like blackened sand dunes. Huge oak rafters had fallen higgledy-piggledy, and were piled on top of one another, crusted with shining charcoal.

The rest was rubble and ashes, well raked over. Harriet could see tracks in the black crumbling dust where men had fossicked for anything worth looting. If any of her clothes had survived the fire, she thought wryly, they were certainly gone. Which meant that her wardrobe was severely de-pleted—she was down to two sets of undergarments, three shawls, two gowns, and a cloak, all of which she had piled onto her body when she had fled from her husband. Rather inconvenient, she decided, but not particularly significant. Otherwise, there was nothing for her here at all.

Everything that had happened to her in this house had been a nightmare, yet it had been possible to admire the old mansion. She turned to the newspaperman, feeling angry.

"Why did you want me to see this?" she demanded. "It used to be a fine house, you know. A hacienda in the traditional style, with a rather nice courtyard in the middle. It had a fountain, and mosaic tiles, and hanging plants."

Mr. Giles was standing in his customary slouch, studying the ruins with a straw in his mouth. He was nibbling at that straw like a rodent, so that his moustaches revolved, and now his eyebrows lifted.

"Why," he said, "perhaps I wanted your thoughts on the subject. After all," he pointed out, "it was your husband the Colonel who lost his life in this fire. How do you feel about being a widow?"

How did she feel? Harriet turned away from the ruins and looked at the meadows and corrals, now empty of cattle and horses. She wondered where all the livestock had been taken, and then

1

thought about how she felt. She was sad about the devastation, she supposed, and certainly angered by the way Mr. Giles had phrased the question. She didn't feel like a widow, but she had never felt like a married woman, either.

Glancing back at Mr. Giles with dislike, she snapped, "You want to record my feelings for a story?"

"Story, Mrs. Sefton?"

"The story you are sending back east—and don't pretend there isn't one."

"Wa-al, of course there's a story in it, Mrs. Sefton, for wasn't your husband the Colonel a prominent figure—in New York society, as well as in the blue-nosed ranks of Philadelphia? He came from an uppercrust family, as you know very well, and was respected in much higher circles than folks like you and me will ever aspire to. And after all, for quite a while people thought you had expired in this fire as well—that is, until you mysteriously materialized out of the hills, in the company of the *Gosling* gold prospecting party. What do you think about your miraculous survival?"

Harriet said, "As you've just pointed out, I was nowhere near here when it happened."

"And neither were you supposed to be, Mrs. Sefton—for didn't your husband the Colonel send you off to his good friend Don Manuel Vidrie and his charming family, right after you arrived here in California? Even though you had been just reunited after more than a year apart?"

Harriet's eyes stung, forcing her to look away. Frank Sefton had humiliated her by sending her away the morning after she had arrived at the hacienda, and now the whole world was about to know that she had been dumped on his Californian friends just one night after getting to his property in the Sacramento Valley.

"You seem to have been asking questions, Mr. Giles," she finally said. "And getting some interesting answers."

"And I have eyes in my head, Mrs. Sefton, and I have ears to listen, too. I might not say much while I am eating, but I watch and I listen, and it didn't take more than one or two courses of that great feast at Don Manuel's dining table before I'd worked out that you had been a guest in his house for a mighty long time, and that you resented it, too. And why else would you have seized your chance to escape while Don Manuel and his showy male relatives were off out riding with your husband the Colonel? You reckon I've forgotten how you badgered me into escorting you out of the Vidries'

2

territory?"

"I don't think you ever forget anything, Mr. Giles."

"You're right again," he said, with one of his sardonic sniggers. "But think, Mrs. Sefton, think!" he went on. "By insisting on coming back to this here house, you could have sealed your doom. According to my deductions, the fire happened only the second night after you galloped here. So how do you feel about your narrow escape from being burned to death, huh? How do you feel?"

"I feel astonished, if that holds interest," she retorted, having no intention of telling him that she had escaped the fire by pure good luck, as she had run away from Sefton earlier that same night. "I'm astonished that it took so long for the fire to be noticed. Why did no one see the hacienda burning? I know it's out of sight of Pueblo San Marco, being over the hill and across the river, but it must have gone up like a torch."

"That's true," he conceded, mumbling at his straw. "Mind you, ma'am, and I apologize that I beg to differ, but those adobe walls were mighty thick. The fire could have smoldered for hours without anyone noticing. It burned like a baker's oven, if you see what I mean. Roasting inside, you understand, but without apparent light and heat."

That could well be so, Harriet thought with a grimace. The chief clerk at Frank Sefton's bank had had just one thing for her— the ring that Frank had always worn. It was a half-melted lump, silent testimony to the heat of the blaze. It had been taken off the corpse, the clerk had said; that was how they had identified her husband's body. She winced even now, thinking that the ring must have been chipped off the finger bone.

Mr. Giles was watching her closely, she saw. "You were meant to be the other victim of the drama," he pointed out.

Harriet shifted uneasily, and said, "Perhaps."

It had been Ah Wong, her Chinese servant, who had made her run away, that night. He had been in a state of utter terror when he had woken her up and told her to her flee—and yet the fire had certainly not started then. Had Ah Wong known that something dreadful was going to happen? She had assumed that he had seized the chance to get her away while Frank was across the river, in Pueblo San Marco. Obviously, Sefton had returned just in time to be killed in the fire. It was unlike Frank to have such foul luck, but it had happened. And, if Ah Wong had not helped her run away, she would have been unlucky, too.

Mr. Giles was saying, "And I do wonder about the identity."

Harriet blinked, dragged out of her preoccupation. "Of what?"

"The identity of the woman who was burned to death in your place."

She flinched with shock. "There was another body?"

"Indeed, Mrs. Sefton. The second body was beside the body of your husband—in your bed. That's why everyone thought you were dead."

"What?" She stared incredulously. "That can't be true! How do you know it was my bed?"

The writer's grin was sly. "Ah, Mrs. Sefton, as you observed earlier, I know where to ask questions, and how to find answers. It was your bed and your bedroom, and the woman's corpse lay blackened beside the equally blackened corpse of your husband, so of course folks assumed the second body was yours."

Harriet stared at him, unable to take it in that Frank should have been found in *her bed*. It was utterly impossible.

Mr. Giles took her elbow, and led her to the oak tree where the bandit Murietas had tethered their horses the night that she had escaped. It was not far away, close to the ruins, and the ends of the branches were scorched, their leaves withered with the heat of the fire. As they walked there, she remembered how she and Ah Wong had hidden in the shadows, holding their breaths for fear that Joaquín Murieta would see them, and drag them inside—that her escape from Sefton's hacienda would be foiled.

There was a broad raked mound under the tree now, with two boards at its head. One board informed her that here lay the remains of Colonel Francis Sefton. He had belonged to Philadelphia and he had been forty-two years old at the time of his death.

So this was the end of Frank, she thought, the miserable end of his devious dealings. All he had wanted was to get back to New York with immense riches, to make a certain Miss Coffin regret her decision to turn down his gallant proposal of marriage. And what had he got? This humble grave.

The other board was blank. "Folks do whisper," said Mr. Giles musingly, "that your husband the Colonel kept a Chinese mistress."

Beautiful little Mei-Mei, Harriet thought, Mei-Mei of the camellia-like complexion and the rosebud mouth. Frank had likened her gold-colored, pouting breasts to pigeons, and had shared her with his friends.

She snapped, "Mei-mei was his ward."

4

"But the feet of the second skeleton were all twisted up, like bird claws. I hear that's what they do to Chinese girls, to make them attractive to men."

Mei-Mei? *In her bed?* It was the ultimate humiliation, Frank taunting her from beyond the tomb. Harriet stared at the reporter, feeling sick.

Mr. Giles's head was tilted as he watched her, so that he looked somewhat like a bird himself. So the whole of the Feather River district knew that Frank Sefton had kept a beautiful, exotic mistress, she thought with shame, and now the whole eastern seaboard of America was due to learn that, too.

She said sharply, "Who told you that Frank had a Chinese mistress? Was it Don Manuel Vidrie? Or Don Roberto?"

"I don't divulge my sources, ma'am."

"Do you not? Then where is Don Roberto now?"

"Who knows, Mrs. Sefton, who knows?" The reporter let out one of his characteristic grunts of sardonic amusement. "No sooner had the alcalde signed the death certificate and looked for his fee than he skipped the territory, ma'am, and who can blame him? He scarpered off for the hills, and no doubt over the border to Mexico, on account of a posse of disappointed gold miners was all baying at his heels, crying out for their gold."

The gold, the vanished gold. No one wanted to find that gold more desperately than Harriet herself. The bank had been the first place she had stopped after arriving in Pueblo San Marco that late morning, for Sefton's bank was where the *Gosling* Company's gold had been stowed after Royal's claim was jumped—by the Murietas.

Instead of gold, though, she and her brother had found a shouting mob outside the door. It had been impossible to tell what all the men were baying about, but after Harriet and Royal had managed to shove through the crowd and get inside, the agitated bank clerk had told them what had happened. All the gold that had been deposited there by Don Roberto—the gold that he had confiscated from God alone knew how many disputed claims—had vanished. When the clerk had come in, the morning after the fire had been discovered, he had found the vaults empty of all the bulging parfleche bags. Thousands and thousands of dollars' worth of gold dust, gold flakes, and nuggets were gone.

Royal had stormed into the vaults, and found them swept clean. Then Captain Jake Dexter had arrived, carrying the documents for twenty thousand dollars' worth of *Gosling* disputed gold, plus Sefton's signed draft for one thousand dollars, repayment of the money Harriet had borrowed for the plot of land she had bought at Sutter's Fort. Jake had listened grimly to what Royal had to say, and then had demanded to see the ledgers. Harriet remembered how nervous the clerk had looked as he had handed them over, and how he had stammered as he said that the last man to write in the ledgers was Colonel Sefton ... who had made a lot of alterations in the lists.

While Jake Dexter was going through the accounts, Harriet had found Mr. Giles at her elbow. Despite her chilly demeanor, the printer had persuaded her to come with him to her dead husband's hacienda ... and here she was, avoiding his insinuating questions while mayhem and panic were still holding sway at Sefton's Bank for Miners. What a waste of time, she thought.

Harriet turned on her heel and set off decisively for the path to the ferryboat. She didn't care if the reporter came or not, but heard his hurried steps as he joined her. Then Mr. Giles was slouching along at her side.

She looked at him briefly, and said, "My brother told me he saw Sefton in Pueblo San Marco, the day after you and I left the Vidrie place. As you know, I arrived here that same night, and was still here that next day—but Frank didn't tell Royal that. Instead, he led Royal to believe that I was still staying with Don Manuel Vidrie. Can you think of any reason he would have lied?"

Mr. Giles was silent a long moment, lost in contemplation. Then he brushed his damp moustaches and said, "No, ma'am, that I cannot guess, other than he wished to keep you and your brother apart."

"Perhaps Royal was mistaken. He said that Frank was very busy in his bank, working away with his ledgers."

"Yep," said Mr. Giles, and nodded emphatically. "That is exactly how your husband the Colonel was spending his last day on earth."

"What? You saw him, too?"

"That I did. Right preoccupied, was he." Then the journalist let out another sardonic grunt, and said, "If he'd known he had only hours to live, he might have been doing something a mite more entertaining."

Harriet ignored this, saying, "What about Ah Wong? You remember Ah Wong, my Chinese servant? Have you seen him at all?"

"No, ma'am. That I have not. I remember him well, but have

not seen him since you and he left me at Don Roberto's fort, after galloping away from Don Manuel Vidrie's estate."

"Poor Ah Wong," Harriet said.

She shivered, remembering how frightened poor Ah Wong had been when she insisted on leaving the Vidrie estate, and coming back to the hacienda. She remembered how she had dreamed that she heard Ah Wong crying and sobbing in the night, and now she wondered if it had truly been a dream, or whether Sefton had been punishing Ah Wong for bringing her back to the ranch.

She had begged her husband not to blame him, saying that it was all her own fault ... that coming back to the hacienda had been her own decision. That Ah Wong had just been following orders. But Frank Sefton's rages had been terrifying.

Forcing her mind away, she said, "What do you think Frank was doing in the bank?"

"But you should know that already, ma'am, because you can work it out for yourself. I recollect quite plainly how we both did wonder about those shares in his bank that your husband was so anxious to sell—and we wondered, too, why he was so strangely willing to lend men the monies for the purchase ... with the shares in the bank as collateral."

Collateral. The last word held more meaning than all the other words put together.

Harriet said, "Go on."

"When he was busily at work with his ledgers, he was converting all those loans he'd made, declaring the debts all bad. With one stroke of the pen he was taking back those loans, and claiming the gold as the security for those loans. It rightfully belonged to others, but there it was in his vaults, and somehow with his legal chicanery he made it legally his. In a word, ma'am, your husband was collecting on bad debts."

The reporter nodded to himself, but apparently not because he was so pleased with his detective work. Instead, he looked world-weary, as if this kind of confidence trick happened every day.

Harriet said bitterly, "I had twenty thousand dollars' worth, you know. I was a major shareholder."

Mr. Giles, for once, looked astounded. "You bought them?"

"No, of course not. That wasn't possible—I had no money of my own, and even if I did, it would belong by law to my husband. No, he presented them to me as a gift. I had to do was sign for them."

"Sign for them?" echoed the reporter. "But that doesn't make sense. Because you were his wife, the shares were still legally his."

"I know," said Harriet wearily.

There couldn't be many women in the world who had fallen for the same trick twice, she brooded, but kept silent. She had no intention of revealing to this inquisitive fellow that Frank Sefton had swindled her once already, in New Zealand, when she had tamely signed the deeds to all his properties, the day before they were married. Just as in California later, he had pretended that he was giving the deeds to her as a present. And then, the morning after their wedding night, he had gone off into town to sell all the properties those deeds represented—at an enormous profit, because they were now in her English name. Because of a loophole in the law, he had made a huge fortune. She had been a fool, a double fool, she bitterly thought, and the prospect that the whole world might get to know about it was mortifying in the extreme.

Like the men who had bought shares in Sefton's bank, she should have taken legal advice, she thought—and at that her thoughts stopped short. The only legal advisor in the district had been the alcalde, Don Roberto.

She said to Mr. Giles, "Don Roberto must have been party to the swindle. He was the one who deposited all that disputed gold in Sefton's bank."

"The way you put it, that makes sense, but who knows, Mrs. Sefton, who knows?"

"He might even have been the man who stole it, after Frank was dead."

"Wa-al, you could be right on both counts, Mrs. Sefton. A lot of the men who claim to own that gold certainly reckon that Don Roberto and your husband the Colonel were working in cahoots, and that's why they are hot on Don Roberto's trail. But it stands to reason, don't it, that he couldn't have carried all that gold away without help. While I've never had much gold myself, I have it on good authority that the stuff is very heavy."

But Don Roberto had six deputies—the bandit Murietas. Harriet stared speculatively at the reporter, and he nodded wisely, and said, "Do you want to know what I think, ma'am?"

"Knowing you as I do, Mr. Giles," she said tartly, "I'm certain you have a theory."

"Ah, Mrs. Sefton," he said, "you know me well," and grunted with cynical laughter. Then he said in a matter of fact voice, "I think Colonel Sefton was the one who carried the gold out of the vaults. I think he got the gold across the river to this ranch here, and then the men who stole that gold from him murdered him and his mistress, either on purpose or accidentally, depending on whether they were dead or not when the house was set on fire."

"*Murdered?*" Harriet could think of many people who would be glad to kill Sefton, but none who would have had the courage to actually do it.

"Murdered," Mr. Giles repeated with satisfaction. "And what could be a better motive for murder than all that confiscated gold?"

"But no one has suggested that the house was deliberately fired."

"No? Wa-al, ma'am, I suggest it now, because it would give us another reason for the long delay in reporting the blaze. After all, if folks who saw it also knew that it had been deliberately torched, their own good sense would advise them to keep shut about it."

Such as Frank's vaqueros, she thought—who had fled, taking Sefton's cattle and horses with them. It was some-thing they certainly wouldn't have done if they hadn't known he was dead. Sefton's iron will and his vicious outbursts of temper had kept them well under control. And naturally they wouldn't have reported either his death or the fire, as the delay gave them time to get away.

So who was the murderer? And who had helped Sefton carry the gold out of the bank and across the river?

Suddenly, the night she had escaped was vivid in Harriet's mind. Again, she heard Ah Wong's terrified gasp as Joaquín Murieta had come out of the courtyard of the hacienda. She remembered how they had cowered in the shadows of a hedge as Joaquín walked to the same tree where Sefton now lay buried, and the red glow as he had drawn on his cigar. She remembered how he had seemed to stare right at her, as she cowered with Ah Wong in the darkness. And Joaquín Murieta had five brothers, all evil, all bandits...

She was suddenly, tragically, certain that poor little Ah Wong was dead. The Murietas would have caught him when he returned with the horses, after taking her to the safety of the hill that overlooked Don Roberto's fort—were probably waiting in ambush as he arrived. She had pleaded with Ah Wong not to go back to the hacienda, but he had been obdurate—because he had to return the horses, he'd said. So it would look as if she had never left the house.

Tears stung her eyes. To hide them, Harriet turned and set off to the ferry landing again.

At the riverbank, to her surprise, she found that the ferryboat was in requisition. It was worked by hauling on ropes and pulleys that were attached to a double line that stretched from the riverbank of the ranch to the embarcadero of Pueblo San Marco, and it had been strictly for Sefton's private use. While it was easy enough to draw it back from the other side of the river by hauling in the line, the villagers had never dared use it. But, while Harriet had been talking with Mr. Giles, some opportunist had evidently realized that Sefton's dominance over the river crossing had ended with his death. So instead of lying on the bank where they had left it, the boat was mid-river and coming toward them.

It was moving very slowly, because it was packed to the gunwales with miners. As Harriet incredulously watched, bearded, weatherworn men in flat, wide-brimmed hats and checkered shirts and buckskin trousers disembarked. After the briefest look around their surroundings, they passed her as they headed off up the slope, with every obvious intention of digging gold-prospecting holes in the land that had once belonged to her husband. Bedrolls and folded tents were packed on their backs, and mining tools rattled around them, and they strode with confidence, because there was absolutely no one to stop them from invading the territory and hunting for the yellow stuff. Some even tipped their hats to her as they passed.

Mr. Giles was watching, too, she saw. He touched his hat to one in return, and then said to Harriet, "Ain't you the rightful owner of all this now?"

"I strongly doubt it," said Harriet, knowing how convoluted Sefton's dealings had been, and how much he had hated her. "But even if I do own it, what can I do to stop them?"

"Nothing," said the reporter, and bent to pluck another straw, which he nibbled. After another meditative moment, he said, "What do you reckon about Don Manuel's fine and fertile property?"

"I beg your pardon?"

"Those miles of Vidrie hills and dales could be invaded by prospectors, too."

"But Don Roberto's fort guards the bridge to the Vidrie lands," Harriet protested—but then she remembered that the alcalde was a long way away from his fort, maybe as far as Mexico. Which meant that the bridge was open to all, and that Don Manuel Vidrie's lush pasture lands and vineyard slopes were now fair game for men who were crazed for gold.

"All it takes is one report of a big find up Cache Creek, and every soul in Pueblo San Marco and further downriver will be fighting to get into these parts," Mr. Giles prophesied. "And it will take more than those showy Vidrie caballeros to stop them."

"You're right," she said, and grimaced.

"How refreshing that you should agree with me," he smirked. Then he took Harriet's arm, and urged her down to the water. The ferryboat, now emptied except for the man who had appropriated the ferrying business, was about to cross the river again.

To her disgust, the new ferryman demanded a fee of two dollars a head, boasting at the same time that he expected to make two thousand this season out of this here venture. However, Mr. Giles paid it with only a token complaint, and the waterman had good reason to be so optimistic, Harriet saw. When they arrived on the other side, there was a packed line of men waiting to board for the next crossing, while many others were settling in for the night, resting up before heading over in the morning. The broad riverbank had sprouted thickets of tents, all the way from the landing place to the junction of the river and the stream that rushed down from the watermill high on the slope above the village.

Mr. Giles was standing beside her as men pushed past them to get to the ferryboat. When he saw her look at him, he smirked again, and said, "What now, Mrs. Sefton?"

She pointed to where the *Gosling* was moored up tight against the embarcadero. Close up, the brig was a sad sight, Harriet thought. With her topmasts struck and her running rigging down, the *Gosling* did not look at all like the dashingly piratical vessel she remembered.

"You're going to live on board?"

The reporter's tone held salacious curiosity. Which meant that insinuations about her adulterous relationship with Captain Jake Dexter were likely to be printed, too.

Harriet gave him one inimical glance. "I'm going to a meeting," she snapped. "And it is just a business meeting, I assure you." And with that, she turned on her heel.

TWO

WHEN Harriet stepped off the gangplank and onto the deck of the *Gosling*, the brig was so silent that she thought that the meeting was over, or had been canceled, and that everyone had returned to their berths. But then she heard voices echoing up the skylight, and realized the *Gosling* Company was holding the meeting in the officers' mess cabin, in the after quarters.

The voices were loud with anger. Bracing herself, she opened the door in the forward bulkhead of poop deck, and stepped down the short companionway, and into the familiar corridor. To her right were the doors to the staterooms that belonged to the mates, the aftermost one being the one where she had slept on the passage to the Sacramento from Judas Island. Now, she supposed, the rightful occupant, Mr. Martin, had reclaimed his territory.

There was another door in the partition that had been built across the sternward end of the passage, which led to Captain Jake Dexter's private cabins. The transom cabin, which was his chartroom and parlor, ran under the lovely old-fashioned gallery of windows in the stern, and his stateroom, where he slept, was on the starboard side of that. Harriet had been happy there, she had been deeply in love, but she would never, ever go in there again, she thought emphatically now. He had made the mistake of possessing her as if she belonged to him — of behaving as arrogantly as her hated husband, and she would never forgive him for that.

In the corridor, to her left, was a pair of double doors, beautifully carved of mahogany, more testament to the old-fashioned tastes of the buccaneer who had built this brig. The noise of men shouting over each other echoed from the other side. She braced her shoulders, opened them, and stepped quietly into the mess cabin — to be greeted by an abrupt silence.

It was a large room, but seemed much smaller than she remembered, because of all the men who were crowded in there. The meeting of the *Gosling* Company was definitely still in progress, she realized. In the past she had considered some of the members her friends, but now, as the seamen and officers turned and looked at her, she saw their faces become hard.

Yet, despite the crowded cabin, she thought sadly, the Company was so greatly diminished. Pablo and Joseph Fayal had been murdered. Jonathan had died of the mountain fever, and was buried back in Bedstead Gully, where the company had prospected for gold. The ex-slave, Davy Jones Locker, had lost his mind after a bout of brain fever, and was living at an Indian encampment near Bedstead Gully, under the delusion that he was an Indian. Two more seamen, Tib and Dan, were back at Bedstead Gully, clearing out the cabin and packing the four llamas for the trek back to the brig, and so there were only eleven men there.

Chips, Irish Cookie and the sailmaker, Abijah Roe, were seated at the big table, in a row on one bench, opposite Charlie and Abner, the first and second mates, and they all had their heads turned to stare at her, their expressions intimidating, because none of them smiled. The late afternoon sun slanted down the big skylight above the table, striking glittering rainbows from the old, fine crystal in the castor rack that hung there between the two hanging lamps, and the prismatic glints seemed inappropriately frivolous in the daunting atmosphere.

Bodfish, the steward, was hovering in the doorway of the pantry, forward, and Valentine and Crotchet, both looking very sheepish, were standing in the corner next to him. Bill, the steerage boy, was there, too. The eleven-year-old had grown amazingly. Perhaps, Harriet thought, that was why Valentine and Crotchet seemed so much smaller. The truth, though, she realized, was that their flamboyance was shrunk by their spectacular loss — and spectacular was the only word for it. After squandering all the company's funds on a café-restaurant, they had lost the lot, café-restaurant and all, in a single game of monte.

When she looked from one face to another, expressions flickered, and they looked away. The only men who met her eyes were her brother, Royal, who was standing at the sternward end of the cabin — and Jake Dexter, who sat in the captain's chair at the sternward end of the table. Royal gave her a small smile that looked like a grimace. Jake merely watched her, without expression but with deep concentration.

Harriet said nothing to fill the awkward silence. She sat down on the starboard bench when Charlie Martin and Abner shifted along to give her room. Then she folded her hands, put them on the table top, and contemplated them while she waited, wondering how far the business of the meeting had progressed.

Nowhere, it seemed.

Abijah Roe was the first to speak, complaining, "But it just ain't possible that we've gained nothing, sir. We come here for a guaranteed fortune — guaranteed! — but we ain't got nothing."

Harriet looked at him. The sailmaker sat like a hunched secretary bird on the other side of the table, his thin cheeks seamed and bristling with stubble, his scant hair gray. His voice was the whine that she remembered so well. But of course he had a legitimate grievance, she thought wryly. The *Gosling* Company was run as a pirate company — which meant no profit, no pay. None of the men were paid wages. Every venture was a speculation, and fortunes were shared out between them all, according to a group agreement.

Then she heard Jake say evenly, "Nonetheless, Abijah, that is exactly the case — exactly as I have described it to you. We have lost everything we invested here. We are no better off than we were when we left Judas Island. But it's no use whining, or looking for someone or something to blame. Instead, we have to decide on a way to turn profit out of disaster, somehow."

"But it ain't right, sir," cried Bill. His voice was breaking, hoarse and shrill by turns. "Captain, sir, they told us in Tombez that the gold lay about in great lumps — so how come we've got nothing?"

"That's right," grumbled low voices. Heads were nodding emphatically.

Irish Cookie said, "How can it be, sir, that our luck be so bad, when others are coming out of the diggin's with a pile?"

"Royal did find a rich vein," Jake pointed out.

"And he lost it, Captain Dexter!"

"That was bad luck, I agree."

Abijah Rose complained, "He might have been the one what found it, sir, him and Joseph Fayal and Pablo, but then it was jumped and our two shipmates was murdered. So was it his bad luck, or ours?"

The spite in his selection of words was plain, and when Harriet looked up at the sailmaker again, his bony finger was pointed to where Royal was standing. "Was it was *our* bad luck that he didn't stake the claim proper, or his?" he demanded.

Royal shouted, "I bloody well did stake it properly!"

"How do we know that, when the stakes was gone?" Then Harriet found that Abijah's finger had swiveled to point at her. "It's both their faults! They talked us into this mess!"

A buzz of agreement ran round the room. Harriet flinched, on the verge of exhausted tears, every nerve stretched to its utmost. Then Jake snapped, "Settle down, the lot of you, or I'll terminate this meeting."

14

"But everything's gone wrong since them Grays came to our brig, sir. *She* comes on board at Judas Island and tricks her way into becoming a member of the *Gosling* Company, and then she tricks us into sailing to Valparaiso with fine promises of half a million dollars for a herd of alpaca, and then we pick up *him* and get thrown out of the port."

Jake barked, "Shut up, Abijah. This is not on the agenda."

"But he's right, sir," objected Chips. "We dassent show our faces in Valparaiso again."

Jake said coldly, "Let me be the judge of that."

"But it's mighty strange, sir," said Irish Cookie. "Royal Gray told us, excuse me, sir, that there was a flock of alpacas up the Tombez, which would make us an ever-livin' fortune when we got them to New South Wales in Australia. And were them beasts there? No, they was not. They had been stolen by the Indians, or so he said, and all we had instead was five llamas, which was nothing but worthless pack beasts. So then he tells us all them far-fetched tales of gold, so we come to California. He told us that gold lay all about here, and he goes and finds a vein of it hisself. But do we profit? No, we do not, sir. Somehow that claim gets jumped, and when he makes a protest, that gold gets confiscated by the authorities, and then when we are told it is safe in the bank while the authorities decide if we are the rightful owners or not, it gets stolen."

Jake snapped, "The tales of gold were told by an American deserter up the Tombez, who called himself Honest Mill Mason. They were not told by Royal Gray. If he said anything about gold in California, he was simply passing on what Mason had said. And we were not the only ones who were cheated of our gold."

"But it was her husband, sir," said Abijah's spiteful voice. "It were her husband's bank where our gold was stowed — and they told us in town that she is the largest shareholder. And she belongs to our very own company, but do we have our gold, sir? No, we don't."

Harriet shut her eyes, feeling weary unto death. When she opened them and looked down at her hands, they were trembling. Then she heard Chips clear his throat. "I don't like to say it, sir, but I must admit that I do agree with what Abijah says. We made our pile, but somehow it landed in her husband's hands, and because of that it got lost."

"*You* made the pile?" Royal demanded in a roar. When Harriet looked round at him he was scarlet in the face. "I was in the party

15

that found that vein, and not you — you scapegoat-hunting bastards! I staked that claim, and I put up a notice, and I left two fine men to dig it while I trekked to Bedstead Gully to report the find to Captain Dexter, and then I returned those two good men had been murdered and my well-staked claim was jumped! I was there, and you were not! I saw their corpses, and you did not!"

He thrust a fist into the air, and then pointed a finger at the bench where Abijah and Chips and Irish Cookie sat — a finger that vibrated theatrically in his towering rage. "Though all murder is foul, this murder was most foul, and strange and unnatural, too — *horrible and more than horrible!* But you haven't a notion of what I am talking about, because you weren't there to see it, as I was. You didn't see my two good friends after they'd been slaughtered — *scalped! Oh God!*" he cried, and shut his eyes, obviously in anguish.

For a moment he visibly trembled, as they all stared at him, mesmerized by his melodrama, and then he opened his eyes, and shouted, "And I also saw the men who had jumped the claim — the bloody Murietas! I protested against the thieving bandit-bastards — I argued as strenuously as I possibly could with Don Roberto, and as sure as Old Scratch it was not my fault, either, that you fools who were left with the simple job of looking after the brig should sink everything and then lose it in a common little gambling saloon!"

There was instant uproar, dominated by Abijah, who was screaming as if demented, "That's exactly it, sir — they brought Old Scratch on board when they come on the brig! It was the devil himself what enticed us to invest in that café-restaurant, for were we not profiting from the devil's tickets in the devil's drawing room? The devil came on board when Miss Gray tricked her way onto the brig, and he laughed with evil triumph when her brother joined the *Gosling* Company!"

Harriet found the strength. She lurched to her feet and ran to Royal and gripped his arm. Royal didn't seem to notice. Instead, he was shouting, "Bloody superstition! Only idiots and little children fear the painted devil! This might as well be a pantomime! For God's sake, Captain Dexter, if Abijah is so determined to find a scapegoat, let him go into an Old Testament wilderness to search for his Satan, instead of cleaving our air with his crazy speech!"

Jake shouted, "Be silent, all of you!" His face was dark, the lopsided eyebrows curled tight down with fury, and he slammed his fist on the table. "Quiet!" he snapped, and the room fell silent as everyone stared at him.

Then his voice dropped to its normal pitch, and he said in a perfectly matter-of-fact tone, "This matter is not on the agenda, and you are all out of order. If you are prepared to listen, and talk sense, then we can discuss what we gathered to discuss — the matter of what to do next. Otherwise, I will declare the meeting adjourned."

"I have something to announce before this goes any further," said Harriet evenly.

He looked at her, one eyebrow lifted, and said, "Yes?"

"I've come here because I wish to tender my resignation. I want out. I want to leave the *Gosling* Company."

Silence, utter silence. The men all stared at her, and then she saw the stares waver. They all looked away restlessly, checking each other's faces for reaction. Only Abijah smirked, and she snapped, "You look pleased at the prospect of my departure, Mr. Roe, but you should think again. You might even miss me when you feel like having a female around to blame when things go wrong."

Even his stare fell away, then, and Bodfish said unhappily, "But a girl, just a girl, alone in a place like this..."

Royal snapped, "I tender my resignation, too."

Good, Harriet thought. She felt warm inside with relief, for Royal was so unpredictable, so unreliable, so apt to go his own merry way.

Captain Dexter's eyes were intent, but his voice was mild when he said, "So what are you going to do?"

Harriet lifted her chin. "Why do you want to know?"

"Because we are looking for ideas about what to do next, and your ideas might be good ones."

"Then I doubt that you'll get much inspiration from me. I have the deed to the land at Sutter's, and intend to build a theater — an establishment for staging drama. I'm a widow now, and own my signature again, so I can safely go into business."

Jake said sharply, "But you borrowed the money to buy the land — from the Company."

"I know that, but the hundred dollars' payment for our two shares in the *Gosling* Company will be a good deposit, and then — "

"The *Gosling* Company is insolvent, madam — or haven't you been listening? The Company has lost everything, and is in no position to pay anything out on shares."

"Then I will borrow more money. I'll find investors, and I will build a theater. It won't take long to find people ready and willing to join me in the venture, and I know it will be a famous success. A

17

theater cannot help but attract customers, not just because it will be a novelty, but because it will be cheap entertainment — much cheaper than the gaming tables. Men gamble because there is nothing better to do, and nowhere to go except the gaming saloons and the café-restaurants, which are just gaming saloons that sell food. I expect to treble my money by the end of the season. And the first profits will go to paying back your men."

"You think finding investors will be easy?"

"I know it will be," she said with calm certainty. "I'll have no difficulty at all in finding plenty of people who are eager to take part in the venture. Believe me, you *will* get your money back. All I need is a little time."

She now felt relaxed, because she knew exactly what she was talking about. There were merchants in Pueblo San Marco with money to burn — men who were raking in so much gold that they didn't know what to do with it. And not only was she naturally eloquent, but she was energized by her utter conviction that a theater couldn't help but do well.

Then she heard Chips clear his throat. "Miss Gray," he said awkwardly. "You don't owe the money to the Company, because Captain Dexter paid it all back to us."

"He did?" The glance she cast at Jake Dexter was dangerous.

Chips said, "But I've got some private cash, and if you need to borrow..."

"Me, too," said Bodfish. His long face was earnest. Irish Cookie was shifting awkwardly, and he said, "I don't have much, but..."

The shipkeepers, she realized with disbelief, were feeling thoroughly ashamed of themselves. It was as if they had only just realized that the company's loss had impoverished her, too.

Then Jake said curtly, "There is no need for Mrs. Sefton to pay me back. She can consider the thousand dollars my investment in her theater."

"That," she said with dignity, "will not be necessary." She saw him flush, and explained, "After all, you may be back in the hills when we make our fortune in the theater — so how will I find you, to give you your dividends?"

"That," he snapped, still angry, "is out of order — for we have still not decided on the Company's next venture."

Harriet frowned, puzzled. "But what else is there for you to do, but go prospecting?"

"I've lost any interest I ever had in prospecting for gold," he said

18

curtly, and to Harriet's distress she heard murmurs of agreement all about the room. Even Valentine and Crotchet were nodding. Only Bill looked rueful at missing out on the excitement of digging in the misty hills, as he had been considered too young to go last time.

Why did the idea that they had given up gold hunting here alarm her so? Then she realized she couldn't bear the thought that Jake and the *Goslings* would sail away from California, leaving her behind. And yet she hated Jake — didn't she?

She swallowed on a tight throat, and then said in a low voice, "Where will you go, then?"

There was a long silence. Then Bodfish said on a tentative note, "There would be a good profit in fetching provisions from the Sandwich Islands, to trade here, or at Sutter's Fort, or even in 'Frisco. In Lahaina, in the season, potatoes cost two dollars per barrel, or so I remember. The price might have gone up because of the gold rush, but I know we could sell a barrel of potatoes here for ninety dollars."

"Good idea," said Chips, and Bodfish wrote it down in the minutes of the meeting.

Silence followed, however. Despite the prospect of making a five hundred percent profit on barrels of humble potatoes, no one looked enthusiastic enough to put it as a motion, and take it to a vote.

Then Bodfish said reflectively, "If we waited a couple of months until the whalemen have finished refreshing, and sailed off to the northwest coast, the price of potatoes would be lower."

Would that be so? Harriet doubted it. Two dollars a barrel was ridiculously cheap already, and the memorial gold rush of 1849 would put the prices up, and keep them high. However, she said nothing, wondering instead what was in Bodfish's mind.

It was Chips, not Bodfish, who spoke, though he talked in the same pensive tone as the steward. "We'd be able to take on more if we rid ourselves of that half-cargo of lumber, and now that we have given up the idea of renting out the hold as a boarding house, we need to take down those berths, and take up the false floor. And there are those bales of heavy calico we've been carrying for trade goods. What do you reckon, Captain?"

Jake's eyebrows were slanted high. He clasped his hands behind his head and rocked his chair back on two legs, and said, "Why don't you tell us what you have in mind, Chips?"

"Wa-al, Captain, I were thinking that a real nice way to use up

19

that timber and cloth would be to build a theater, just to get Miss Gray and Royal a-going, so to speak."

Silence. Harriet gazed at Jake, wondering why she had an obscure feeling that this little discussion had been stage-managed. She could tell nothing from his face, as he merely seemed lost in thought.

Then all at once he sat up straight, rocking his chair forward again. "Why not?" he said. "Want to put it to the vote, Chips?"

And as quickly as that the affair was decided. Even Abijah voted for it, though he looked around at all the other raised hands before he did. Jake gave out orders to get the brig ready for the downriver passage to the Embarcadero at Sutter's Fort, and the meeting was called to a close.

The men left the cabin, off to their rightful quarters. Royal went with them, to the forecastle, his expression sardonic. Even Charlie and Abner went, evidently to see to jobs on deck.

Harriet waited until she and Jake were alone. She watched the door to the passage close and listened to the feet disappear up the companionway, and then braced herself to turn and meet his inquiring stare. Her breast felt heavy with the knocking of her heart. It was the first time they had been alone since she had run away from him. She had been careful to avoid his company, and with good reason, so why was she so vividly conscious of his scent, his presence — his aura, so beset with sensual memories?

He said, "Harriet?"

"Yes." She had to swallow before she could speak again. "I want ... wish to ask a favor."

"What, another one?"

She felt herself flush, and said defensively, "It's not for me."

Silence. She watched him unfold himself from his chair and stand up straight. Then he came over to her, his eyebrows high. When she still didn't speak, he put out a finger and tipped up her chin and said promptingly, "Well, Harriet?"

She edged away from his disturbing touch, and said, "Davy ... I'm troubled in my mind about Davy."

Jake sighed, and put his hands on his belt. "So am I. But what can I do? I tried to speak to him, but it did no good. You know that he was determined to stay with his Indian friends."

"But I wondered if there were any spare provisions?" she ventured. "Surely the shipkeepers didn't sell them all? Isn't there something that can be sent to him, before the brig sails from Pueblo San Marco? The Indians live on acorn-meal cakes. I've tasted one, and they are dreadful. There won't be much game, for the miners shoot it all, and ... and..."

"Consider it done."

The sentence was so abrupt that Harriet felt taken aback. Awkwardly, she said, "Thank you," and turned for the double door to the passage and the companionway to deck. Then, so abruptly that she jumped with fright, he was beside her, his hand on the door, holding it shut.

Jake said, "And where do you think you are going?"

"On shore, of course." Her tone became defiant. "I don't belong here any more."

"I didn't hear the Company accept your resignation."

"But you did hear them blame me for their troubles. I can't stay on the brig, knowing what they think of me."

She stared up at him. He was close, too close, and she could smell his familiar scent of soap and warm leather.

Edging away again, she snapped, "If you're wondering if I am going to sleep in the street, then you can set your mind at rest. Mr. Giles is going to find me a lodging room."

And if she had to share it with Royal, it wouldn't be a problem, as they had shared rooms before. Hopefully, her thoughts ran on, Sefton's half-melted gold ring would be enough to pay for it.

"Giles?" Jake's brows had lowered, but then they lifted again, as he muttered, "That meddling printer." Then, more clearly, he said in a perfectly businesslike tone, "I'll send him a message, because you're staying here."

And with no more ado he opened the door, and guided her with an inexorable hand on her shoulder across the passage to the stateroom where she had lived on the brig.

Shock and disbelief took her that far, but then she stopped dead, and exclaimed, "I am not staying here!"

"But you are," he said with perfect certainty, and swung her round and muffled her furious exclamation with a hard kiss on the mouth. Then it was over. It was over as fast as it happened. He gave her a little push and she sat with an undignified bump on the edge of the freshly made up berth, while he frowned at her, the creases about his mouth very tight.

Without another word, he moved back, and she watched the door slam shut. She was alone. After a long moment she stopped shaking with rage and consternation. Then she reached up and pulled the latch string through to her side of the door, so that no one could come into her room.

It took Harriet a long time to fall asleep. She was angry and hungry and the brig felt strange. It lay unnaturally still, moored tightly to the embarcadero with the topmasts struck down.

There was also a constant hubbub from the town as men roistered away the night. The racket lasted till near dawn, and then the bells began to sound — bells for breakfast, bells to summon workmen, and bells to signal that the doors of shops and stores were open, because no one slept the whole night through in California, sleeping being no way of making money, and the day began before the sun came up.

When she did sleep, she had nightmares. She dreamed of the Murietas and Don Roberto, galloping off to Mexico with all the stolen gold ... and she dreamed of Ah Wong, poor Ah Wong, the little man who had saved her life, because he had made her run away the same night that Sefton's hacienda had caught fire.

And then she dreamed of poor Davy. She dreamed that he was in trouble.

Davy slept, too. He was asleep when the horsemen thundered in from the mists of dawn. He was a stretched out on a blanket in the shelter of his house, and his wife lay asleep beside him. The baby slept too, in the cradle-board that was slung on a post.

The baby never cried. Davy often wondered about that, in the daytime when he was awake. On the plantation in Guyana where he had been born a slave, raised as a slave, and worked as a slave until he escaped, babies and children cried and whined all the time, even though they had attention and affection. Indian babies, it seemed, had plenty of good care, but no affection, and yet they never cried.

They were trained not to cry, he understood in the end, because crying babies attracted animals. If a baby persisted in crying, he was taken out and his board slung from a distant tree branch for the night. Then, if he still lived in the morning, he had learned not to make a sound.

So Davy's baby made no noise to wake him and warn him of the danger that was crashing down.

Davy woke with a lurch, with a howl of fear, to a nightmare of shots and shrieking, the pounding of hooves and the desperate sound of running bare feet, and the swish and crunch as clubs and hatchets swung. Davy sprang up, shaking with uncomprehending terror, and the elk hide that closed the opening to his house was torn to one side.

The red glare of flames, a vicious silhouette, fire shining on the wet gleam of an ax blade, and behind that the crying out of women and the shadows of people — Davy's people — fleeing in horror and panic. Children, old men, horses rearing and screaming as their riders clubbed the fleeing helpless.

At that hellish moment Davy cringed, weeping, whimpering, and couldn't understand who he was or what he should do, and he cried out, terrified, "Oh, Captain Dexter, help me!"

And the man in the doorway laughed, and swung his ax.

THREE

IN the morning, Bodfish tapped on the door of the transom cabin. Jake answered impatiently, because he had a headache, and had slept badly, and the bells had wakened him long before dawn.

Bodfish needed to know what should be broken out of the hold, for Abner to carry to the Indian encampment on the Bedstead Gully trail, to be given to Davy and his friends. Quenching a sigh, Jake followed the steward into the bright light of the open decks.

Valentine, Crotchet and Abner were aloft, setting up the topmasts with Charlie Martin supervising, and when Jake went down the ladder to the hold, it was just as busy there. Bill and Abijah, supervised by Chips, were prying apart the berths that had been constructed for the passengers the brig had carried from Tombez to California, and stacking the timber to one side, with a lot of shouting and clatter.

Holding a lighted lantern, Jake followed Bodfish down the ladder that led into the hold proper, where the provisions were stored — or what was left of them, as he grimly saw now. For the first time, he realized the full impact of the disastrous café-restaurant venture, because most of the provisions had been used up. There were just four barrels of salt meat left, and six bags of flour. Though there was the flour that should be waiting at the mill up the hill, he remembered — if it had not been stolen. The miller had told him that Sefton owned the water-mill, which meant that Jake's grain might have gone the way of Royal's gold.

There was no rice at all. Like the beans, it had been cooked for the meals in the café-restaurant. And there was nothing in the way of fruit or vegetables — no potatoes, no pumpkins or squash.

Jake bit back another sigh. Back at the Tombez River, when he'd had the idea of charging the Ecuadorean Argonauts provisions for their passage, he had envisaged the huge profit the Company would make from selling them in California. But the provisions had gone down the throats of the café-restaurant customers, instead, all save the remnants down here. However, there was no point in saying anything. It was too late for remonstrance.

Then he saw that Bodfish was watching him and waiting. The steward's expression was anxious.

Obviously, he had been brooding about the small supplies left, as well, because he said, "Captain, how much do you think we can afford to send the Indians?"

Jake paused, remembering the Indian encampment the first time he'd seen it, on the way to Bedstead Gully, when a chief who had been killed was being cremated. In his mind he could smell the stink of the burning corpse, and he remembered the food Davy had given the young widow. Instead of eating it, or putting it aside, she had thrown it into the fire as an offering.

He said shortly, "I certainly can't afford to send any flour."

The Indians would have to manage on their traditional acorn meal, despite what Harriet had said. It would take several days to get the brig ready to sail downriver to Sutter's, and then God alone knew how long to build Harriet's theater, and he knew the men wouldn't consent to leave until the theater was finished. And then there was the passage to Lahaina...

Bodfish nodded, looking relieved — as well he should, he being the man in charge of baking the daily bread. He said, "So what about the meat, sir?"

Jake thought about it, studying the four barrels of salt meat, each of which would fetch five hundred dollars here, because the pork, as he remembered, was so very fine.

He said with decision, "One barrel will do. A hundred pounds of meat should keep them going for quite a long time."

Bodfish nodded. Again, his expression held approval. Then he said tentatively, "Which one?"

Jake, surprised, turned his head to study the steward's face. Did it matter? Then he looked at the barrels again.

They all looked the same, just as they had when the six Murieta brothers had brought them to Bodfish's store on shore at the Tombez River — except that there had been twenty barrels of pork, back then, enough to pay for their passage to California. These four were all that were left. So which one should he send to the Indian encampment? And why had Bodfish asked him to choose?

And yet, as Jake suddenly remembered, it wasn't the first time Bodfish had been reluctant to point out one of the pork barrels. He wondered if Bodfish recollected that hot late afternoon by the sugar cane field as vividly as he did — whether he remembered the loud squeak of wooden wheels as the barrel-laden cart had come down the track to the old barn Bodfish had used as his store. The low sun had struck on the fat rows of casks, and on the ghastly bloodstains that smeared the Murietas' greasy shirts and calcineros. Their wide hats had been well pulled down, but still Jake had seen their thin, cruel grins.

Bodfish had explained his system of opening one barrel at random, as a spot-check on the rest, and they had seemed to find it amusing. Joaquín Murieta had smirked even more widely when Bodfish had finished, and then he had said, "We open ... which one?"

And instead of answering, or pointing at one of the barrels in his usual manner, Bodfish had hesitated. Why? Because the bandits intimidated him so? The silence had dragged on, while the Murietas waited and smirked, and Jake had watched, puzzled. Then the tense quiet had been abruptly broken by the thud if a thrown knife. Jake remembered how Bodfish had flinched with shock. It had been Joaquín Murieta who had thrown the knife, and it had sung as it quivered in the side of one of the fat casks.

And Joaquín had pointed at the barrel with the stuck knife, and said, "That one?"

Jake remembered how Bodfish had shaken his head. Rather wildly, the steward had pointed at a different cask, choosing it at random. It was as if he had been too scared to open this one — this particular one, the one that still bore the scar of that knife, the one that Jake was looking at right now. A spear of dusty light fell over his shoulder from the hatch above his head, and illuminated the dusty arrowhead mark in the side of the cask where Joaquín Murieta had pulled out the knife.

Jake shrugged away memories, and pointed at the cask with the arrowhead mark. He said, "That one," and turned away.

He went up to deck, leaving Bodfish to organize hoisting the cask out of the hold, and after he spoke to Charlie Martin, Abner was detached from rigging duties. By the time the second mate had arrived at the gangway with his bedroll, the barrel was ready. Then the two of them headed down the plank to the embarcadero of Pueblo San Marco.

The waterfront was more suffocatingly thronged with men than ever. Many were greenhorns, fresh from a four-month Cape Horn passage, while others were seasoned miners, the experience of a summer in the hills behind them. However, as Jake forced a route through the crowd for Abner and the barrel, it occurred to him that they looked remarkably alike, whether fresh or experienced, for they all looked weatherworn, and they were all dressed the same. He meditated that it was almost as if there was a miners' uniform, which had come into being all by itself.

It was a uniform of stained and torn buckskin trousers, with checkered woolen shirts, and tight double-cleated boots that reached to the knee. The men all sported Spanish-looking sashes and scarves in bright colors, and they all wore wide-brimmed leather Californian hats with a plaited cord around the brim — but none of them, as far as he could tell, were speaking in Spanish.

Last year, when Jake and his prospecting party had headed into the hills, Spanish had been the *lingua franca* here, but now all he heard was United States American. Even the old Californians — the traders, the merchants, and the gamblers — were speaking English. They had all learned English in a hurry, he supposed, so they could make great fortunes out of these men as they passed on to the hills.

And the touts, who had been advertising women, liquor, goods and gambling in a mixture of English and Spanish last year, were now yelling out their enticements in plain, unadulterated English —

"Come and see the fandango, see the Spanish women dance!"
"Abrigo's café-restaurant, the best game of monte in town!"
"Boots, boots, best mining boots, you'll curse yourself if you pass 'em by!"
"Mule train, mule train, train to Don Roberto's fort, gateway to the hills!"

Jake followed the sound of the last shout. "Ten cents a pound for yer baggage," the mule driver said, and Jake sighed. Tib and Dan were taking a long time to come back with the llamas, and if they had been more swift about it, it would have saved him some money. He paid over the required ten dollars, and watched the train and Abner trudge off. The young man had to walk, because hiring a riding mule for the half-day trip would have cost sixteen dollars. When he arrived at Don Roberto's fort, he would have to improvise.

The best Abner could do, Jake meditated, was to leave the cask at the fort, and continue on the trail to Bedstead Gully, in the hope of meeting up with Tib and Dan with the llamas. Then, after they had collected the cask from the fort, Abner and one of the llamas could be detached to pack the cask to the Indian encampment, while Tib and Dan came on to the brig.

But Abner was resourceful enough to make it up as he went along, Jake thought, and forgot it as he watched the muletrain disappear around the first uphill bend.

Instead of contemplating further, he put his mind to his next mission.

FOUR

JAKE Dexter found Giles sitting on the balcony of one of the hotels that faced the busy waterfront.

The journalist's feet were cocked up on the rail as he wrote notes on a pad that was propped on his knees. Jake set a brandy bottle and two glasses on the table at his elbow, and then leaned on a pillar, studying his quarry while he waited for a reaction.

The newspaperman took his time, scribbling a sentence before he looked up. Then he brushed his moustaches away from his mouth, and looked at the bottle with a hoisted eyebrow.

"I'm usually the one to oil men's tongues," he observed.

Jake merely flicked one eyebrow.

"However," said Giles, and sat up straight. He opened the bottle, filled a glass, lifted it appreciatively to the light, and then sipped. "Thank you," he said. "How much did it cost?"

Jake was surprised into a laugh. "What does it matter?"

"Why, nothing at all, since you are the fellow paying the bill. Call me curious. Last week a glass of what passes for brandy was a pinch of dust, but yesterday it was half a teaspoon, so it could well have been a whole teaspoonful of dust today. God knows what a whole bottle will fetch by tomorrow."

"I paid coins," Jake said. "Twelve Chilean silver dollars. I got a better bargain by paying cash."

"Ah." Giles nodded as he sipped again. "So Colonel Sefton was talking sense, after all."

"Sefton?" Jake echoed. All amusement had fled.

"It was one of his arguments for buying shares in his bank. He said he had plans for establishing a mint. He reckoned that gold is getting debased, and coins will put everything back to rights."

"And where did you hear this?"

"At a fine old hacienda up Cache Creek, about five hours' ride from Sefton's rancho. It's owned by an old California identity, Don Manuel Vidrie, and is quite a sight to see, something out of old Spain. It's an estate in the real old Spanish California style, complete

29

with its own vineyard and press house, its own pueblo, its own church, and its own bear pit."

"Bear ... *what?*"

"Bear pit. An arena where a wild bear fights it out with a wild bull, while the people watch and cast bets."

"Jehovah," said Jake. A shiver touched the back of his neck. He remembered the bear that had attacked Harriet, back at Bedstead Gully, and how it had snarled and swiped at branches as it had pursued them; he remembered the rank smell of its hide and its breath. He had been frenzied with terror for her, shoving her along frantically as they ran. They had escaped only by sheer accident, by tumbling down a hole into the fern bed of a gully, and after the bear had pounded on, clearing the hole and then crashing through the trees until it was out of hearing...

With a deliberate effort, he tore his mind away from the memory of Harriet's trembling body, and returned his attention to Giles.

"Colonel Sefton carried me along to the Vidrie hacienda," the reporter was saying. "Along with a couple of Yankee merchants by the name of Prenderwhite and Chaffey. Don Manuel entertained us with a bull and bear fight and after that treated us to a great feast about a great table, all very old world and courtly. The food was dominated by garlic, but the wine was excellent. The bear won the bull and bear fight," Giles added. "Rather to the colonel's disappointment, or so I noticed. He told us he had done better at Christmas, when the bull won the fight."

Jake said rather blankly, "He'd placed his bets on the bull?"

"The colonel was very keen on bulls. A strong black bull appeared to be his favorite kind of animal. He talked about the future of the California market being a rising one, like a bull that tosses the bear into the air, and then gores it to death. Have you heard of Chaffey and Prenderwhite before?"

Jake shook his head. "Never."

"I arrived in California in their company. We rode to the Feather River from Sonoma, and called at Sefton's rancho, as Chaffey had a letter of introduction to the colonel, writ by someone with a significant name who resides back in Philadelphia. The colonel greeted us politely enough, but didn't seem too keen on entertaining us in his own home. Instead, he took us to Don Manuel Vidrie, so his good Californian friend could provide the board and lodging and entertainment."

"That was very neighborly of Don Manuel."

"A neighborly man altogether, Captain Dexter. Why, he hosted Colonel Sefton's wife for several months, just about all the time she has been in California. Her husband the colonel sent her there the very next day after she arrived at his hacienda, or so I heard — but maybe Mrs. Sefton told you that herself?"

Jake pressed his lips together.

Giles quaffed his glass as he waited for an answer, and when Jake remained silent he went on in perfectly matter-of-fact tones, "So I reckon Sefton must have had some sort of hold over Don Manuel Vidrie."

"Blackmail?" said Jake alertly. "On what grounds?"

"Who knows, Captain Dexter, who knows? Probably it was a matter of money, since Don Manuel was repaying the colonel in hospitality — paying in kind, as it were. How do you reckon Don Manuel felt when he got the news of the tragedy, huh? Sad, or glad?"

Jake said incredulously, "Are you inferring that Dan Manuel Vidrie *murdered* Colonel Sefton? And then fired his house to cover up the murder?"

Giles's eyes widened, and then he shook his head and laughed. "Now, sir, that would really be a story." Then he refilled his glass, then lifted the bottle with a brow raised in Jake's direction.

Jake hesitated, but then nodded, and the journalist filled the second tumbler.

Jake sat down on the chair on the other side of the little table, picked up the glass, saluted Giles, and then sipped. He didn't drink often, but this looked as if it was going to be a long and interesting conversation.

He nodded at the journalist's pad, and said, "But there is a story?"

"Colonel Sefton belonged to an old and prominent Philadelphia family, Captain Dexter. Of course there is a story."

"So tell me about him."

"Hasn't Mrs. Sefton told you enough already?"

Jake was silent. Instead of speaking, he sipped brandy. He found Giles amusing and exasperating by turns, and right now he found him irritating.

"An interesting character, Colonel Sefton," said Giles, not at all deterred by this lack of audience response. "Very wishful to better himself in the financial way, and return to high and flighty New

York circles most enviably rich, to make the men and women wonder greatly about his admirable resourcefulness — one woman in particular. But I am sure Mrs. Sefton has mentioned that I knew her husband the colonel in New York? Though the word should really be *observed*, because I certainly observed him in New York — and observed him with interest up Cache Creek, too, particularly when I found that he didn't remember me. He had a little habit that I found intriguing," said Giles, and drifted off into silence, drinking instead of explaining himself.

Jake waited, and then said, "What?"

"Oh, it's just that it seemed so womanish. In California the men smoke cigars at the dinner table, just as they do in Spain or South America."

And North America, Jake thought, but didn't comment.

"Do you use tobacco yourself, Captain Dexter?"

Jake shook his head, and the journalist laughed. "You should, according to the colonel. It seems that cannibals avoid the meat of men who have used tobacco. So smoking, according to his logic, lengthens life."

"I don't see what difference it makes whether you have smoked or not, once you are dressed for the table," Jake objected. "Your meat might be rejected, but still you are dead."

"A very good point, sir! Or perhaps cannibals smell the victim's breath before deciding whether or not to dispatch him. Is it possible that cannibals are choosey?"

"I've heard what is supposed to be a true story of some cannibals sparing a whaling captain because he was so thin it didn't seem worth the trouble to kill and cook him," said Jake, and sipped meditatively. Then he said, "And you think this is why Colonel Sefton smoked cigars?"

"The point of my story is that he did not smoke cigars, sir. The cannibal comment was just an instance of his rather ghoulish style of speech — for I surely did notice how he liked to grab the audience and dominate the conversation." Then, after a pause to refill both glasses, Giles continued, "The Californian women make miniature cigars by scraping tobacco flakes into a scrap of paper, rolling it up, twisting both ends, and then putting one end between the ruby lips, and setting fire to the other end. They call it a cigaretto. Is that the right word, do you reckon?"

"It's a good enough word, since I understand what you mean," said Jake, adding shrewdly, "And I assume that Sefton's womanish custom was to smoke these cigarettos, rather than cigars?"

Giles nodded in appreciation, then said, "And to make them, Captain — to *make* them. The impression I had was that Sefton smoked them because the manufacture of one of these cigarettos gave him time to think."

"While he chose his words?"

"Exactly, Captain Dexter! And Sefton chose his words very carefully indeed, or so I noticed. He was uncommon wishful to sell Chaffey shares in that bank of his, so wishful that he was willing to lend him the money to do it, and his whole conversation was designed to that end. I saw you looking at the bank ledgers, Captain. Tell me, was Chaffey's name in the list?"

Jake shrugged. He couldn't remember. "It was a very long list."

"Of men who'd bought those shares? And borrowed the money to do it?" Then, when he saw Jake's nod, Giles pursed his lips in a silent whistle. "He was a persuasive man, the colonel."

"Obviously, it was too good a deal to be easily turned down," Jake said, and sipped again, judiciously, because he could feel the brandy going to his head. "And when you think about it, the investors haven't lost their money, even though the shares are worthless, because they don't have to repay what they borrowed to buy the shares in the first place."

"How right you are, sir," said Giles with vast approval. "It's the disappointed miners who had their gold all confiscated who are baying after the alcalde in the hills."

Jake's brows shot up. "After Don Roberto?"

"Wa'al, he's the fellow who put all that gold in Sefton's vaults, ain't that so?"

"In the hills, you say?"

"As far as Mexico, I'd hazard. Don Roberto is both a Londoner and a Mexican citizen, too, or so Mrs. Sefton told me."

"She told you that?"

"We had quite a conversation, Captain Dexter."

"At the Vidries'?"

"And at Don Roberto's fortification, at the junction of the Feather and Cache Creek. As I am sure you know already, his fort guards the bridge to Vidrie lands — though I would hazard that doesn't stop the miners now, the alcalde being absent in the hills. An interesting old customer, Don Roberto, don't you agree?"

"You find everyone interesting," Jake remarked, and drank more of the brandy, which was definitely going to his head. He slumped back in the chair and cocked one ankle across the other knee, surveying the parade of miners and touts past the balcony rail.

"I certainly find Mrs. Sefton interesting," said Giles.

Jake narrowed his eyes. "You do?"

"I do indeed. You could've struck me down with the proverbial feather, Captain Dexter, when she informed me that she is nothing more than a poor strolling player."

"But everyone knows she's an actress, surely. The Gray family," Jake told him rather broodingly, "is famous."

"So I learned, Captain Dexter, so I learned. I've asked around about the Gray family since, and was told a great deal, there being quite a number of Englishmen here."

"Englishmen?"

"They've been hearing the news of the gold there, too, you know, and have responded with the same enthusiasm as Americans. What do you think Colonel Mason would have to say about that, huh? His intention was to dilute the alien influx with more Americans, not to bring in more aliens — and while he might be able to countenance the French, wouldn't he consider Englishmen his traditional enemies?"

Jake didn't answer. Instead he waited, not wanting to betray his interest in whatever the reporter had to say about Harriet. Giles drank more instead of talking, however, so in the end curiosity drove him to say, "So what did you learn about the Grays?"

"Charles Gray was very fond of horses, a good bottle of port, and comely women, not necessarily in that order, and Mary Sissons, who was Mrs. Sefton's mother, was considered one of London's great beauties. Thousands mourned when she died, including a prominent banker and an earl or two. However, in case you are wondering," he added with a smirk, "I was also told that Mrs. Sefton takes after her father's family in looks. And good looks, they are, too. Charles Gray's aunt, Diana Gray — Mrs. Sefton's great-aunt — was a famous creature in her time, an exquisite beauty — or so I was told — and a great favorite in the more informal gatherings at court. Books were written about her, and ballads penned in her name. Her lover and protector was one of the princes of the realm."

Good lord. Jake took a larger mouthful of brandy than he had intended.

"So, having learned all that rather sensational background, it seemed even more amazing to me."

"What did?"

"That Colonel Sefton, the high and mighty scion of a blue-blooded Philadelphia family, should have stooped so far as to marry Miss Harriet Gray."

Jake said coldly, "I beg your pardon?"

"Face it, Captain Dexter, she's an *actress* — and, what's more, an actress with a sensational background. She might be beautiful, but an *actress* is hardly the kind of woman a man like Colonel Francis Sefton would want hanging on his elbow when he attended social events in New York — and not the kind of woman a man like Colonel Francis Sefton would want to introduce to his friends in Philadelphia, either. Not as his wife, at any rate."

Jake was getting angry. "Harriet has impeccable manners."

"And a loud and ringing voice, Captain Dexter."

Jake was silent, unwillingly remembering the demure dovelike murmuring of New England women. Harriet definitely had a ringing voice — trained to reach the back walls of a theater, he supposed. When in the throes of a tantrum, she could be quite deafening.

"And remarkably lovely legs," Mr. Giles added, and watched Jake's expression with ill-hidden satisfaction.

"How the devil do you know that?"

"Not from personal observation, unfortunately. She was a very popular Principal Boy, or so I hear. Her impersonation of Dick Whittington drew huge crowds to wherever she was playing."

"Principal Boy?" said Jake blankly. "But she's a girl."

"It's usual for a girl to dress in tights and play the Principal Boy in pantomime, and a man in a gown and wig to play the Old Woman — Mother Hubbard is a popular role. Or perhaps you've never seen pantomime in New England?"

Jake had never even heard of it. If a girl in boy's tights was a regular part of pantomime, he doubted it would be *legal* in New England.

"I haven't seen pantomime anywhere," said Mr. Giles, looking regretful. "But from what I hear, it seems to be a remarkably ancient art, harking back to the *commedia dell'arte* of old Italy, and the story of Columbine and Pierrot, the star-crossed lovers who are in constant flight from the wicked villain. Mrs. Sefton could play Columbine to perfection, don't you think?"

Jake looked at him for a long moment, his glass neglected in his hand as he thought about this. "And the villain?"

"I had the strong impression that she hated and feared her husband — which makes me wonder still more about the marriage."

Jake said, "It was an arranged marriage." Then he remembered that he was talking to a journalist, because Giles's eyes sharpened. He was definitely drinking too much, he thought.

"Arranged?" Giles echoed. "And how old was Miss Gray at the time?"

"Sixteen, I think," said Jake reluctantly. "The Grays had just arrived in New Zealand."

"So she was a minor. Any arrangements would have had to be co-signed by her father, who should have made sure that the colonel was paying out large for the lovely ingénue. And yet, I gather that the lovely ingénue didn't benefit from the marriage at all ... and even now is an impoverished widow, in great need of your protection. Which you, I assume, are extending?"

For the second time that day, Jake remembered Joaquín Murieta. This time, he remembered the Ecuadorean's insolent query — back on the brig, on passage from Tombez to San Francisco. *She is yours, the pretty gray filly, you are her protector, yes..?*

Yes, he thought. He should have said yes, back then. If he had said yes, Joaquín Murieta would not have cut her cheek — would not have tried to take her by force. He remembered the feel of Harriet in his arms, the scent of her body, and said nothing, leaving silence for assent.

"So, how did it come about, do you reckon?"

"What?"

"How was the lovely ingénue finish up so poor, when the man who married her was so rich?"

Jake hesitated, but then shrugged. "I gather it was because of a loophole in the law."

Giles stared at him a long moment, then sipped, and said judiciously, "Wa'al, that would be typical of Colonel Frank Sefton. Tell me more."

"He had speculated in New Zealand land before the British annexed the country — and once the British were in control, a law was passed saying that Americans couldn't benefit from their investments. That they had to sell their property to British nationals, at the price they had originally paid. So, the day before the wedding, Colonel Sefton signed over everything to H... to Miss Gray, so that it was in English hands. Then, once they were married..."

Again, he shrugged.

"Aha, I see it. Once Miss Gray became Mrs. Sefton, the land was

36

back in *his* hands, but with the advantage of being held in an English name. So he sold it all, at a profit?"

"So I believe."

"And sailed to Canton, or so I was told."

"He didn't take her with him, if that's what you are wondering."

"I knew that already, Captain Dexter."

"He left her without a penny to her name."

"I knew that, too, Captain Dexter." Giles paused, contemplating Jake, and then said, "So what did the ingénue do next?"

"She went back to the stage."

"Under her stage name?"

"Of course."

Which was why she had boarded his brig under her stage name, Jake brooded. Which was why he hadn't known until he had arrived at Sutter's Fort that she was married — and that Sefton had the legal right to claim her. Because Harriet had never bothered to tell him her story, he'd had no way of knowing that she belonged by law to another man.

The old bitter jealousy rose, and he drank brandy to quench it.

Then Giles said, "So where was Charles Gray while Sefton was selling all his investments at a profit, and taking all that profit off to China?"

"He died."

"What? When?"

"He was killed in an accident, two days after the wedding," Jake said shortly.

"Well, well, well," said Giles, and pursed his lips in a whistle. "How very, very convenient for the colonel."

FIVE

FOUR days later, the brig was ready for the downriver passage to Sutter's Fort. The casks where the sails had been stored had all been broken out of the sailroom, and the retrieved sails had been bent onto the newly braced yards and stays. The rigging had been overhauled, and was taut as it ever had been ... but Tib and Dan and Abner had still not come back.

Obviously, there had been a problem getting the cask of meat from Don Roberto's fort to the Indians. Jake found this worrying, as it implied that Abner had not met up with Tib and Dan and the llamas, and that there might have been an accident. However, he was certainly not going to send more men after them, as his crew was reduced enough already.

The best he could do, he decided over supper, was to leave a message. The three men were perfectly capable of joining the brig at Sutter's, he thought. Then, as he drank his coffee and contemplated Harriet's silent, averted profile, he heard the frantic cries from the embarcadero.

Abner's face was a pale blob in the dim evening light. Dan and Tib were there too, with one llama and a mule — and there was a body lying across the mule's saddle.

It was Davy. As the boys wearily explained, they'd had to exchange two of the llamas for the mule, as all the llamas had all refused to carry the burden of a man. And they had lost another llama when it had run off in terror. Maybe someone would report it.

Very carefully, Tib and Dan carried Davy up to the deck, and down the companionway into the afterquarters. Then they put him in the second mate's stateroom, which had been hastily vacated by Mr. Martin. Jake lit a lamp, and winced at the state of the rags that Abner had bound round the poor boy's head. Then, he sent Bodfish off for hot water, his medicine chest, and his medical book.

It was a mercy that Davy was unconscious, as when he unwrapped the improvised bandages it was to find a ghastly, weeping, bloody gash underneath the rags. It seemed impossible that he still lived. Then Jake sensed Harriet come in, even before he heard the rustle of her skirts.

He said quickly, "Don't look" — but too late. He heard her sharp intake of breath. She didn't go, but handed him clean rags and rinsed them in hot water as he handed them back, calling out for more water as she did it. Over their long separation, and the silent days since, he had forgotten her courage, but now he was grateful for it.

Tib and Dan had been sent to the galley to get supper, but Abner was hovering in the doorway. He was holding the glass of brandy Jake had told Bodfish to give him, but not drinking. The one time he had tried to swallow some, his teeth had chattered on the edge of the glass. Jake had told him to go with Tib and Dan, but he was too anxious about Davy to leave, he said. And he wanted to talk about the dreadful things he had seen at the ruins of the Indian encampment, as if talking would get them out of his head.

"They were all dead, all the old men, all the babies and children, all the women, and the huts were all on fire ... and the smell rushed at me as I came along the valley. It hit me like a blow." Abner's voice was ragged. "Then Davy began to crawl out of a heap of corpses, I saw that heap of bodies move, and dear Jesus how it scared me, Captain, but he was the only one alive. The rest were all slaughtered, Captain, they'd been slain just horrible. Then while I was dragging Davy away from the fire Tib and Dan arrived on the trail from Bedstead Gully, and they looked too, making certain sure there was no one else left alive — and all the people had been scalped. They were all scalped, women, children, babies, them all. And the blood, all that blood, Captain, and the *smell*. That's why the llama run away, but we managed to keep the others."

Scalped. Jake saw Harriet shut her eyes. Then they both looked again at Davy's wounded head. His peppercorn hair was matted with water as well as thick with blood, but it had not been torn from his skull.

Then Harriet whispered, "The administrators of Chihuahua and Sonora pay a bounty for Indian scalps."

"Oh my God," said Jake, and winced. "Who told you that?"

"Either Sefton — or Don Roberto. I don't remember which, because it was a long time ago, and they were both talking to me at the same time. But I do remember that the bounty is two hundred dollars for the scalp of a man, but only one hundred for a woman."

And babies and children had been scalped, too.

Jake said, "*Christ.*"

Sickly, he wondered how much an Indian baby's scalp was worth. He was warming a bottle of oil of turpentine over a lamp, and the hand that held the bottle shook.

Harriet nodded. She was very pale. Then she looked down at the long, clean rags she was laying out, and she said, "But even though the conversation happened a long time ago, I do remember asking them how the administrators could tell the difference."

"And the answer?"

"They didn't know."

Jake took a deep, steadying breath. Then, slowly and evenly, he poured the warm oil onto the cloths. It would prevent the bandages from sticking to the gash in Davy's head and work against putrefaction as well, he hoped.

Charlie Martin, his features stiff with horror, held Davy's poor head while Jake wound bandages, and Harriet handed over another clean rag as Jake came to the end of each one. Then it was done. Davy's head was lowered gently back to the pillow and Jake looked down at him.

The ex-slave was deeply unconscious, snoring on a choking note, his eyes not fully shut, so that Jake could see the rolled-up whites. He doubted that Davy would last the night. It was a miracle, he thought, that he'd survived not just the attack but also the journey from the Indian camp. Men would take turns to sit with him — as seamen had done for sick shipmates since the beginning of time. But there was little more that could be done.

Harriet had her head bent as she gathered up the filthy rags. Charlie and Abner had both left for the steerage, while Bodfish had taken the pitcher of hot water away, so for the first time in four days she and Jake were alone. He wanted to hold her, and take comfort from her lithe, warm body, and give her comfort in return, but knew he couldn't. Because he had to wait.

He had had so little contact with her over the past four days that he watched her with intensity. Her hair was always a mess, as most of her pins were lost, and most of it was tumbled untidily to her shoulders, but he still wanted to gather it in his hands. Over the months of winter she had grown thin, so that the brown gown she was wearing sat loosely on her body, but still he thought she was beautiful.

Jake said, "Is there something that you should be telling me?"

"What do you mean?"

"I feel as if you are holding something back."

She was quiet for so long that he thought she hadn't heard, or had decided not to answer. Then she looked up at him, and her eyes met his for the first time in four days.

She said, "Chihuahua is part of Mexico?"

"So I believe," he said.

"I thought so." Another pause. Then, "Mr. Giles told me that Don Roberto ran through the hills to Mexico, with the men who'd lost their gold from Sefton's bank hot on his tail."

"Yes." Giles had told Jake that, too.

"And the Murietas. They've gone, too."

So they had. Jake's eyebrows tilted, because he hadn't thought of that.

"They were his deputies. But they were also the men who jumped Royal's claim after Pablo and Joseph Fayal were murdered."

"Yes, I know," he said.

She paused to take a deep breath, and then said, "Pablo and Joseph were scalped, like Davy's Indians. That's what Abner told me at Bedstead Gully, and Royal has confirmed it. Pablo was Spanish and Joseph was Portuguese, and they both had black, straight hair, so their scalps could easily pass for Indian scalps. Unlike Davy's," she added.

And they both looked at Davy again. Davy, whose peppercorn hair had not been sliced off.

Dear sweet lord, thought Jake with horror. Like Royal, he had watched with shocked disbelief as the bodies of Pablo and Joseph had been hauled out of their tent; like Royal, he had seen the obscenity that had been done to their heads. Tib and Dan had been there, too, and he remembered their grunts of sickened revulsion; he remembered that Royal had cried out wordlessly, but he couldn't remember what he had said, himself.

When she looked back at him, he said in a shaking voice, "Harriet, do you really think the Murietas sold their scalps — for the bounty? Pablo? Joseph? *My men?*"

She sighed and picked up the last of the rags and put them in the basin.

"I don't like to think about it," she said. "I can only guess, and I don't even want to do that."

She was about to leave. Without any preamble at all, or even knowing he was going to say it, Jake said, "Harriet, how did your

41

father die?"

She stopped dead. Her face went blank with shock at the unexpectedness of his question. He saw her eyes go shiny, and knew she was holding back tears.

Her voice, however, was perfectly steady when she said, "He was murdered."

"*Murdered?*"

"Frank Sefton either killed my father himself, or paid someone to do it."

Then, without another word, she left the stateroom.

To everyone's amazement, Davy survived the night, and was still snoring in the morning. There was no point in hanging about Pueblo San Marco, so Jake ordered the *Gosling* unmoored, and jibs and topsails flown for the passage downriver to the Embarcadero at Sutter's Fort.

It was late April, and a perfect spring day, and the breeze was fair for the downriver passage — for perhaps the last time until October, as the season of the upriver wind was coming fast upon them. Though the air was crisp, the sky was pale, with a promise of afternoon heat. Far beyond the terraced streets of Pueblo San Marco the purple mountains were rimmed with eternal white, but here, on the village embarcadero, the men who were crowded to watch the departure of the brig *Gosling* wore the sleeves of their checkered shirts rolled up to the elbow.

Jake wondered why something so routine as unmooring and setting sail should draw such an audience. Then they started to shout out jovial taunts, solving the mystery by making it evident that they had all come to marvel at men who were crazy enough to sail downriver, when this was the start of a new mining season. What the hell were they thinking, these men on the *Gosling*? — or so they hollered. The goddess of fortune was in the hills, not down the river at Sutter's Fort!

Harriet was at the port rail of the after deck, and for a wonder she was laughing, looking relaxed and at ease as she listened to the jibes from shore. Leaving Pueblo San Marco, obviously, was a reason for happiness. Jake shook his head, smiled, and turned back to work.

He looked up and around, and then said to Charlie Martin, "Loose topsails."

"Lay out and loose!" cried Charlie, running to the foredeck, and the response was instant. The pretty way was to have both topsails set at the same instant, without one creeping up more slowly than the other, and the *Goslings*, like Charlie Martin, were determined to show these saucy miners on the embarcadero how real seamen could do it. "Sheet home, and hoist away!" he cried, and men heaved on lines, and parrel straps squeaked as the yards swung. "Haul taut!" he shouted, and, as smooth as melting butter, the *Gosling* moved out into the stream.

Jake watched with approval, and nodded as he shouted, "Set jibs." The *Gosling* heeled slowly, like a dog remembering old tricks, and then the current seized the hull, and *away* she sailed.

Thank God, thought Jake, and did not bother to look at Pueblo San Marco and the misty mountains any more. There were nothing but bad memories there, and he, like his ship, was back in his proper element. Everything was going well, for a change, and it would be a short, swift passage to Sutter's Fort.

The men seemed remarkably happy, too. Davy might be gravely ill in the second mate's stateroom, and the horror that had happened to him might have been a shock to them all, but it was also an eloquent reminder of what dangers and miseries they were escaping.

Because of that, perhaps, they sang merrily as they set the decks to rights, and moved about aloft. "In California lived a maid," sang Valentine, the ship's shantyman —

> *Mark well what I do say*
> *In California lived a maid*
> *And she was mistress of her trade*
> *I'll go no more a-roving, with you, fair maids —*

And the *Goslings,* as remembered well, picked up the refrain with gusto —

> *A-roving, a-roving*
> *Since roving's been my ruin,*
> *I'll go no more a-roving*
> *With you, fair maids!*

The current was rapid, the long ripples curling like green and gold serpents about the dappled hull, so that the scenery scudded by quickly, and Pueblo San Marco was soon far behind them. And gladly did they see it go. It was eight months since they had come up this river — eight months of winter, San Pueblo, the mountains, horrible deaths, and many disappointments. It was very good to get away.

Because of those eight months, it took a little while for the river to seem familiar. The oaks that stood along the banks of the Feather grew as thick as Jake remembered, but the steep grassy slopes of the banks themselves looked different. Then he realized that it was because they were bristling with the slender stems of myriads of oak seedlings. The Indians, who usually harvested the acorns along these banks in the fall, had been driven away, or had gone of their own accord into the mines. Jake saw one elk where he remembered seeing bounding herds.

Perhaps, he thought, the elk had taken for the hills, though it was more likely that they had been slaughtered for food. Waterfowl had become exceeding scarce, perhaps also shot for rations. In the water huge fish hovered, all turned the same way, nosing the scent of the eternal hills — the miners, it seemed, preferred not to eat fish. And then, from downriver, from the direction of the junction of the Feather and the Sacramento rivers, came...

An armada. All coming this way. Schooners beat against the current, while boys hauled manfully at the oars of whaleboats, or paddled madly in canoes. The whaleboats, elegant gigs and awkward dinghies were all moving upstream, on the way to Pueblo San Marco, all packed with boys who were dressed up like miners in checkered shirts, but who looked like greenhands. Their shining faces were agog with the prospect of adventure, and they all bore the true, eager look of untried prospectors.

Half of those in the overloaded small boats were engaged in madly baling out the scud thrown over the gunwales with every forward surge, just to keep afloat. And, like the men back in Pueblo San Marco, these argonauts were amazed at the sight of a brig going in the wrong direction — downriver, instead of upriver to Pueblo San Marco, the gateway to the mines.

"You tarnation fools!" one fellow hollered. "You're goin' the durn-wrong way!"

"What news of the mines?" cried another.

"Hard enough!" shouted Abner. Which was greeted with a roar of disbelieving laughter.

Undoubtedly the newcomers believed that the *Gosling*s had made their pile already, and were off to Sutter's Fort to spend it, because many of them back-paddled to ask for hints, which were freely given.

"*Oh, the gold, they say,*" sang Valentine. He was back to high spirits, now they were out of sight of Abrigo's café-restaurant, that humiliating reminder of how he and Crotchet had persuaded the shipkeepers to sink all their money into the café venture, and then lost everything, café and all, in a game of monte —

> *Oh, the gold, they say*
> *Is brighter than the day,*
> *And when it's mine,*
> *Oh, won't I shine,*
> *And drive dull care away — suh!*

And the boys, as the boats pulled on, were roaring out the chorus as if they had been singing it all their lives. Jake could hear Tib and Dan laughing about it from aloft, hollering to these greenhands that this gold rush business was a wonderful lark — until the seven thousandth bucket of dirt had been dug, panned, and washed, with not a single fleck of gold to show for it.

Jake himself, more practically, wondered where all these boats had come from. Surely not San Francisco, he thought, or even Sonoma. The boats were too small for a voyage like that. They must have put out from Sutter's, he decided, so he thought that the Embarcadero might look a little different from the day back in September when the brig had left the mooring.

Then Tib and Dan cried out in wonder. Jake climbed the main shrouds swiftly, hauled himself over the top, and stood hanging onto a shroud with one hand and shading his eyes with the other, equally amazed.

The Embarcadero had become the front street of a large town! Where the three army lieutenants had marked out straight streets last fall, there were ragged clusters of calico houses and thickets of tents, thronged all about with people. It had turned into a calico city.

Then Jake looked at the river. At once, with more than a little urgency, he hollered out orders and skidded down a backstay. The lookouts had forgotten what they were about, which was to watch for hazards and oncoming traffic. While Jake yelled and Charlie Martin ran about frantically, the brig almost ran afoul of five whaleboats, four canoes, and a dinghy.

Then Jake shouted to his first mate to make sail again, for the departure of this miniature fleet had left a space in the packed mass of moored shipping, and Jake was determined to beat another brig to it. Mr. Martin hollered and the men shifted themselves even more quickly, while Jake went back aloft to issue directions — and the *Gosling* got her nose into a gap behind a moored schooner while the other vessel was still two dozen yards away.

Of course, thought Jake with great satisfaction. Despite a winter at Pueblo San Marco and in the mines, his crew had not forgotten old tricks. He braced himself to drop down from the mast again — and then froze, as he recognized the schooner.

Sefton's schooner. It was tied up in the same space at the Embarcadero where the fancy vessel had been moored in the fall. *Sefton's schooner*. How had he forgotten it — and how the hell had it come here from Pueblo San Marco? And when? It hadn't been moored at the upriver town when he'd arrived from Bedstead Gully, but he hadn't paid attention at the time. Jake cursed himself softly as he slid down to the deck.

The instant the gangplank dropped, he beckoned to Tib, Dan, and Abner, and led them on shore. His last glimpse of the brig was Harriet's frown as she watched him over the rail. As she turned her head to scowl at her dead husband's schooner, she was nibbling the tip of one finger in the attitude of deep thought that he knew so well. Then Jake led the way along the Embarcadero.

It was all so different. The great patch of muddy meadow the three lieutenants had marked out with stakes and strings the year before was unrecognizable, now. Houses made of cloth tacked onto wooden frames stood in long rows along the imaginary streets they had labeled with numbers and letters, and there were dozens more a-building. Tents were clustered like toadstools under the huge old trees that had been left to stand along the waterfront — round tents, square tents, tents made of old shirts pinned over heaps of branches. Hammers banged, saws grated, and men shouted — and all the shouting was in United States American. Both Colonel Mason and Captain Mervine should be highly gratified, Jake mused, because the Embarcadero, which had been so Mexican just last August, was now indubitably American.

Then he reached the gangplank that linked Sefton's vessel to this muddy bedlam. With Tib and Dan and Abner close behind, he strode up onto the schooner.

There were men lounging about the decks, but they backed off

46

in haste the moment he began to ask questions, and they soon disappeared into the calico town. The two deck cabins were empty. Despite the possibilities of the schooner as a lodging place, there was no one below decks, either.

Jake stared around at varnished walls and varnished benches — empty, empty. The hold, when he went down there, was another yawningly empty cavern. Nevertheless, he issued orders to the three *Gosling*s to search the ship thoroughly, every inch from tops to bilges.

They found nothing — nothing but an air of neglect. Her small crew had left long ago, and there were certainly no bags of purloined gold. The men who had been lounging about on the open deck had just been passing through, and had left no trace of their presence.

It was impossible to tell why no squatters taken the vessel over. Other craft that were moored up to the Embarcadero were doing a roaring trade as lodging houses or trading posts, their galleys turned into cafés and their deck-cabins leased out as shops, but the schooner had been avoided. Perhaps, Jake thought, it was something about the forbidding air of the vessel, because though it was nicely varnished, it was also full of daunting shadows.

Giving up, he returned to the brig, and checked that Charlie had snugged her down and moored her up tight. It took ten more minutes for him to realize that a member of the company was missing.

That Harriet had vanished.

SIX

BODFISH, who was sitting with Davy, said had not seen Miss Gray since she had called to check on Davy, half an hour earlier. She was nowhere in the cabins, and nowhere about the decks.

Jake found Royal, and barked, "Where is your sister?"

Royal looked about, his air irritatingly vague. "Could she have gone to check the bit of land she bought for a theater?"

Of course, thought Jake. He said urgently, "Where is it?"

Royal grimaced, trying to remember. He led the way down the brig's gangplank, looked up and down the Embarcadero, scratched his head, and turned right. Jake followed him.

Calico City was very crowded, full of men and bordered by their strange habitations. The broad street that ran along the waterfront was thronged with men and pack beasts. Jake, following Royal, had to dodge teams of horses and oxen, mutinous mules, and galloping riders. Dogs yapped at his heels.

There were hand-lettered signs everywhere, propped up against trestles and dangling from calico walls, silently roaring their messages — SALOON ... TAVERN ... CAFÉ FRANÇOIS ... ITALIAN CONFECTIONERS ... SALOON ... TAVERN ... SALOON. Trestles set out in front of tents were piled with boots, saddles, gold-washing equipment, mining shirts, bottles and medicine chests, all for sale. Nothing looked familiar, and everything seemed strange.

Then Bill came hurtling out from behind a dray, yelling, "Cap'n, Cap'n!"

He appeared blinded by his rush. Jake grabbed him as he flew by and said, "What is it?"

"Miss Gray ... she run off, sir, off after a Chinese man. She screamed out, Ah Wong! And then she run off after 'im."

Ah Wong. Who the hell was Ah Wong? Jake snapped, "Which way?" — and Bill whirled about and dashed off into the crowd again. He moved like a ferret. Jake was hard put to it to keep up with him, and when he looked over his shoulder Royal was out of sight.

Bill's fleeting feet led the way up the street the lieutenants had called L, and from there onto the trail to Sutter's Fort, where it stood on its inland rise. This road was dryer, because the fort was on a rise, and was almost as crowded as the Embarcadero. Tents were springing up here, too, many of them taverns, saloons, stores, and restaurants, with notices that shouted out the same kinds of blandishments for customers as the structures on the Embarcadero — though one, standing almost under the walls of the fort, bore the enigmatic message GOOD NEWS FOR MINERS. Then they were over the bridge, and almost at the entrance of the fort. But, instead of turning through the gate into the compound, Bill dashed onward, heading for the adobe barracks that stood halfway up the next slope.

In contrast to the Embarcadero and Sutter's Fort, the barracks seemed much emptier than Jake remembered. Last fall, though there had been no soldiers in evidence, there had been a lot of lodgers in the army quarters, and a few horses in the semi-circular corral. Now, the corral appeared quite empty, and no men were leaning on the long, narrow balcony that overlooked the horse enclosure. There was no sign of Harriet on the path that wound past the stout fence that hemmed in the corral, and very few men. Then Jake saw a familiar uniformed figure marching down the path towards him. Bill turned around and came racing back, but Jake stood still.

It was Captain Mervine, looking just as Jake had seen him last — in Monterey, when he had left the frigate *Savannah*. Oddly enough, perhaps because he had been thinking how American this place had become, Jake felt no surprise at seeing the frigate's commander.

Mervine, he noted, was not surprised, either. Instead, he marched right up, stamped to a stop, and barked, "And what do you think of it all, Captain Dexter? Ain't it all amazing? Ain't it a monument to American drive and energy? Tarnation, Captain, I would not have believed it if I had not viewed it myself. I arrived with a small force, after deserters, you understand, two weeks back. This place was quiet enough then, nothing but a few wayfarers at the fort, and what do you see now, huh?"

Jake interrupted, "Have you seen Mrs. Sefton?"

"Missus who?"

"Miss Gray."

"Two ladies, are there? Right uncommon, in these parts. No, I can't say I've seen either."

"I was told she came this way after a Chinese man."

"Chinese? Then that explains it," said Mervine with mysterious disapproval. "Come and have a look for yourself."

And he swerved around, and marched back in the direction he'd come from.

It was the right direction, so Jake followed him. As he came up with the frigate's captain, he heard Mervine grumble, "It's a scandal, and stripe me if it ain't un-American."

It was as if the intervening months since their last conversation hadn't happened, because Mervine appeared to be laboring under much the same grievances.

Jake said cautiously, "It is?"

"Yes, Captain, and never a truer word did I speak. I brought a small force only, caught some deserters right away, had to send 'em back with some of my men to San Francisco to the frigate. And you know why? Because there ain't no soldiers here. The barracks have been taken over, Captain Dexter, the army quarters have been requisitioned by the rancheros and the restaurateurs."

"It was used as a hotel the last time I was here in the fall," Jake pointed out. "So the soldiers didn't have it then, either."

The soldiers, he remembered, had gone to the mines with Colonel Mason, to find out what kind of riches there were really there — the soldiers, that is, that hadn't stayed here to lay out the streets at the Embarcadero.

"Well, now it's full of Chinese coolies, sir, all brought in as indentured labor by the rancheros and the restaurant keepers!" Then Mervine stopped, and barked, "And what d'you think of that, huh?"

Jake looked around, puzzled, because he could see nothing out of the ordinary. The stout high wooden fence of the corral rose up on his left side. Ahead was the entrance to the army building, and above the entrance and the corral, the balcony. There were two tall and weather-beaten characters standing either side of the door to the barracks. Neither of them was Chinese, and neither of them was a soldier.

Then, just as he was about to ask what he was supposed to be looking at, he heard Mervine say, "Did you say Mrs. Sefton? You can't mean Colonel Frank Sefton's wife, for he ain't got one. He's a settler here, done right well, mark my words, he has, but he ain't got a wife."

Jake said carefully, "You know him?"

"Of course I do! Met him twice, at least."

"The big schooner moored down at the Embarcadero was his."

Mervine stared. Then he tut-tutted. "Dearie me," he said. "That was the vessel where I found six deserters from the *Savannah*. Jumped ship right after we dropped anchor in August — I told you about it, I'm sure. Well, turns out they was here, ensconced on that schooner. Found them lounged about below decks as easy as if they had crystal-clear consciences. I arrested them on the spot, sent 'em back to the frigate, and they'll make spread-eagles of 'em all, as an example to the rest. But I thought better of Colonel Sefton than that he employed runaway navy-men."

"Did they have any gold?"

"Gold?" Mervine stared again, and then guffawed. "Nope. They didn't look the lucky sort to me. Worse luck for the United States treasury, too, for I would've confiscated it if they'd had any." Then he said, "Who is this Mrs. Sefton you asked after?"

Jake was glancing all about, his hands clenched with tension. There was no sign of Harriet, and Bill had disappeared, while Royal had made no appearance at all. Where the hell was Harriet?

There were people in the barracks, he abruptly realized — the Chinese coolies? He could hear strange sounds from inside the building, a kind of soft chanting, and his nape crawled with a sense of danger. There was a faint smell in the air, an aura of violence and death, mingled strangely with the smell of burning tobacco.

Mervine was staring at him. Jake said, "Mrs. Sefton is Colonel Sefton's widow."

"What? He's dead? My God," said Mervine. He seemed very shocked. "Truly in the midst of life we are in death, Providence can seize any one of us all. Has he been dead long?"

Jake had to think. "About three weeks," he said. "He died when his house burned down."

"Dearie me." And Mervine clicked his tongue. Then he demanded, "Where is he buried?"

Jake blinked, startled by the question. "I don't know — on his ranch, I suppose."

Then his voice faded, as his thoughts stopped short. He had just glimpsed movement inside the corral. He could see the outline of a well, and the little roof over it, and beside it, on the brown ground, something darker brown moved...

"But that's a scandal," Mervine expostulated. "We'll have to fix that! Do something more decent! He came from a prominent

Philadelphia family!"

Jake hardly heard him. His attention was riveted by the movement in the corral. Then he said, "Oh my God," as the creature stood up on its hind legs. It was a bear, a huge bear. He had to fight the instinct to recoil, despite the stoutness of the fence.

He said, "What the hell is *that* doing there?"

"Terrible, ain't it," said Mervine.

"My God yes." The beast was enormous. He could see the long claws and smell the rank fur. It was like the bear that had menaced Harriet, chased them both. It could have been the same animal.

He said violently, "Why don't you shoot it?"

"Because it ain't mine to shoot," Mervine said in a very cross tone. "It was here when I came, so we couldn't even quarter our horses here, let alone us, ourselves, in our rightful accommodations. The barracks is full of coolies, and the corral's full of bear. Those two men, there, they captured him and brought him here, and only Providence knows how they did it. They put that there bear there, and they keep watch over it to make sure no one interferes with the beast."

Jake looked at the two men again. They were mountain men, judging by their remote, narrowed eyes and the fringes down the seams of their dirty shirts and trousers. They slouched each one against one side of the entrance, and they had long-barreled Kentucky rifles longer than themselves leaning against the wall within reach. Why? In case the bear escaped? Or to shoot any man who might be mad enough to steal it?

"They say they'll get good money for that bear when they sell him," Mervine said. "And who am I to get in the way of American enterprise? Providence knows how they'll get the bear there, but they say that they'll sell him to Don Manuel Vidrie, up the upper Feather..."

But Jake had stopped listening. Harriet had run out onto the balcony — so precipitately that for a ghastly second he had thought she was going to topple over the rail into the corral. She caught herself with both hands on the rail, but in imagination he saw her fall, heard her scream, heard the crunch of terrible jaws.

He cursed under his breath, and shoved past Mervine, past the mountain men and through the entrance, and then through another doorway.

The room beyond was full of Chinese coolies. They were seated about rough deal tables playing some sort of table-top game. Jake heard clapping and weird syllables cried out, "*Aie, aie, san sze!*" The yellow sun slanted in the long, barred windows, and lit up smooth Oriental faces, lips drawn back as the men called out the words. "*Aie, sze ... san!*"

It was like some ancient incantation. Jake's mind was full of incoherent pictures of frigid eastern deserts and the tough little horses warriors like these had ridden. It reminded him of the paintings on old Chinese scrolls of armies going to battle, even though in his mind he knew that these Chinese men were gambling.

Then the sounds trailed off as the coolies saw him. Row by row, the faces turned. But the chanting continued in another room. Jake set himself into a run again.

He called out Harriet's name as he ran. At the front end of the third room he found stairs, narrow stairs, winding steeply up a bastion. He dashed up, round and round, and then spun out onto the balcony, to lurch up to the rail with his momentum, just as Harriet had done.

He caught himself. The bear looked up. It was still standing on its hind legs. Harriet was looking at him wide-eyed. He could hear her fast breathing.

She gasped, "I saw him, Jake. I saw Ah Wong! He was terrified. He shouted at me to run away, run, run, and then he ran away himself. I thought he was dead, but he is alive! I followed him, I'm sure I didn't lose him, I'm sure he came here, but those men down there, they just stared and wouldn't understand me and then they went back to their gaming..."

Jake stopped listening. He reached out and gripped her upper arms with hands that were still shaking, and he said, "Don't ever do that again."

She flinched, and then he saw the anger in her eyes. She said coldly, "I beg your pardon?"

"Don't ever leave the brig without telling me or Charlie Martin where you are going."

"I have to have your permission before I can leave the brig?"

"Yes, if you want to put it like that. But Harriet, I'm just trying to..."

She snapped, "I see."

Then, without waiting for him to explain, she turned, and with head high, with dignity, she walked along the balcony to a doorway that led to another flight of stairs. Jake followed her, feeling helpless, trying to assemble words to explain his intense need to watch over her, to keep her safe from ... from... He wished he knew what.

The Chinese men in the room at the bottom of this second flight of stairs had also been playing their game. Why? What was its attraction? Was it the craze of the moment? Jake had no way of asking. The men watched them walk through the room in open-mouthed silence, their white teeth very big in their small faces.

Mervine was still outside the entrance. He said, thunderstruck, "Miss Gray!"

"Captain Mervine," said Harriet. She inclined her head graciously.

Then Jake saw Royal come up the track.

Just she had at Bedstead Gully, the day the bear had chased them, and ... Harriet ran over to her brother, and put her hand in the crook of his arm. Then she turned and stared challengingly.

Jake shut his eyes. He had never felt so helpless in his life.

SEVEN

HARRIET went to live at Sutter's Fort. She borrowed money from Bodfish, giving him Sefton's half-melted ring as security, and rented lodgings in the house where she'd stayed last autumn. It turned out to be the same room she'd slept in the one night she had stayed here — the night before the morning that Frank Sefton had caught up with her.

Not only was it the same room, but it was the same bed too, and apparently had the same corn-shuck mattress. It was as if time had rolled back. Accordingly, Harriet felt no surprise whatsoever when her old companion in this room, Mrs. Marchant, opened the door and came in.

Mrs. Marchant, however, looked utterly astounded. "Miss Gray!" she cried, and threw out her arms. "So you returned with spring, like a joyous thing!"

"Thank you," said Harriet, rather weakly. While she certainly hadn't forgotten her erstwhile roommate's ebullient figure and abundant black hair, the woman's strange rhyming manner of speech had somehow slipped her mind.

"And how romantic and fitting," the flamboyant lady cried, "that I should be the one to say, Mrs. Sefton, welcome to Sacramento City, today!"

The Embarcadero, it seemed, had grown a new name, along with its uprush of tents. After all, many lesser places had an embarcadero, and even though the Embarcadero at Sutter's had always been graced with a capital E, that wasn't sufficient any more, or so Mrs. Marchant conveyed.

"But pray tell me," she went on in a theatrically hushed tone, "what are you doing here? Where is your husband, the handsome colonel?"

Harriet said demurely, "You can call me Miss Harriet Gray now."

"You have at last escaped from your husband — to the man who had already claimed your heart?"

"Not exactly," Harriet said, adding, "Colonel Sefton is no more."

"He ... has gone away?"

"No. He..."

"To the diggin's, perhaps?"

"Good lord, no!" The idea of the urbane and pompous Colonel Frank Sefton digging for gold in the hills was quite comical.

"Then what, Miss Gray?"

"He's dead."

"*Dead?*" It was a shriek.

"He died when his house caught fire."

"He was burned to *death*?"

"I'm a widow, Mrs. Marchant."

"Merciful heavens," said Mrs. Marchant. It was clear that she was not sure what kind of expression to assume.

She went on rather hesitantly, "You weren't there at the time?"

"No — I was quite a long way away." According to Harriet's reckoning, she would have been passing Don Roberto's fort at the time — or even, perhaps, on the trail to Bedstead Gully.

"Then thank God for that."

Again Mrs. Marchant paused. Harriet could almost hear the questions that were racing around in her head. Then she was saved by the ringing of the bell for the first sitting of the midday dinner.

Just as they had done last autumn, Harriet and Mrs. Marchant went down the outside stairs and walked across the great compound of Sutter's Fort, where men lined up to buy bread from men working at beehive-shaped ovens, and collops of cooked meat from other men with grills set over little fires, while others queued at the well, holding pitchers and pails. In the dining room, the same rows of long deal tables were lined with very similar looking men, who hammered on the tops with their jackknives in just the same way, impatient for their food to come.

The portly form of Mr. King arrived out of the doorway to the kitchen. He stopped and looked around, the lord of all he surveyed — which meant, just like last year, he was making an enormous profit out of selling meals to the lodgers. Then he came over, and greeted Mrs. Marchant affectionately.

Mrs. Marchant said, "You do remember Miss Gray?"

"Of course," he said, though his expression became so vague that it was obvious to Harriet that he didn't remember her at all. He was as avuncular as ever, though, and as talkative.

Booming pleasantries, he escorted them both to a table at the head of the room, which was crossways to all the rest. Chairs were fetched, and Harriet sat down by Mrs. Marchant, with Mr. King on Mrs. Marchant's other side.

Then, for a moment or two, it was impossible for even Mr. King to make himself heard. Men hollered as sweating Chinese cooks carried in huge platters of meat and saucers of molasses, vying to be served first. Down slammed the trays and platters, and suddenly silence reigned, as the men ate with silent voracity, intent on getting as much as possible packed down before the next bell rang to send them off, and signal a second sitting.

Mrs. Marchant said, in a voice that rang out in the uncanny quiet, "Colonel Sefton is dead."

Mr. King blinked. He said, "Colonel Frank Sefton?"

"Yes!"

"Then a mercy on the departed soul," he said. "How did the sad event come about?"

"His house burned down — around his head!"

"Who told you that?"

"Mrs. Sefton." And Mrs. Marchant pointed a dainty finger toward Harriet.

"Mrs. Sefton?" said Mr. King blankly, then looked at Harriet with light dawning in his eyes.

"Yes," said Harriet, and smiled politely. Evidently he had remembered her at last.

He turned to his lady love, and hissed in what he undoubtedly thought of as a whisper, "So why did you call her *Miss Gray*?"

"It's her stage name," said Mrs. Marchant.

"Ah." But Mr. King still looked puzzled. Then, remembering his manners, he put on a somber look and said to Harriet, "My sincerest commiserations."

"I thank you for the kind sentiment."

"Colonel Sefton died when his hacienda caught fire?"

"I'm afraid so," said Harriet.

This, it seemed was even more saddening than the demise of the ranch house's owner. "While I never had the privilege of calling on Colonel Sefton, I heard that the hacienda was quite magnificent," Mr. King said mournfully. "I was told quite often that it was a particularly fine specimen of old Californian architecture. I also believe he owned some very interesting furnishings that he brought with him from the Celestial Kingdom. It is all quite destroyed — all of it?"

"It was a very intense fire, Mr. King."

"A pity ... a pity." Then he cheered up. "But his lands were vast, I believe, truly vast ... And they're now all yours?"

"I'm afraid not."

His smile vanished. "But...?"

"Everything was stolen."

He looked more puzzled than ever. "But..."

"All I own is a plot of land I bought in my own name last autumn."

"But Mrs. Sefton, surely Colonel Sefton's lands — "

"A plot of land here — on the Embarcadero," Harriet said firmly, and then remembered the various name changes. "On Front Street. In Sacramento City," she amended.

This silenced Mr. King, but not for long, as he soon rallied to demand to know the exact whereabouts of this plot.

"Between J Street and K Street, across the Embarcadero from the brig *Gosling*," she said, and he slammed his fist on the table, sending echoes around the vast room.

"Then we are neighbors, Mrs. Sefton!"

"We are?"

Her theater site, she learned, was only two spaces away from the lot he had bought to invest his all in the accommodation business. Mr. King had made an ever-living fortune out of selling one-dollar meals in this dining room, to which he had just added a neat round sum by selling his interest in this business to another man. And now, as he informed her, he was devoting all his time and money to the building of a grand hotel, which he confidently expected would make him an even greater pile.

Harriet said quickly, feeling alarmed, "So who will run the dining room here, Mr. King?"

"The man who has purchased the business from me, Mrs. Sefton!"

"But when will this happen?"

"Tomorrow, Mrs. Sefton! Many people say," he confided in a bellow, "that without a word of a lie my business sense is renowned as infallible — and between you and me I made a nice little profit — a very nice little profit! — from selling out. And I intend to prove those people right, with the building of this hotel!"

"So where will you and Mrs. Marchant be taking your — ?"

"And it will be a grand one," he sailed on. "Such a mighty edifice, you've no idea! We drew up great plans over the winter in

'Frisco, for a hotel that would not disgrace New Orleans — with a veranda, a balcony on the second storey, and the principal rooms below, two of them very spacious — one complete with billiard table, and the other a great dining room, offering epicurean feasts. No more one-dollar meals for me, Mrs. Sefton!"

"So, after tomorrow, will you and Mrs. Marchant — ?"

"Kitchens at the back, of course. To one side there will be three lesser saloons, devoted to gaming, each of which I will let out at the rate of fifteen hundred dollars a month, and not a penny less. And there will be two well-supplied bars, one in the entry, and the other in the billiard room, where I will stock the best liquors the market can supply. I intend to cater for the higher class of client — the drinkers of iced champagne, Mrs. Sefton! And they will have accommodations to suit! Bricks cost forty-five dollars per thousand here, and yet I pay without complaint, for I have great faith in the future of this here Sacramento City."

"Wonderful," said Harriet. "But — "

"I expect to make a net profit of sixty thousand dollars a year from the bar trade alone," he beamed. "I'll provide offices, too — chambers for lawyers, physicians, and money-lenders. The lawyers and physicians are bound to be nothing better than clerks and apothecaries come to reap a fortune, but having an office with a notice on the door will give them credibility, Mrs. Sefton, so they'll pay three hundred dollars a month rental with pleasure. But it's the accommodation business that will be my bread and butter! It will all be on the second floor, with an omnibus apartment for second-class guests, who will pay twenty-five dollars a week, each, twenty dollars extra for two meals a day, and a tier of eighty-dollar staterooms for the superior class, those who have made their piles of gold. With bathrooms!"

"Bathrooms?" Harriet echoed rather wildly.

"Attached to the staterooms, Miss Gray, so my guests won't have to walk down the hall."

"Merciful heavens, how wonderful." She remembered that Mr. King had boasted a great deal about the bathroom furnishings during a very similar conversation last fall.

"With long baths?" she asked, and watched the great entrepreneur lose his ebullience. Even the shine left the ruddy, plump face.

"Long baths are a scarce commodity here," Mr. King mourned. "In fact, I must confess it, I ain't been able to buy a single one, on account of there ain't any to be had."

"Oh dear," she said. Then, grabbing her chance to insert her pressing question, she said, "So where is the man who will be managing this dining room from tomorrow?"

"There he is, Sam Young!" he said, as if she should have known, and flung out an arm to point at a weathered looking miner in stained buckskin trousers and checkered shirt who was lounging the doorway that led to the kitchen, picking his teeth with a straw.

"Oh dear," said Harriet. Sam Young, undoubtedly, was a miner who had done well in the hills, he having the manner as well as the clothes of someone who had spent months at the diggings. Evidently he had the sense to know that catering to the emigrants was going to make a lot of money, and also the intelligence to realize that providing one-dollar meals was probably the extent of his talents.

She said to Mr. King, "But you and Mrs. Marchant will still be eating here?"

"No, of course not," he said, as if the very idea of patronizing the man to whom he had just sold the business was unthinkable. Then, with scarcely a pause, while she was still contemplating this new problem, he asked Harriet how much she had paid for her plot of Sacramento City land.

"One thousand dollars," she said distractedly, and then winced at the enormous price.

"One thou'?" Mr. King looked very thoughtful. "I wouldn't mind a look at it, I wouldn't."

"I intend to look at it myself," Harriet said — which was exactly right, as she planned to set out for the Embarcadero and the brig as soon as she could escape from this unpleasant dining room and this disturbing conversation. Not only was it her turn to sit with Davy, but she needed to talk to Bodfish. And looking at her property on the way might bolster her rapidly descending spirits, she thought.

A bell rang, and bedlam broke out again, as all the men stood up in a crashing of boots and benches. Chinese stewards rushed into the room with trays and cloths, hurrying to clear the tables and wipe them down before the next sitting stormed in. Harriet, drawn along by Mr. King's hand on her elbow, joined the mass exodus into the courtyard, then through the big, square gateway with its overhanging wooden portcullis.

Two motes in a torrent of men, they fought their way along the packed road that led downhill to the Sacramento River and the

Embarcadero, while Mr. King talked on about his plans. But, though he was bellowing right in her ear, Harriet hardly heard a word he said.

Instead, her mind was fully preoccupied with the unpleasant fact that eating in the dining room at the fort was no longer an option for her. She doubted that Sam Young was any kind of chef, but that wasn't the problem, because it was very likely that the Chinese cooks would carry on as if there had been no change in ownership. The unpalatable fact was that without Mrs. Marchant to keep her company, she would be the only female in the room. And, while she might be just an actress, and was probably considered by many to be an adventuress, too, even she couldn't commit that kind of impropriety — even to defy Jake Dexter.

Then, she was distracted. As they passed a solid-looking square tent with a notice blaring GOOD NEWS FOR MINERS over the front, to her surprise she recognized Mr. Giles. The front flaps were drawn back, so she could see the journalist standing by an ancient-looking printing press. Even more intriguingly, Bill the steerage boy was with him, and they were talking animatedly as they both peered into a shallow tray that undoubtedly held type. What the devil were they up to?

However, she didn't draw Mr. King over to introduce him to the printer, or to ask Bill what he was doing. Instead, she kept on walking.

EIGHT

THE changes in California, declaimed Mr. King, were beyond human comprehension.

And they were indeed, thought Harriet silently, listening at last. At the bottom of the road, where it suddenly became L Street, some men were building fences by the simple but smelly means of stretching wires and then hanging half-cured hides from them. They were enclosing a space for a corral, or so said Mr. King. But why a corral, right here? Because there was a bear in the army corral, Harriet supposed with a shiver.

As Mr. King was swift to expound, the corral at the barracks wouldn't have been big enough, anyway, because this here corral was being built in response to a sudden huge demand. Mules were arriving in abundance, and needed somewhere to be stowed. They had been brought in by the men who'd come overland, but who couldn't afford to keep them any more — not at the rate of five dollars a day for forage. The mule traders who were building this corral bought up the pack beasts for the sum of fifty dollars each, and then either sold them on at the base rate of sixty dollars, or fattened them with the view of an even higher profit later. This, it seemed, was yet another of the multitudinous ways of making a fortune out of California.

"Merciful heavens," said Harriet, and wondered if the extempore enclosure would ever be replaced by a proper corral, with proper stables. Probably not, she mused, land being so valuable here. Would another year see a hotel on this site — or even a mansion? An arcade of stores? A rival theater?

The Embarcadero was busier than ever, packed with hurrying men, many riding horses or mules, others striding about on foot. Carters hollered, and whistled deafeningly for the crowd to make way, and there were mule trains, too, so Harriet had to step carefully to avoid piles of steaming manure. Heaps of lumber and bricks were piled here and there on the riverside edge of the promenade, and the air rang with hammering and sawing as calico tents were replaced with stone and clapboard buildings. New ventures were springing up by the hour.

Here, it was easy to see why Mr. King had decided to sell off his interest in the catering trade, simply because there was so much competition. Cafes, taverns, and restaurants were mushrooming everywhere, with bold notices proclaiming fanciful names — TONTINE'S, THE ALHAMBRA, JACKSON'S, KEARNEY'S CAFÉ. Vendors of coffee, cakes and sweetmeats had set up stands under the magnificent old trees, to tempt the appetites of men who had just arrived up the river, or miners who had come down from the mountains. Harriet saw one establishment that was the most ad lib yet, being a mere roof made of branches with the leaves still attached, with two long tables set out underneath, four benches made of logs for the customers to sit on, and a log at the back that was stacked bottles of various lurid-looking liquors, and which served as a bar. But it did have a name — PADDY'S.

Some of the restaurants had dead wild fowl strung up over the door, still wearing their spectacular plumage, while others suspended quarters of young elks, or portions of bear, as an even more exotic enticement. And they all had slates propped by their doors, advertising tempting menus. SOUPS, offered one, with a choice of Mock Turtle soup at seventy-five cents a bowl, or St. Julian for one dollar. Salmon — presumably straight out of the river — cost one dollar, seventy-five cents, while customers with less epicurean tastes could feast on mutton with caper sauce, or corned beef with cabbage, for the price of just one dollar.

An excellent fillet steak of beef, garnished with potatoes, with mushroom sauce and a cup of good coffee or chocolate, would be just one dollar in total, Harriet saw. It would be easy enough for her to get three good meals a day, she thought wryly — if it was respectable for a woman to dine alone, which it wasn't, and if she had money to pay for it, which she didn't. So which of these restaurants did Mr. King intend to patronize? Harriet meditated that if she knew which one, and could borrow some more cash from Bodfish...

But she didn't have a chance to ask.

Her escort bellowed, "Do you remember a settlement on a bend in the river what was called New York of the Pacific?"

Harriet blinked. New York of the Pacific? Then she remembered the poor place, and how funny she and Royal had found it. The grandly misnamed settlement was fifty miles upstream of San

Francisco Bay, located on a level plain, and backed by a range of barren mountains. When the brig had glided past it on the upriver voyage to Sutter's, last August, this New York of the west had been composed of two huts and two grounded riverboats.

She said, "Is it still plagued with mosquitoes?"

"You wouldn't believe it now!' Mr. King exclaimed, with his usual facility for ignoring her questions. "Seven big ships a-moored there now, most of 'em whalers gone into the boarding trade. There's even a post office! — in a building called the Junction Post Office! And there's a large hotel a-building there, too, made out of the heaps of brick and lumber which right now are all heaped up on the bank of the river."

"Merciful heavens," Harriet said. She couldn't conceive of a single reason why the town should flourish.

"Like all of this here California, New York of the Pacific is goin' ahead with railroad speed!" Mr. King assured her. "And all because of the steamboats. They're shipping them around the Horn, you know, and assembling them in 'Frisco. Sturdy enough to withstand the choppy waters of San Francisco Bay, but small enough to navigate the river."

"Steamboats?" said Harriet. So, she thought, events would have soon spelled an end to Frank Sefton's grand plans for making a fortune out of ferrying men up and down the river in his schooner — the same schooner that was now lying, mysteriously deserted, at the Embarcadero.

"Steamboats," confirmed Mr. King. "The steamers will call regularly into New York of the Pacific to wood up — to fuel their engines, you understand. And so the wooders who have claimed preemption rights to the timber are chopping down the trees, in readiness for the great trade. They expect to get between twelve and fifteen dollars a cord!"

"Oh dear," said Harriet, feeling shocked and sad. She remembered the great oak and sycamore trees that lined the Sacramento River, and how they had framed spectacular glimpses of distant mountains. She remembered, too, how the foliage had glistened when it was washed with rain. But now, she deduced, that grand landscape was about to be fatally ravaged.

"This be the land of progress, Miss Gray!"

"So it seems, Mr. King."

Then, she felt him grip her upper arm, as he drew her across the road to a place nearly opposite the landing. Then he urged her to a stop — to gaze at a patch of land with posts sticking out of the mud. This, Harriet realized, was nothing less than the beginnings of Mr. King's hotel.

Mr. King showed her over the site, as proud as Punchinello. "Piles for the foundations," he pointed out, beaming. Many of the foundations were the stumps of trees that had been felled to make way for the great hotel, which was odd enough, Harriet thought. Naturally, though, she kept a tactful silence — and then, moving a little further on, they arrived at the theater site.

The patch of mud was trampled and littered with stray rubbish, but otherwise was empty — except for three young men who were earnestly digging up the dirt. They wore city suits and patent leather boots, and they had shining bright trowels with varnished mahogany handles, and they were most definitely panning for gold.

For a while they refused to believe that the land was owned by anyone at all, let alone a female, particularly one who found what they were doing so amusing. But luckily Harriet's stake and notice were still there, and so they were forced to pack up and move off.

Then, as they trailed away, Harriet realized that Mr. King was breathing heavily.

"Building lots at New York of the Pacific are going for five hundred dollars," he meditated aloud. "Tell you what," he went on, lowering his voice to what he doubtlessly regarded as a mutter. "I'll give you two thou' for it."

She stared, amazed. When she didn't reply, he nudged her with a salacious elbow, winked, and said, "Or p'raps I should convey my offer to Cap'n Dexter. What do you reckon, sir?" he demanded in his usual bellow — but Harriet had already known that Jake Dexter had joined them, because of the warm tingle in the back of her neck.

Jake didn't look at Mr. King. Instead, he looked at her with his wry eyebrows slanted.

He said, "Harriet?"

She said quickly, "Is Davy...?"

"Davy is alive. He's just the same. He — "

Mr. King roared, "Captain Dexter, I'm right glad to see you!"

With every appearance of disbelief, Jake said, "You are?"

"I've been making this little gal an offer, sir, but she don't pay attention, wimmen not having the head for business that men do. Three!" he roared.

"I beg your pardon?"

"Three thousand, for this little bit of land here."

"Three?" Jake blinked, and turned and looked at the theatrical lot.

Judging by his expression, it was the first time he had looked at it properly. While Harriet and Mr. King watched, he stepped onto it, and paced out the boundaries. Then, after crouching to study the tattered notice, he stood in the middle and looked up and down the Embarcadero.

His expression was so assessing that Harriet looked around herself, but the landing looked just the same as it had when they arrived. There was the same crowd pressing back and forth, as busy and rowdy as ever. Many of the men were gathered under the big trees that lined the waterfront. These ones, the ones on the Embarcadero in front of the junction of Front Street and J Street, had been spared for a particular duty, which was luggage stowage. Bags hung down from the branches like exotic fruit. Perhaps, Harriet thought, the first luggage had been hung there to keep it out of the way of boots and hooves, and when it had turned out to be as safe there from robbers as it was from being trampled, hanging one's property in trees had turned into a local custom. Or was someone raking a huge profit from renting out the branches? That, she thought, wouldn't surprise her at all.

Jake arrived back from his survey, but before he could open his mouth, Mr. King gave him one of his meaningful nudges.

"Beautiful woman, lovely," he said, in what he perhaps thought of as a conspiratorial whisper.

Jake pushed back his hat and studied Harriet in much the same way he had studied her piece of land, while she scowled back at him, irritated into meeting his bright hazel-green eyes.

Then he looked back at Mr. King and said in a matter-of-fact sort of voice, "Yes, she is."

"A woman is worth her weight in rubies, I allus say."

"Or gold dust."

"True, Captain Dexter, very true. It's the prime disadvantage to this Sacramento City, the mournful lack of women. A widder here is not a widder long. It's the washing, you know."

"The ...?"

"The laundry. The merchants in 'Frisco were paying one dollar a piece to have their washing done when we was there this last winter — one dollar! Per piece! Can you credit that, sir? Many a man who has failed to wash out a fortune at the diggin's has found that his wife has washed out a fortune for them both."

Mr. King laughed immoderately at his little jest, and then said, "Four thousand."

"I beg your pardon?"

"For that land. A four-fold profit. Why not grab it?"

"Or why not think about it?" said Jake dryly. "Who knows what it'll be worth if I wait a week? Or even just one hour?"

"But can you afford to wait? Surely you don't intend to build! Do you know how much that hotel over there will cost me? One hundred thousand and not a cent less. I don't do things by halves, I don't. Tell you what, I'll give you five."

Jake was silent, looking about again, while Harriet gazed at him, fraught. She knew, she *knew,* that a huge profit could be made from a theater, and she had no idea what she would do if he sold the land. But, if he did take the offer and accept the cash, the *Gosling* Company would make a small profit from her purchase, which was a lot better than a loss.

Then Jake looked back at Mr. King and said, "No."

"No?" Mr. King echoed in tones of great astonishment. "You say no, and don't even take the time to ponder? Reconsider, Captain, reconsider!"

"No," said Jake, and shook his head. "I've made up my mind to build a theater."

NINE

LATE that same afternoon, Jake was relaxing in his transom cabin with a glass of brandy when there was a knock at the door that led from his private quarters to the mess cabin.

The door opened when he called out, to reveal Bodfish, who was wearing a most peculiar expression. The steward always made a magisterial figure, with his bald head and sheeplike whiskers, but his long face conveyed unusually deep disapproval.

Jake, immediately curious, said, "Yes?"

"You have a visitor, sir," said Bodfish with a sniff.

Who the hell? King, Jake supposed, come to renew his offer for the piece of land Harriet had so unwisely bought last fall.

He sighed, and said, "From shore?"

"No, sir. A supplicant."

"A — *what?*"

"A member of the *Gosling* Company, Captain Dexter."

Jake frowned. "Not Mr. Martin?" Charlie Martin, as his first mate, didn't need any ushering in by the steward, and would only bother him at this time of day if there was trouble with the crew that he couldn't sort out by himself.

Bodfish cleared his throat with a harrumph, and said, "It's Miss Gray, Captain."

Harriet? Jake's brows shot up. It was indeed an unexpected pleasure for Harriet to seek out his company — but that was surely no reason for Bodfish to be so stuffy about it?

As neutrally as he could, he said, "Then send her in."

Harriet, obviously, had been hovering about behind Bodfish, because she came in right away. She didn't look like any kind of supplicant, being flushed and rebellious.

What the devil, Jake wondered, had she done to offend Bodfish? The steward, however, said nothing more, merely heading back to the mess cabin.

Jake said, "Harriet?"

She was delivering an inimical look at Bodfish's retreating back.

When the steward closed the door with a loud snap, she turned, and said, "Yes."

Her tone wasn't friendly in the slightest. Jake said, "What have you done now, Harriet?"

"Nothing!" Her dark eyes flashed at him, but just as quickly she looked away. When he told her to take a seat, she perched on the edge of the chair at his chart desk as if ready to make a bolt for it.

There was a long silence, while he waited, and she gazed down at her hands folded in her lap, and he watched the the wayward tumble of her hair down her bent neck, sensual awareness coiling inside him. She was up to something. He could feel it in his bones.

Then she looked up with one of her most radiant smiles — which definitely meant she was being devious — and said, "You're really determined to build a theater?"

"That's what the Company voted."

"But you said to Mr. King that you're determined to build one! So you see the commercial sense of it now? That I wasn't really so stupid when I invested in that lot of land?"

In truth, he still thought it was a brainless purchase. One good survey of the terrain had been enough to convince him of that. The Company had voted to build a theater, though, and in this case he was happy to bide by their majority decision. However, he couldn't resist drawing her out, as any emotion, even anger, was better than being coldly ignored.

He drawled, "Isn't the Embarcadero rather muddy for a theater?"

"It was muddier last autumn."

"And is going to be under water," Jake mused on. He sipped brandy with a judicious air. "The street being lower than the level of the river, flooding is inevitable."

"Lower than the river?" Her expression went blank.

"Look for yourself," he invited, but he was only being rhetorical, because when she looked up at the wide gallery of stern windows behind the sofa where he sat, the river vista was hidden by the hulls and rigging of the vessels that were moored behind the *Gosling*.

Jake said, "A week of solid rain, and every single building on the Embarcadero is doomed."

"Surely not," she said, dismayed.

"If the river floods the way it did last winter, this so-called Sacramento City will be twelve feet under water by December."

"Oh!" she said, and smiled. "No pantomimes, then."

"Pantomimes?' Jake blinked, and then remembered his conversation with Giles. Harriet in tights as Principal Boy... Again, that tug of sensuality, bringing a memory of what her body felt like, under his...

She said, "Pantomimes are traditional at Christmas. But," she added musingly, "if the theater is twelve feet underwater..."

Christmas in Sacramento City? It was impossible to imagine. Last December, Jake and the *Gosling* prospecting party had been living out the winter in the log cabin they had built at Bedstead Gully. They hadn't even noticed Christmas Day passing, not until a couple of days later, when someone had pointed it out.

"With luck, the theater will be high and dry," he said, relenting. "All that's needed is for this city to get some levees."

"Levees?"

"Of course," said Jake. "With levees, this city has a great future."

"But won't that be expensive? And who will build them?"

"The city fathers, of course — once Sacramento City has voted in a crew of city fathers, which I bet will happen before the end of summer."

"You've been talking politics," she accused.

"Of course. Apart from gold, politics is the major topic of conversation around here. Men who understand the potential of Sacramento City will line up to be voted in."

"Then they will certainly understand the potential of a theater!" she exclaimed, her dark eyes sparkling.

"Well, the men were actually talking about the potential of Sacramento City as a river port," he said, and then became enthusiastic. "Just today, I counted between fifty and sixty sail of vessels at or off the Embarcadero. And men told me that steamboats will be plying the route from here to San Francisco within weeks, if not days."

"I've heard that, too."

"From whom?" he demanded at once.

"Mr. King told me — if it is any of your business."

King. Of course. Jake shut his eyes briefly, wishing he had kept his mouth shut, then decided it was high time he took control of this conversation.

He said, "Why did you want to see me, Harriet?"

She flushed, and snapped, "Bodfish made me!"

So she and the sniffish old steward had been fighting, he realized, though it must have been in mutters, because he hadn't heard a thing.

He said, "Why?" — and waited in some suspense, but instead of answering she changed the subject yet again, with yet another brilliant smile.

"You're reading Captain Schouten's book," she said.

Jake looked down at the old journal on his knee. The original owner of the scrapbook had been the builder and owner of the brig, a gold-seeking pirate by the name of Schouten. Jake had found the book in a secret drawer when he had torn down the fancy mahogany bookcases in the mess cabin, and had become instantly fascinated by the strange collection of tales, all to do with pirate gold, that Schouten had copied into this journal in his precise, old-fashioned hand.

They were enticing tales, too, many with hints and clues for the whereabouts of treasure, others with ideas of unusual ways to turn a profit. What strange adventures he'd had because of this book, he thought, one of the strangest having been the hunt for Henry Morgan's lost treasure on Judas Island. That search had turned up nothing but old, old skeletons, but other quests had been quite lucrative.

Then he was brought out of the brief reverie. Harriet said, "Why did you put that book in my basket, before Sefton took me away?"

Why? His brows slanted. It had been an impulse, one that had come quite unexpectedly, in the midst of his rage and hurt when he had found out that Harriet had forgotten to inform him that she was married. Now, his actions after he had learned that Sefton was on the way to the Embarcadero to claim his wife were a blur, partly because he had got drunk, and partly because of his fury.

He remembered stalking through the passage to the companionway to deck and seeing one of the two champagne baskets Harriet used for luggage standing by the door. He'd had this journal in his hand — why? Jake couldn't remember. And he couldn't remember why he had opened the basket and slid the book into it, either. He had done it without premeditation, and with no apparent motive.

So he merely shook his head, and sipped brandy.

"Because it was very kind of you," she said soberly. "Reading it saved my sanity, I think."

He was surprised. "You read it often?"

"Every day, while I was living the Vidrie mansion. You know

that Sefton sent me there, almost as soon as I arrived at his hacienda? The women observed siesta, you understand — not that they napped. They simply gathered together in one of the bedrooms, and gossiped and primped. Not my bedroom, never," she said broodingly. "I sat alone, in my own room. It wasn't considered proper to go out, so I was — trapped there, I suppose. In the mornings — except for Sundays and holidays, when we all went to the chapel in the pueblo — I went riding, and in the late afternoons I walked in the garden. And in the early afternoons, in siesta time, I sat in my room with Captain Schouten."

Jake paused, watching her, remembering how they had pored over this book together while on passage from Judas Island to Valparaiso, and then from Valparaiso to Tombez. That was when he'd started to fall in love with her — and that, he realized now, was why he had surreptitiously given her the journal. It had been the link to her that he needed, despite his fury at her deception.

He finally said, "You must have been very lonely."

"Very lonely." She nodded emphatically. "But Captain Schouten was good company."

"I'm glad."

"But then Sefton stole the journal."

Jake frowned. "How?"

"He paid only two visits to Don Manuel's hacienda, and on the second visit he caught me reading the book. I tried to hide it, but the next morning I found it was gone. He must have stolen it in the night."

In the night. Jealousy stabbed hard.

"I didn't hear him creep into my room, but that must have been what happened. I made him return it, though, which is very lucky, as otherwise it would have been burned in the fire, along with all my clothes," she said. "Returning it was one of the two conditions I made before I agreed to sign for those shares in his bank."

Those goddamned shares, which had given Sefton the pseudo-legal right to confiscate the twenty thousand dollars' worth of gold that rightfully belonged to the *Gosling* Company.

He said, "And what was the other condition?"

"That he should return the deed to the land over there." She jerked her head in the direction of the Embarcadero. "The land I bought for my theater."

The theater. Jake's lips tightened. Always, the conversation returned to her theater.

He said sharply, "Why were you and Bodfish arguing?"

Her dark eyes flashed. "He refused to lend me some money."

"Money? Again?" Jake winced. "What for, this time?"

"And he told me that you gave him the money I had borrowed for the room at the Fort, so it is you I owe the money to, now," she said, more angry than ever. "I wish you hadn't done it, and I can't pay you back until the theater gets going, so here's the collateral, which I made Bodfish give me back."

Collateral? Jake frowned, puzzled, and then saw the lump of gold that she was holding out to him.

He took it, and looked at it. "Where did you get this?"

"It's a ring, only it's half-melted. It was taken off Sefton's corpse. That's how he was identified, by this ring he always wore," she said. Then she added meditatively, "I suppose they had to chip it off."

"Oh my God," said Jake. He reached across and opened one of the drawers in the chart desk, and threw the ring inside with some force. Then, slamming the drawer shut, he said, "Why do you need more money?"

"For food!"

"*What?*"

"Meals used to be included in the boarding price at Sutter's Fort, but they aren't any more, as Mr. King has sold the catering business. So I was going to find out which restaurant he and Mrs. Marchant are going to patronize, and buy meals there at the same time that they did. But when I told Bodfish about it, he was furious! He said it was an aspersion on the good food he sets on the cabin table!"

Jake opened his mouth to bark at her, but then amusement took over, and he said, "The poor fellow."

"*Poor?* He was rude to me!"

"You insulted him greatly."

"He was stuffy about it! He said my rightful place is here, on the brig, and he said you would say the same."

Jake paused to sip more brandy, while he contemplated her cautiously. Bodfish was absolutely right, because he would certainly say the same, but Harriet had fire in her eye.

Finally he said, "So that's why you're here — to find out what I would say?"

"There's no point in that," she said with spirit. "Because I know exactly what you would say."

"So," he said with a knowing grin, "you've come to ask if you could please have your meals on the brig?"

"Jake Dexter, you're the most infuriating — "

"You don't need to ask, Harriet," he said. "The pleasure is yours by right."

And with wonderful timing, Bodfish tapped on the door, first to announce supper, and then to add firmly that he had set a place for Miss Gray. As usual, thought Jake as he rose to his feet, the old steward had been eavesdropping.

TEN

NEXT day, Jake Dexter had just returned to his transom cabin from dressing Davy's head when there was yet another tap on the door that led to the mess cabin.

And again it was Bodfish, who cleared his throat and then said, "You have another visitor, sir."

Jake felt surprised, as he had noticed nothing unusual at either supper the night before or at breakfast that morning. Harriet had been rather silent, and her glances at both him and Bodfish had been resentful, but that was just as he had expected.

He said, "Miss Gray, again?"

"It's Bill, sir."

"With Mr. Martin gripping his ear?"

Charlie was as capable as Jake was of giving the boy a swat over the breeches, but sometimes Bill's crimes were too great for such minor punishment. Not only was he inconveniently intelligent, but his mischief could be astoundingly inventive, so Jake waited in some suspense.

"No, sir," said the steward, his expression rather odd. "Bill asked for you himself — on a very important personal matter, or so he conveyed to me."

"Good lord," said Jake. "Send him in."

Bodfish went out, and pushed the boy inside. Then the door shut, leaving Captain Dexter alone with the youngest member of the crew.

Most unusually, Bill was clean and tidy, with his hair brushed. Jake said in his most forbidding tone, "Yes?"

Bill said brightly, "I want to leave the brig, sir."

"You do?" Jake thoughtfully considered the young Polynesian face with its oddly blue eyes. "I suppose you have a good reason?"

"Oh yes, sir. A very good reason, sir. I have plans."

That word *plans* was spoken with great emphasis. Jake snapped, "Not to go prospecting in the hills, I hope, because I won't allow it."

"Oh no, sir. I have much greater ambitions than that."

"You have?" Jake's eyebrows shot up. Digging a fortune in the hills was the greatest ambition of any man or boy in these parts, as far as he could tell.

"Yes, sir. I have great ambitions to be a scrivener."

"A ... *what?*"

"Mr. Giles has offered me a position as a printer's devil, sir, and he assures me that once I've served my time and become a journeyman printer, the world is my oyster, sir."

"Oyster?" echoed Jake, feeling even more astonished.

"The world will be my oyster, sir," repeated Bill. "Shakespeare said it first, or so Royal Gray told me, and he knows Shakespeare inside and out, like no other man living. And he assured me that it means that my future will be glowing and bright. Once I am a journeyman printer, I can call myself a scrivener, he says. Which means I can write stories, and see them printed on paper. Then I will become famous."

"You will?" said Jake. Then, abruptly remembering some of the adventures of the *Goslings* while Bill had been on board, he said suspiciously, "What stories?"

"Stories of adventures, sir," said Bill, confirming Jake Dexter's fears, but then went on, "The stories men have told me here are more marvelous than anything I have ever read, sir, even better than *Robinson Crusoe*, sir, and truly beg to be put down in print. Mr. Giles says that the stories of the California gold rush will equal the stories of the Great Crusades in their magnitude and peril and adventure, sir, when people get to read them."

Good lord, thought Jake. "And," he inquired, "you reckon you're going to be the fellow who becomes famous by writing these gold rush stories that are bound to become legend?"

"Only if Mr. Giles doesn't beat me to them all, sir. He's already beaten me to the story about the company of miners who spent one hundred and four days at sea, the passage round Cape Horn being so uncommon arduous. When they finally run into San Diego, they voted to sell their ship, being so very tired of their voyage, and headed this way on foot. They walked the whole length of the Californian Peninsula, just because they were tired of the sea, imagine that, sir!"

Jake thought he didn't want to even try to imagine it. Instead, he said, "He's published this story already?"

"Aye, sir, and it has been printed in New York, too, or so he told me. But," said Bill with great animation, "I don't think he's talked yet with the poor fellows who came the Gila route, over the Great Desert to the west of the Colorado River. Do you know that their path was marked out by the bones and corpses of those who had come that way before? Hundreds of mules, all dry and rotting, and the bodies of humans, too, lying half-buried in the sand."

"Oh, dear Jehovah," said Jake.

"So will you let me go, sir? What do you think?"

"What I think," said Jake Dexter very firmly, "is that I need a talk with Mr. Giles. Alone," he added, even more sternly. "I'm sure Mr. Martin can find something for you to do while I'm gone."

As Jake walked along Front Street, he had to push through a group of men who were gawping at the sight of a small Italian with a barrel organ and a performing monkey. It was as if they had never seen a Savoyard before. As for his monkey, the animal was such a novelty that the cup it carried around was soon filled with coins and little lumps of gold. Columbine and Pierrot, Jake thought, remembering his conversation with Giles in Pueblo San Marco. They would do equally well here — for hadn't Giles said that the old comedy was Italian in origin?

Another crowd was gathered about an itinerant artist who sat at an easel and sketched the scene. The men were paying five dollars — or the equivalent — to have their faces drawn in with the rest. As Jake watched, the artist finished the painting with a flourish, then auctioned it off for a little bag of gold dust. This was the entrepreneurial spirit of California, he thought, as he shook his head in wonder.

And suddenly, completely without expecting it, he felt convinced that Harriet's theater was bound to do well. That he wasn't staying here in Sacramento for the wrong reasons, after all.

Giles's tent was a good walk away, being set under the walls of Sutter's Fort. It was a more solid affair than most, square in shape, erected on substantial poles, and covered with a double layer of calico cloth. Once Jake ducked under the notice over the entrance that read GOOD NEWS FOR MINERS, he found a surprisingly tidy scene. Even larger on the inside than it had looked from the outside, the structure housed a cot, a table with a couple of chairs, several small crates that served as benches, and a stout wooden contraption.

This last was in the form of a squat scaffold, with a narrow table top projecting from it, which stood on a couple of narrow legs. At the scaffold end, there was an iron plate and a press with a handle.

Giles was standing over the table part of this machine in a slouched, contemplative sort of attitude, a glass of brandy held in one inky hand, and the handle of an ink-drenched mop in the other. With every appearance of deep concentration, he was studying the contents of a shallow box.

"Captain Dexter," he hailed, without looking round. "I'm told you're going to build a theater."

"I am," Jake acknowledged.

"Aha." The printer straightened and turned, looking animated. "You'll be needing posters printed — not to mention programs, and broadsides, and tickets."

"Will I?" said Jake. With a wince, he remembered the parlous state of the *Gosling* Company's finances — which meant he would have to stump up the money himself. How much was Harriet's hankering to establish a theater going to cost him?

"My rates are very reasonable, I do assure you of that, Captain Dexter. I print tickets at the rate of just twenty dollars per thousand, and programs and posters in proportion. And of course I publish advertisements in my paper, also at very reasonable rates. Join me in a drink."

Jake accepted a glass. However, he firmly declined to discuss printing tickets and placing advertisements, saying it was far too early to put his mind to something he had just thought about for the first time. Instead, he walked over to the contraption and studied it with interest.

It was a printing press, he deduced, partly because the shallow box held columns of metal letters. "Front page of this week's edition of the *Placer Times*," Giles confirmed. "The banner head looks a trifle rough, perhaps, but I had to carve it myself, with a pen knife, out of wood."

"It looks fine to me," said Jake, though it was hard to tell, the flourishing letters being inside-out.

"This issue contains a sensational story, Captain Dexter, one that has only just come to my attention. Would you like to hear it?"

Jake lifted his glass and sipped brandy, at the same time wondering if Giles had beaten Bill to the story of the corpses and bones on the Gila Trail. He said, "If it saves me buying a newspaper, why not?"

"Why not, indeed? You remember Colonel Mason and his news of the gold, which was supposed to bring American hordes to California, and dilute the Spanish population?"

"Of course I do — and I believe the ruse worked."

"Well, sir, the good colonel and his retinue took passage to Panama on a steamer. During the passage, one of his corps heard two of the seamen discussing something in low voices, and one of the sailors said in meaningful tones, *Half past one.*"

"The time when the watch changed?" Jake guessed, feeling some seamanlike interest. "They were at the helm, perhaps?"

"You would know better than I do, Captain Dexter," Giles conceded. "But when the mysterious *half past one* was talked over in the cabin, they all jumped to the conclusion that the sailors were going to stage an insurrection at that hour of the night. So Colonel Mason organized the passengers into two parties, and muskets and pistols were handed out, along with a bottle for courage."

"That can't be the truth," said Jake, with a shout of laughter.

"I assure you I heard it from an excellent source, Captain Dexter."

"Then it must be so, incredible as it seems. How many passengers were there?"

"Sixty."

"And how many seamen?"

"Five."

"And the captain? And a couple of mates? That adds up to eight — against a force of sixty?"

"I told you it was amusing, Captain Dexter. But to continue with the story, Colonel Mason's party took the first watch. One of the sailors spied the colonel as he sat on the quarter deck with a double-barrel gun at his side and a cavalry sword beneath his cloak, and *he* jumped to the conclusion that the passengers were about to take over the ship. So he and the four other seamen shut themselves up in the forecastle to save their skins, which left the two mates to steer the steamer — under sail, of course, all the fuel having been used up."

"And?" said Jake, riveted.

"In the morning the farce became apparent to all, and the captain, who had been sleeping soundly throughout the affair, took charge, and steered the steamer into port."

"Good lord," said Jake, and looked at the box of type again, marveling that all this sensational stuff should be encapsulated in just a few mysterious columns of metal. There was a wonderful kind of miracle involved in the creation of a newspaper, he decided.

"That tray is called a coffin. Did you know that?"

Jake tipped back his hat, and studied the tray more closely, because he hadn't known that at all. These letters were all as backward and inside-out as the banner head, like letters seen in a mirror. And how did those letters get onto paper? With the press, he deduced.

Standing back to contemplate the contraption in all its solid glory, he said with some awe, "How the hell did you get that machine here?"

"By ship, Captain Dexter. How else?" Giles sat down at the table, and waved Jake to the other chair, and they saluted each other and drank again.

"It was a schooner, actually, and a rather small one," the printer amended. "The *Dice me Nana.*"

"I wonder what that means?"

"So do I, Captain Dexter — but it got the press safely here from 'Frisco. It's a Ramage," Giles elaborated.

"The press?"

"Ramage had a printing press workshop in Philadelphia. He made American printing presses famous."

"So how did you get this press to California?"

"I found it in San Francisco, Captain Dexter, in the office that was vacated when the staff of the *Alta California* took themselves off to the mines. No one was using it, and it was in a damaged state, anyway, and after I appropriated it I put it in the charge of the captain of the *Dice me Nana*, and he duly delivered it to the fort, where Captain Sutter kindly stored it until I arrived. Then I retrieved it and fixed it up, and here it is."

"So why didn't you come with it?"

"Aha." Giles contemplated his glass, and brushed his moustaches. "Chaffey had that letter of introduction to Colonel Francis Sefton, and when he invited me along I accepted without a hint of hesitation, sir, even though it meant I had to make hasty arrangements for the transport of this here press. As I've already told you, I'd had some previous acquaintance with Colonel Francis Sefton, and I was mighty curious to see what he was up to in California."

"You saw a story in it," Jake guessed.

"Exactly. And I will travel far, sir, when I scent a story."

"So what did you have loaded on your mule?" Jake asked curiously. When he had seen the miserable animal in Pueblo San Marco, it had been well weighed down.

"Cases of type, paper, ink." Giles shrugged. "The type came from the *Alta California* office, too, but it is expensive and irreplaceable, Captain Dexter. Once I had hold of it, I couldn't afford to let it out of my sight — men steal it, you know, to melt down the lead for bullets for their guns. Imagine, legendary prose melted down to be fired at some harmless bird or beast!"

Jake couldn't imagine that, either, so he sipped more brandy, while he mused that Giles was better organized than he looked.

"So to what do I owe the honor of your company, Captain Dexter?" asked the printer, adding meaningfully, "Since you're not prepared to talk business yet."

"My steerage boy, Bill, reckons you have offered him a job."

"I have indeed."

"But why?"

"I need someone to dampen the paper before I feed it into the press, Captain Dexter, and a multitude of other things. In short, I need a printer's devil. I can't do it all myself, the life of a printer being not being an easy one." Giles drank brandy, and then waved the glass at Jake, and said, "Is the lad strong?"

"He's hauled quite a few lines over the past two years."

"Two years? That's how long you've had him on board?"

"Aye. We took him on at Capricorn Island, in the eastern Pacific. His real name is Wahamu," Jake added.

"He's a Kanaka?"

"Half-Polynesian. His father was a Yankee beachcomber and his mother was a girl who'd somehow got to the island from Tahiti. As far as I know, the girl died when Wahamu was about seven. The boy's father jumped his responsibilities by joining the crew of the next Yankee whaler to drop anchor in the lagoon, so the local mission was left to look after the boy. That's when his name was changed to Bill. And that is where I found him."

"Two years ago? He must have been — what? Ten? Eleven?"

"Who knows? Whatever, the missionary couple begged me to ship him, as a favor."

And Jake had agreed. Not only had he felt sorry for the elderly couple, but he had needed a cabin boy. It had taken only a couple of weeks to understand why the missionaries had been so desperate to get rid of Bill, but he decided to keep quiet about that.

"Well, well," said Giles, and sniggered. "And there was I under the impression that the boy was yours."

Jake treated this with the silent contempt it deserved, concentrating on his brandy instead, and Giles said, "Can he spell?"

"Bill?" Jake laughed, and said, "He was taught to read and write by the missionaries, so I imagine his spelling is immaculate — though I'm not sure if it's good enough for him to spell words inside-out. And I taught him his tables," he added.

"Then he can manage the shop's finances."

"That I would not recommend."

"He ain't trustworthy?"

"Oh, he's keen enough, so he's unlikely to cheat you. But he also likes making money, so he might be a bit sharp with your customers."

"A most suitable fellow for California, Captain Dexter!"

"Indeed," Jake agreed. "So what are you offering him — apart from the hard work of a printer's devil? I must warn you that he has great expectations of being a journeyman printer and then a famous writer."

Giles laughed, and then said, "I need a boy to run around and paste up notices, and look after my mules, and I'll teach him the trade, certainly. If I take him on, it's at apprentice rates. After he's a qualified journeyman, it's up to him — as I told him, the world is his oyster, if he writes the kind of stuff that people like to buy."

"I'm sure he will. He's intelligent — too bright for his own good — and very determined."

"Then he should do very well indeed in the scrivening way, most of the writers and printers I've encountered being too bright for their own good. He'll need to start work at sun-up, and he will have to be willing to keep the shop clean and tidy. Is he capable of that?"

"All seamen are capable of getting up early and washing the decks."

"Once he learns to set type, he'll be compositor, folder, and distributor, too, as well as soliciting job work for me. The only thing I won't print is books — I don't have enough type to set big jobs like that — but he'll have to learn to quote for all other kinds of work. And edit and proofread, too." Giles added rather broodingly, "You'd be amazed at some of the rubbish I've been asked to turn into print, Captain Dexter. The higher a man might be in society, the lower is his ability to construct a decent sentence with proper spelling — or so has been my experience. And then there's the little sideline I'm going to establish. Miners like to buy stationery, I notice — sheets of paper with fancy pictures of the diggings and elephants at the top, where they can write down their adventures, and send them to the States to impress the folks at home. So I'll keep a stock of that, which means my apprentice will be running this tent as a stationery store. But most of all, I want him to watch the shop while I go out after stories, Captain Dexter, because every moment I spend here might satisfy my journeyman's heart, but it is also a moment when I might be missing the story of the year — and this here California is as full of stories as a walnut is full of meat."

Jake paused, thinking that printers did a lot more than he had imagined. Then he said, "Bill could be a master of whatever he wants to master. In fact, it has been surprising what I've caught Bill mastering over the past two years. You'll get your money's worth, I know. So what do you intend to pay him?"

"*Pay* him?"

"Aye. After all," Jake pointed out, "you sound as if you need that apprentice rather badly."

The printer emptied his glass in one vast swallow, came up for air, and said, "You're right, Captain Dexter. Send the boy along, and I'll give him five dollars a day, with his board — a regular compositor's rate, even though he's unqualified. I might even buy a mule for him to ride on."

Surprised at Giles's generosity, Jake decided to be munificent himself. He said, "You can have a llama, if you want, and then he can ride on your pack mule."

For once, the journalist looked astonished. "I beg your pardon?"

"We were given five llamas by the Indians, back at the Tombez River — in place of the herd of alpacas we were expecting," said Jake, rather broodingly, and drank more brandy. "We lost one when it was killed by a bear on the way to Bedstead Gully, and another ran away when it was scared by something else. And two were traded for a mule by my seamen, a mule that we sold in Pueblo San Marco — but we do have one llama left. Bill, being the youngest, had the job of looking after them when we were on passage, so it seems logical that if you take on Bill, you can take on the surviving llama, too."

"Well," said Giles, and refilled their glasses. He seemed lost for words.

"And I'll send along some wood and rope and a carpenter, so he can have a cot to keep himself out of the mud at night."

"That's mighty civil of you."

Jake lifted his tumbler in another salute, feeling he had done the best he could by Bill, whose talents were definitely wasted on board ship.

Then, with no preliminary at all, he said, "What do you know about a man by the name of Ah Wong?"

This time, Giles betrayed no surprise. It was almost as if he was expecting the question. However, he said, "Why do you ask?"

"Harriet — Mrs. Sefton — reckons that she spied this Ah Wong when we moored here — and that when she chased after him he told her to run away."

"He did?" The journalist's eyes sharpened, and he said, "I surely do wonder why he would say that."

"So do I," said Jake broodingly. "So, who the devil is he?"

Giles contemplated his glass with his eyebrows high. "Ah Wong is — or was — Mrs. Sefton's servant. He accompanied Mrs. Sefton and me to Don Roberto's fort, the day we left Don Manuel's estate ... the day she disobeyed her husband by refusing to stay with Don Manuel's family a single hour longer. Ah Wong was very nervous about going back to Colonel Sefton's ranch. Well, I suppose he was really Colonel Sefton's servant, so he had reason to be worried." Then he added, "Mrs. Sefton seemed very fond of him."

Jake frowned, and said rather sharply, "Fond? What is he like?

Giles looked at him with a small, secret, knowing grin that was somehow salacious. However, he merely said, "He's Chinese, so you know already what he's like. Her husband sent Ah Wong along with her when she was ushered off into Don Manuel Vidrie's care. He was her groom, as well as her servant."

"Groom?"

"I gathered they went riding every morning. They seemed companionable — as if they had shared the same scenery for a very long time."

"Yes," said Jake. He remembered what Harriet had told him.

"Mrs. Sefton seemed very anxious about what happened to him after he returned to Sefton's hacienda."

Jake frowned. "He went back?"

Instead of answering, the printer drained his glass, contemplated it as if he was choosing his words, and then remarked, "Providential, don't you think, that Mrs. Sefton wasn't burned to death in that fire, too?"

Misgiving hit Jake in a jolt. "What?"

"She left the house the very same night it caught fire."

Oh, dear lord. Jake was remembering fragments of what Harriet had said after she had joined him at the log cabin in Bedstead Gully. He had been feverish at the time, which was why the memories were so remote.

Finally, he said with awful certainty, "You think Ah Wong is dead."

"Why?"

"You said *was* her servant."

"Ah, Captain Dexter, so I did. My impression was that he had died the night the house caught fire, after he went back to the ranch. It seemed logical."

"But Harriet — Mrs. Sefton — saw Ah Wong here, so he can't have died in the fire."

"There's a good chance the man she saw was not Ah Wong. There are a lot of Chinese men in the barracks. It's a very new kind of Californian business, the bringing in of indentured labor from China, and to most people all Chinese men look alike."

"Perhaps you're right." Though Jake remembered that Giles had just told him that Harriet and Ah Wong had spent a lot of time together.

"But," said Giles, "even if the man she saw was not Ah Wong, yelling at her to run away seems an urgent kind of warning. One that she should take notice of, perhaps?"

"Yes, definitely yes," said Jake. He drank the rest of his brandy in one gulp. It helped to stifle the foreboding inside him.

ELEVEN

"YOU'RE going to build a theater?" Mrs. Marchant demanded.

Harriet nodded, thinking that gossip got around very fast in California.

"I've been hearing so much about it — that you plan to provide culture in this uncultured place, an alternative entertainment for the miners."

Harriet surveyed her, gathering her thoughts. She had spent the day sitting with Davy, putting warm bottles to his feet and cool cloths to the nape of his neck, feeding him soup and soothing potions that Jake Dexter had mixed. Davy had muttered a lot, and tossed and turned. He had seemed feverish, but for the first time he had moved of his own accord, so Harriet allowed herself to feel some hope for his recovery.

She was also slightly puzzled. Bodfish had materialized beside her as she descended the brig's gangway when she left the *Gosling* after supper, and had insisted on accompanying her all the way to the fort. Throughout the long walk she had wondered why he was there, as he had made it plain that he was still very cross with her. But after delivering her, he had gone off with no word of explanation.

"Ah," said Mrs. Marchant. "Aha!" And, when Harriet blinked blankly at her, she announced, "My epic drama, Miss Gray, be about complete."

What the devil was the woman on about? Then Harriet remembered. It seemed so long ago, but she recollected an unlikely story of a poem Mrs. Marchant was writing, about a young miner bringing his wife to California. Or maybe it had been a number of miners, bringing their wives? And something about a baby?

If Mrs. Marchant noticed Harriet's vagueness, she didn't let it worry her. "My poetic tragedy begins with the courtship, Miss Gray, so wonderfully adaptable for the stage. I've named my heroine Malvina," she said. "*Malvina was fair and of a tender heart*, runs the first line."

"She was?" said Harriet. Men in the attics above the ceiling were shoving and cursing. By the sound of it, there were ten too many and they were fighting each other for room. Harriet expected to hear the firing of pistols at any moment, but Mrs. Marchant did not seem to think that this was a highly inappropriate accompaniment to her romantic saga. No matter how the floor boards rattled, she stood poised with her hands clasped before her ample breasts, lost in the wonder of her poetic creation.

"The hero is named Bert," she intoned. "Malvina prized Bert's noble spirit, so full of loving notions."

"Merciful heavens, did she?"

"Of course!

> *Malvina was fair, and of a tender heart,*
> *Who loved a stalwart swain; she prized*
> *His noble spirit, full of loving notions*
> *And warm devotion, her chosen mate and friend!*

"The next scene shows the happy nuptials, Miss Gray. Then, drama intervenes, with his fatal announcement that he is off to the land of gold, Calafia's Kingdom, the wondrous coast, Miss Gray! Malvina cries, *No, ah, woe no!* But does he pay a blind bit of notice?"

Harriet, sitting on the edge of her bed, was trembling with her inner struggle to quell half-hysterical giggles. "I suppose not," she admitted at last.

"And you're not wrong, Miss Gray, you are right! So, Malvina declares her intention to go, too —

> *A marble pallor o'er her features came*
> *And when it fled, left the strong intention there*
> *To go with him*

"She speaks with hard purpose, and when, Bert, our hero, tries to dissuade the sweet girl, there are scenes of great emotion. He pleads, his mother pleads, but she remains obdurate, Miss Gray! And so Malvina braves the pitching deck and the pirate-ridden Carib sea, to disembark at Aspinwall. Then — the awful crossing of the Isthmus of Darien to the ancient city of Panama, a city of pirates and also the precinct of priests, Miss Gray — priests in enormous black hats! Fleeing this decayed, ivy-clad port, they tempt the raging

87

main again, braving storms, tempests, thunderstorms, to arrive at 'Frisco. And from there they journey up the river, to arrive at Sacramento City, and then trek onward to the diggin's. Malvina sickens, and expires with great passion, leaving a helpless babe and a grieving swain. Bert toils on, digs his pile, makes his way home with his little son, while Malvina's tender ghost looks on — a most happy apparition, for we must have a ghost, don't you think? And Love Conquers All, Miss Gray!"

"Does it?" Harriet said wryly, but that, she saw at once, was not the response the poetess wanted.

"Give me your opinion,' Mrs. Marchant begged. "Do you think it could do on the stage? Do you think it might live? You are an actress, Miss Gray, a famous actress, so be truthful and honest, I pray."

Harriet paused. Then she said, with perfect honesty, "In this place and at this time, I think it would do very well indeed. You can tell Mr. King that I think it would make a great deal of money."

To Harriet's surprise, when she descended the outside stairs next morning Royal was waiting for her. "Is something wrong?" she said at once.

He shook his head. "Jake sent me to warn you that the men have requested a meeting of the Company."

"Oh dear! Are we in trouble again?"

"No, no. They're all fired up about the theater . And," he said after a dramatic pause, "they want us to help them decide what they're going to stage."

"*They* want to stage something?" she said incredulously.

"So Jake Dexter told me," Royal said. His expression was sardonic. "Suddenly, they're all for seeing for themselves just what their grand theater can do, once it's built. And for some reason, Jake seems very much in favor of it."

Harriet stared at her brother, coping not just with this completely unexpected development, but also with the realization that she could be spending much of her time in Jake's disturbing company for months, not just weeks.

It was bad enough that she had found herself enjoying their teasing conversation in the transom cabin — a place she had sworn never to visit again. She had simply intended to request permission to take her meals on the brig, as haughty as only an actress could be, but somehow it had got out of hand.

She had also found that the old magnetism was still there, that there was that same wicked impulse to creep into his arms, and snuggle against his hard body. It was no use reminding herself that Jake had possessed her without a word of love after the bear had chased them at Bedstead Gully, just intent on satisfying his own pounding need ... because she still found him enormously attractive, despite her deep anger and disappointment.

Harriet bit her lip, but then saw that Royal was contemplating her with his head on one side, his eyes narrowed.

Her brother knew her too well, she thought. Turning away quickly, she said, "Excuse me a moment," and ran back up the stairs.

By the time she rejoined Royal, she had gathered her composure. Ignoring his inquiring look at the papers she was carrying, she said, "Do you think the *Gosling*s have any idea how much it costs to stage a play?"

"I'm sure they don't have a notion."

"That's what I thought," she said, and nodded.

"You don't seem worried. About that," he said with emphasis.

"I do have alternatives," she said, ignoring the last.

"What, dear sister, are you cooking up?"

"You'll find out in due course, dear brother."

On the Embarcadero, at the bottom of the brig's gangway, there was a drama of another kind being staged. Harriet and Royal were forced to come to a stop, because Valentine and Crotchet were hassling up custom for an auction of the *Gosling*'s gold mining tools, and a crowd of curious men had gathered, blocking their way.

"Come and make your biddings, suh!" Valentine was crying. "Cast your shrewd blinkers on the first item in the memorial *Gosling* mining effects sale, which be this proud and battle-scarred gold-washing cradle, señors — the identical cradle where a lump of gold weighing three ounces even, twenty-four carats fine, was discovered by the fine tall fellow standing by the lovely lady under that there tree over there."

"Goddamnit," said Royal in Harriet's ear. "The young scoundrel's right! I know that confounded cradle well. And it wasn't one nugget — it was five!"

"But don't expect him to exhibit those self-same nuggets, suhs," said Crotchet, who was holding up the cradle in two muscular arms.

"They being hidden so well that no one knows where, on account of the ill-famed state of lawlessness here."

This was received with a loud roar of laughter. "He be Crotchet, from lower Carolina," quoth Valentine, "and my name is Valentine, and I hail from old Virginny, and we are the auctioneers, at your service, suhs! Gentlemen traders, get ready to place your bids."

Then he started the bidding at a hundred and fifty. "Which I will take in gold dust," he announced, "at the standard rate of fourteen dollars the ounce, or at a discount of ten per cent, if any one of you gentlemen traders is willing to settle in broad silver pieces."

"Damn it," hissed Royal in Harriet's ear. "That cradle cost less than seven to make!" But it sold, within minutes, for a hundred and ninety-nine.

"The very essence of California," philosophized Harriet, as a second battered gold washing cradle was placed on the block.

"Do you know what I saw, just the day before yesterday, just in the course of a short wander along the Embarcadero?" Royal said passionately. "There, Hat — over there! — was a fellow selling off the one dozen bowie knives he had brought with him from the States, five dollars apiece, no bargaining permitted. He sold them in a blink, because of their so-called scarcity value — and picked up his bench, took it along to another tree, and presto, he had another one dozen bowie knives to sell, that original one dozen having been renewed by some kind of magic.

"I tell you what, Hat, his supply was endless! Yesterday, I saw him again, performing the same trick of selling off one dozen knives, swearing they were his whole stock in trade, and because he was under yet another tree, nobody seemed the wiser. And there was another man..."

Harriet didn't know whether to laugh or shake her head. While Royal had been talking, Valentine had sold off the second cradle for an even two hundred, and was embarking on the sale of a shovel. She had no idea what the shovel had cost originally — a dollar or two, no doubt — but within two minutes it had been handed over to a happy purchaser for the magnificent sum of twenty dollars in Chilean silver coin.

"And this man was selling the garments off his back!" Royal was saying. "First his coat went, then his jacket, and when he was down to his drawers, he beat a retreat to a tent — to reappear fully equipped, to start selling the clothes off his back again."

"Dear me," said Harriet, but had to laugh. "This really and truly is California." Then at last the crowd thinned out, and they were able to board the brig.

TWELVE

AS the weather was hot and sunny, the Company meeting was held on the poop deck.

The auction was well and truly over, so the first item on the agenda was Valentine's accounting of the proceeds of the sale, followed by a careful counting up of gold and coins by the secretary, Bodfish. Then, when they had all finished congratulating Valentine and Crotchet on the immense profit gained, and then congratulating themselves on the coffers being reasonably replenished, it was found that the agenda had only one more item on it.

This, however, was a grave one, being no less than the taxing decision of what they were going to do once the theater was built.

"I thought you were going to Lahaina," said Harriet. She was wearing the straw hat one of the men had made her, still decorated with the ribbons Captain Dexter had bought her in Valparaiso. They were sadly faded, and the hat was somewhat battered, but it provided a welcome speckled shade as she gazed about at the *Goslings*.

Chips said, "We've been thinking and talking about your prognostications for your theater, Miss Gray, and how you reckon it could be a little goldmine."

"I do believe that it could make a lot of money," she said, choosing her words carefully. "But I've been proved wrong in the past, as you know all too well. It could be a complete failure. The grog-sellers and gambling house proprietors will certainly do their utmost to ruin the project, because they will fear that it will take away their custom. But I also think that the men flooding in and out of here will come very eagerly to see a drama, because I think many of them are driven to their wits' end to find some kind of entertainment that doesn't risk their hard-won gold. They're mad for novelty, and — in particular — anything that reminds them of home."

"Miss Gray is right," Bodfish said with animation. "Why, just the other day, I heard a barrel organ — a barrel organ in

Sacramento City! For me, it was almost like being back in a park in New York, and the little Italian who was turning the handle was the most popular fellow on the Embarcadero. With my own eyes, I saw him go off with a hatful of money."

"I heard it too," said Abner. "And truly like home, it was."

"So what do you reckon we should stage?" said Chips.

"*We?*" Harriet tipped her head on one side as she gazed at him with her brows arched.

"That is, if the Company do decide to do it. So what would you propose we stage, Miss Gray? That is," he said again, "if we do decide to do it."

"Ah," said she. "I've dreamed of doing Shakespeare."

Royal hooted with derisive laughter. "*Shakespeare? Here?* You dreamed, Hat, you had a vision rare? Oh dainty duck, dear dreaming Hat, for Shakespeare in Sacramento City is the silliest proposal I e're did hear, it kills me. Even Italian opera would do better!"

"But miners are dreamers, dear Royal."

"Nonsense, Hat, nonsense! Culture in Sacramento City, presented for the edification of toughened, roughened miners? They don't want Shakespeare, or Sir Roger de Coverley! They want jigs, and music they can sing along to, memories of home, and stories about themselves."

"So what do we stage?" Chips persisted, adding yet again, though not with any great emphasis, "If we decide to do it."

"What the audience wants, of course!" Royal grandly declared. "For the stage but echoes back the public voice! The drama's laws the patrons give, and we actors who live to please, must please to live!"

"Such a way with words," sighed Bodfish, that great admirer of theater. His hands were clasped together.

"Such gammon," Harriet derided. "However," she said, "I have to admit that Royal is right — that we have to judge what the miners want. And I do have a suggestion that fits exactly what he describes — a drama with songs, dances, remembrances of home, and a California story. And, because it fits the bill so exactly, I believe it can't help but make money — perhaps a great deal."

The men looked at her in expectant silence, though she did think she heard a mutinous mutter of *Alpacas, again* from the direction of Abijah Roe. Then Jake Dexter prompted, "Yes?"

"It's a poetic melodrama, fresh from the pen of the poet."

"Which poet? Who?" said Royal suspiciously.

"Mrs. Marchant."

"*Who?*"

"Abiah Marchant. Mr. King's light of love. She's a poetess, among her other talents. She also teaches painting on velvet," Harriet added.

"My God," said Royal. "*Her.* But you reckon it will work?"

"Oh, most definitely," Harriet assured him. "Just wait until you hear about it."

"We're waiting," prompted Chips.

They were all looking quite eager, she noted with continuing disbelief, even the sailmaker, Abijah Roe, who could be relied on to be grouchy. As she unfolded the papers she had borrowed from Mrs. Marchant, she was aware of their deep attention, and the waiting silence.

"Mrs. Marchant's poetic saga," she began, "tells the story of a miner's voyage from his native hills of New England. It starts with his decision to go to California, and then describes his voyage through the stormy Atlantic to Portobello at the gate of the Isthmus of Darien, complete with sounds of cannon, fired from the castle walls."

"Castle?" said Jake, his eyebrows very high.

"Yes. The old castle of San Lorenzo, which crowns the great cliffs that overlook the river Chagres. It was supposed to be impregnable, but it was seized by Henry Morgan after he and his buccaneers scaled the walls. So fearsome a sight were he and his bloodthirsty band, that many of the defenders leaped from the walls, rather than face their pistols and swords."

The *Gosling*s were gazing at her, more spellbound than ever.

Then Captain Dexter said, "That's all very well, Miss Gray. But cannon — fired on stage?"

"Along with much noise and not a little smoke," she assured him. "Every melodrama has to have a ghost and cannon, and believe me, this poetic melodrama has both. And lightning would be very good, too — broad flashes of lightning, so that the castle, painted on the backdrop, leaps out of the gloom at dramatic intervals."

"Backdrop?"

"Of course! Though a panorama would be both the most effective and the most economical," she amended thoughtfully. "A moving backdrop would work very well indeed, there being so many changes of scene."

"Panorama," said Jake. His voice had gone flat.

"They're all the mode in London," she assured him.

"Panorama?" said Chips.

"A big length of canvas, as high as the roof, which is wound between two great rollers."

"Ah," said Chips, and nodded. As boatswain, and in charge of ship's gear, he could be expected to look alarmed, so Harriet was intrigued to see that he did not.

"But to continue with the story!" she said, when Chips said nothing more. "Arrival at the Chagres River is followed by his frightful journey through marsh and jungle to Panama City on the Pacific side. Then the hero sails for 'Frisco through wild seas, gets to the port, goes up the river to Sacramento City, and slogs onward to the diggings, with his faithful wife at his side."

"Wife?" said Jake, astonished.

"Of course — for we must have romance! But then Malvina dies, leaving a helpless babe. Bert makes his pile, and heads off home in solemn triumph, where he is greeted by his adoring mother, with Malvina's ghost watching benignly over them."

"Dear Jehovah," said Jake, sounding stunned. Then he said again, "A panorama?"

"Yes. Fifty feet long, say — with scenes of home and sea and Portobello and the castle, then lots of jungle, Panama City, San Francisco, the Sacramento River, and the diggings. The rollers stand in the wings, and the canvas strip is drawn back and forth with a handle."

"Back and forth?" said Chips.

"Yes," she said. "For the return journey the panorama only needs to be wound backwards, which means a big saving in canvas and paint."

"Jehovah," said Jake again. He was shaking his head, but his men didn't seem daunted in the slightest.

"We have plenty of old canvas, sir," Abijah Roe said, his tone reproving.

"And Valentine is quite an artist, when he puts his mind to it, suh," said Crotchet. "And I'm always happy to do a little daubing."

"And there's paint, sir, quite a few colors of paint," said Chips, back to his role as boatswain. Then, in his role as carpenter, he added, "And it will be an interesting challenge, making them rollers with a handle. Two handles, if we're winding it backwards."

"And I must confess I like the idea," said Royal, with sudden animation. "For this place, at this time, it's perfect. Let's have a look," he said, and grabbed the script.

"Malvina! Love!" he cried in ringing tones —

> *Fain would I marry and place you in a home*
> *Lofty, such as you deserve.*
> *But — if I venture out, for just two brief years*
> *To the land of hidden gold*
> *That wondrous coast, that place of dreams*
> *It will make us rich!*
> *— if I but go!*

"Blank verse, by thunder," he said. "There's the culture you seek, Hat! And the miners will love the effects."

"*Effects?*" echoed Jake.

"Sights and sounds, waterspouts, hurricanes, and that lightning and those cannon, of course," said Royal, more enthusiastic than ever. "That is what our patrons will pay good gold to see — excitement, equestrian processions, tempests to make the sea journey more awesome, the clink and spark of prospector's pick on gold-bearing rock!"

Jake pushed back his hat. "What the devil is an equestrian procession?"

"Actors on horses. It's called Hippodrama. Harriet once played Cordelia on a horse in Bristol. Though I assure you, Captain Dexter," he added, rather hastily, "my sister would never, ever stoop to playing Lady Godiva."

"But we haven't any horses!"

"We do have one llama, sir," said Tib, and looked around vaguely, as if he wondered where the llama had got to.

"No, we haven't," said Jake. "I gave it to Giles, so that Bill would have a mule to ride on."

"Giles, sir?"

"The newspaperman. He came here from Pueblo San Marco not long before we did, and set himself up as a printer. Bill wanted to be his apprentice, and so I let him go."

"But we should have had a meeting about that, sir," Chips protested.

"He was only the steerage boy," said Bodfish. "So I don't think he counts. Or counted," he amended, and peered at the page in his minutes book that listed the regulations of the Company.

"We passed Mr. Giles's tent this morning," said Harriet. "It's beneath the walls of Sutter's Fort, and has a notice saying something about good news for miners."

"It's good news for him, I reckon," said Royal. "Every story going out of this town has his name on it, I hear, and the editors in San Francisco are baying for more. He'll be in equally great demand when his stories get to the eastern States, too, without doubt. It's a success story, in the great Californian tradition!"

"And maybe he will let us borrow his mules, for our equestrian procession," said Jake. He started to laugh at his own joke, but then sobered as he saw his men's reproachful expressions.

"But it's a romance, Captain Dexter," Bodfish expostulated. "A romance! And Miss Gray would make such a fetching Malvina."

"As long as she consents to be a ghost," said Royal. "Nothing succeeds these days without a convincing specter. Chips, do you think you could devise a phantasmagorium?"

"Chips can do anything," Jake said with blithe confidence.

"You reckon it will do, sir?" said Tib.

Jake shook his head, and laughed again, but then he said, "Yes, I'll vote in favor. Miss Gray is right — the miners are dreamers. They're all caught up in their dreams, and a spectacle about themselves and their dreams of gold and the adventure they've chosen is exactly what they would want to see."

"It's just a fair-time fit-up," warned Harriet.

"But a fair-time fit-up is exactly what they want," said Royal, and so the motion was put and the vote taken, and not only was the Lahaina venture postponed, but the decision to put on the epic drama was passed.

Unanimously, Harriet noted. Even Abijah put up his hand.

"But," she said, as Bodfish wrote it down in the minutes, "there will be costs. Money will be needed. Lots of investment."

Blank silence. Bodfish stopped writing. Like all the others, he stared at her as if she was spoiling their fun.

"Tickets and programs have to be printed, and posters to advertise each production — Mr. Giles's paper might accept advertisements, and if he does, that will cost money, too. And actors have to be hired, because Royal and I can't do it all. Backstage hands will be needed, to work the cannon, the curtains, and the effects. Musicians — we will have to have musicians, to get the audience in the mood, and keep them swinging along. And that means singers, too."

"But we can do the backstage work," said Chips. "And Valentine

97

and Crotchet can sing."

"Nevertheless," said Harriet, and paused, while everyone stared at her. Then she smiled complacently, and said, "But I have good news."

"You do?" said Royal. He sounded deeply wary.

"I have a sponsor who will put up the cash. I told him I would need twelve thousand dollars, and he has agreed to invest that amount."

Silence. No one looked as pleased as she expected.

"But that means he'll take all the profits that you said we could make, Miss Gray," Bodfish objected.

"Not at all," she said. "He is investing in the production, not the theater itself. The Company will still own the theater, and so he will have to pay a rental. Royal and I will be paid, Valentine and Crotchet will be paid, and Chips and his gang will be paid, as well — and that will all go into the Company coffers. And as well as that, the Company will get a percentage of the takings."

Chips said incredulously, "We do what we want, what we voted for, and someone will *pay* us to do it? And we get to keep the theater after the production is finished?"

"Exactly," she assured him. "That's how theater works."

"But who the devil — excuse me, Miss Gray — would sink good gold when we were willing to do it for nothing?"

"Someone whose commercial judgment is infallible," she said demurely.

Royal snorted. "It's Jed King, isn't it."

"How did you guess?"

"Because the poetess who wrote the drama is his light of love, his beloved mistress. And also because he informs the world so often that his commercial sense is infallible. But, I also warrant," Royal went on heavily, "that there are conditions attached."

"Of course there are," said Harriet.

"Conditions?" said Chips, looking very suspicious. "What kind of conditions, Miss Gray?"

"Well," said Harriet, "Mr. King does insist on being billed as the producer of the drama, but who can blame him, when he is putting up the money? The important point is that he is willing to invest the twelve thousand dollars we need. Which means we will have plenty of funds, so that we can lash out on your beloved effects."

"And," Royal said flatly, "his lady love, Mrs. Marchant, is to play a major role."

Harriet grimaced. "You're guessing well today, brother."

"Then I'll guess further, my sister, that she plans to be the Grieving Mother."

"Again you are right, Royal," she said.

But Harriet was smiling as she looked at them all. Her heart was lighter than it had been in a long time — not because the *Goslings* were looking at her with approval, not because they were so unexpectedly alight with this new excitement of staging a real production in a real theater, not even because the meeting had been like the old times, but lots of banter and good humor ... but because Jake had called her *Miss Gray*, instead of the humiliating *Mrs. Sefton*.

She told herself it was illogical, but it was still amazing what a difference it made.

THIRTEEN

WHEN Harriet arrived on board the brig next day, Davy was up and about.

For the first time, everyone understood that Davy was going to get better. It was a miracle. As the weeks passed, however, it became obvious that though his full strength was coming back, his mind was not going to mend. His eyes were open but sometimes he walked into obstacles that at other times he would avoid like any other man. When he attempted to speak all he managed was agonized grunts, as he tried, it seemed, to talk about what had happened to his tribe on that nightmare night. He seemed happiest when he was watching the theater being built, so Harriet spent a lot of time standing beside him at the port rail of the brig, watching the men at work, just the other side of the broad street.

Watching Jake. It had proved easier to take her meals in the after cabin than she had expected, because Jake was perfectly relaxed, talking to her just as if she were another member of the Company. When he dropped the Miss Gray and went back to calling her Harriet, she scarcely noticed. As the weeks went by, it was even possible to forget that horrible day at Bedstead Gully.

The weather became very hot as the season moved to high summer, and the men rolled up their sleeves as they worked. When Jake took off his leather weskit there was a damp patch on his shirt between the broad shoulder blades. He had kept clean-shaven, so that the creases in his face had tanned again, the way Harriet had seen him first. Did he know that she watched him? He worked very hard, she thought. The theater might be made of lath and calico, Sacramento City style, but it was built to last, with care and attention.

It was a big task, as Chip's design called for a building one hundred feet in depth by nearly sixty wide, using the whole extent of the lot, except for narrow alleys at one side and at the back. The front wall was like a lopsided triangle, so that one side wall was higher than the other, and to match this fancy shape, it had a fancy double door. This led to the foyer where tickets would be sold, and which had more doors on the inside wall, leading to the amphitheater. This theater-proper was a long shed, the same shape as the foyer but with a higher roof, so that it could accommodate a mezzanine that was reached by a stairway, and which was where the privileged people would sit. Altogether, the theater would provide seating for three hundred, crowded together on benches. The stage was to be built of solid wood, and raised a full two feet above the pit, and there would be a tumblehome at the front of the stage, sailor-style, to shelter the whale-oil lamps. And, of course the backstage area would be big enough for all the fittings that would deliver the dramatic effects.

The height of the digging season was upon them, and migrants were streaming into Sacramento City, pitching their tents in dense thickets in the meadows around the town, where they refreshed for a few days before heading to the mines, either taking boats to Pueblo San Marco, or making the trek by horse, mule, or on foot. Many had come overland, their faces lined, their bodies prematurely aged, all looking worn-out, weather-beaten and poor.

And yet Jake revealed at the dinner table that he had spoken to two overlanders who were judges back home, five more who were ex-governors, three who had been lawyers, and as many doctors. Bodfish, joining the conversation in his usual democratic fashion from the pantry door, commented that though he had not been as favored, he had been astonished enough to find blacksmiths, tailors, tinkers, and drapers among the constant stream of migrants.

Many came in large parties, with teams of oxen, three or four yoke to every wagon, and at times the Embarcadero was packed from one end of Sacramento City to the other with beasts and wagons fighting for passage. Women came with the teams, too, looking tired but not nearly as weatherworn, having ridden the wagons much of the way, and they attracted much attention from the longer term residents of the city.

For their part, they watched Harriet, obviously curious that an Englishwoman should be living in this place. When she walked from the brig or the theater site up the road to Sutter's Fort, she was very aware of the women's eyes following her — scandalized perhaps, she thought, because she wore a battered straw hat, with ribbons, instead of the bonnet that decent American women wore when in town.

She walked back to the fort in the late afternoons, because that was the time for rehearsals. When time allowed it, she would stop at Mr. Giles's tent, and chat with Bill or the printer, just to keep track of their ex-steerage boy — or so she told herself. Bill had adapted to the life of a printer's devil with wonderful ease, she found, and then thought that no doubt there really was a bright future beckoning for him, complete with his own byline. He certainly had a good example to follow, in the form of his mentor and master. Mr. Giles's stories were not just in demand in San Francisco now, as Bill boasted — they had reached the eastern seaboard of the United States, and were getting a lot of interest.

However, if she was honest, she also stopped there because she enjoyed the view. From the front of Mr. Giles's tent Sacramento City was clearly visible, spread out on the plain, surrounded by meadows where cattle and horses grazed, and with the lofty peaks of the Sierra Nevada mountains as a spectacular backdrop. The tents and wagons of the newcomers made a distinct district, often a mile in extent, with most of the migrants clustered under the high, spreading trees that had been left unfelled, providing shelter from the midsummer sun.

In the city itself, the houses were arrayed in neat rows, so Harriet could easily distinguish the streets and squares that the three lieutenants had been laying out with stakes and strings the previous fall, and marvel at the changes. Now, there were some handsome buildings on I Street, and a few more on K, L, and M. The greatest business, however, was done on J Street and Front Street, where the wood and brick buildings had verandahs with graceful balustrades, to shelter the customers from the rain and sun. And there, on Front Street, close to the junction with J Street, her theater and Mr. King's hotel were taking shape fast, as if each building was striving to be built faster than the other.

Harriet certainly didn't talk to Mr. Giles and Bill because she lacked company — because she always had an escort. It was odd, but every time she came down the gangplank on her way to the fort, she could guarantee that someone would fall in step beside her. Usually, her companion was Royal, because he was going to rehearsals, too. If Royal was doing something else, Bodfish would turn up, though occasionally the steward was forestalled by either Captain Mervine or Mr. King, who just happened to be going the same way.

There was no problem holding conversation with any of her escorts. She and Royal discussed Mrs. Marchant's failings — her grand attitudes, her horrible propensity to ignore cues, and her lapses of memory, which were ridiculous, as Mrs. Marchant was the one who had written the script.

Bodfish, being Bodfish, gossiped, so that Harriet learned a lot about Abner's success with the dark-eyed Californian girls. Another day, he confided, "Valentine and Crotchet are being propositioned by the owner of one of the gambling hells to sing at his doorway, and entice custom to the tables."

"Good lord," said Harriet. "Who?"

"I don't know his name, but the establishment is called The Plains, and it's in K Street."

"Oh dear," said Harriet. Valentine and Crotchet were famous shanty singers, but they also had a fatal propensity for gambling.

"He's offering them an ounce — each! — for each performance!"

"Good lord," she said again. "Don't they think they have enough to do already?"

"The energy of the young, Miss Gray, is boundless," said Bodfish. "Those two young gentlemen don't seem to need any sleep at all."

Which, she supposed, meant that the two young gentlemen had succumbed to the owner's blandishments, something that was confirmed when Bodfish went on, "They tell me that the walls inside are quite tremendous, having been painted by one of the overlanders with scenes from his great journey — Independence Rock, Fort Laramie, the Wind River Mountains..."

Bodfish sounded a little plaintive, she thought. "You haven't seen them for yourself?"

"But it's a house of dissolute gambling..." he mumbled.

"Oh, go on, have a look at the devil's drawing room," she urged, trying not to laugh. "I'm sure you're immune. As for Valentine and Crotchet, providence only knows what they are doing with the ounces they're earning."

"But we can comfort ourselves with the reminder, Miss Gray, that *this* time they are not playing with *Gosling* Company money."

"That," said Harriet, "is definitely something to feel glad about."

When she was escorted by Captain Mervine or Mr. King, Harriet seldom needed to speak, as all she had to do was listen. Mr. King boasted about his commercial acumen, complete with facts and figures, and Captain Mervine prophesied a great future for

California, which was now definitely American, for though flags of many nations floated from the forest of masts that filled San Francisco harbor, Old Glory was predominant.

Harriet listened to this a little cynically, because Mr. Giles had told her that there was a crafty system in operation, to make sure that the American proportion of the population increased with every ship that came in. The instant the anchor was dropped, a customs house officer boarded the ship, to charge each passenger a poll-tax of one dollar, and then register him as a citizen of California before he was allowed to disembark. Naturally, however, she made no comment.

On the occasions when he wasn't being eloquently patriotic, Captain Mervine complained about the bear in the corral, and the coolies in the barracks. Harriet often wondered why the bear was still there, and why the Chinese men, who were certainly badly used, never tried to run off to the diggings, but she kept her questions silent, as she had theories of her own.

Don Manuel, she thought, might not be in the market for a bear any more, as the miners had continued to flood across the river onto Vidrie land, there having been great tales told of the gold discoveries up Cache Creek. And she was convinced that the coolies were scared of Captain Mervine's uniform, and his reputation for making spread eagles of all the deserters he caught.

Then, Captain Mervine announced that he had been called back to the frigate *Savannah*. He could afford to leave Sacramento City without a force to hunt down deserters, he said. Though the ships were still flooding into San Francisco harbor, the problem of runaway seamen was becoming less pressing. There was a significant United States Navy presence, now, with a navy yard being laid out at Benecia, and several frigates keeping the *Savannah* company, which was a deterrent for would-be deserters.

And, as well as that, he said, the rainy season had arrived early this year. The skies were heavier and grayer than usual, and the wind blew steadily from the south, which was an unfailing sign for old California hands that winter was nigh — or so Captain Mervine had been told. In few weeks the roads into the mines would be impassable, and fewer men were willing to over-winter in the hills this year, as the incomers had heard so many grim tales of what it had been like last winter. Or so he reckoned. Most importantly of all, an army headquarters had been set up at Benecia, so that the river traffic was regularly inspected before the vessels were on their way upriver, so there was little need for a force to police the vessels as they came into the Embarcadero.

Perhaps, thought Harriet silently, after Captain Mervine and his men had gone, the Chinese would seize their chance to run away from the barracks. She could easily imagine the hardy little men spending the winter hunkered down in the hills, being more willing than their European counterparts to endure unspeakable privation until it was time to set up their own gold mining operations in the spring. Would Chinese settlements spring up in the diggings, complete with Chinese restaurants, where only Chinese was written and spoken?

One enterprising Chinese family — who had evidently contrived to get to California without pledging their bodies and souls to some European master — had set up an eating house on K Street, which had become quite famous. While Harriet hadn't visited it herself, Chips had revealed that it was universally recommended, both for its cleanliness and for the tastiness of the curries, hashes and fricassees that they served up in little dishes.

Bodfish had listened to this with his face quite blank, and the next time he had escorted Harriet to Sutter's Fort he had commented meaningfully that not one of the men who lauded the place had been curious enough to ask about the ingredients.

"Have you noticed there are no cats and dogs on the Embarcadero?" he asked.

In the early mornings, Davy escorted Harriet from the fort to the brig. The ex-slave was straight and strong again, even if his mind was feeble, and every morning, rain or shine, dark or light, Harriet found him waiting patiently at the bottom of the stairway from the second floor, where she slept.

This, too, was odd. Over the weeks, she had become convinced that Jake was making sure that she never walked alone between the brig and the fort. Why? There were many rough men among the swarms of miners and migrants, but no one had offered her a crude word, let alone a physical insult. And she resented it, because he had no right to be so jealously possessive of her — so arrogant. Jake Dexter might be the king of the brig, but he was not the ruler of her life, she emphatically thought.

There was something more to Davy's loyalty, though. If she watched the building from the deck of the brig, Davy was always nearby, and if she crossed the Embarcadero to get to the theater site, he was always quick to follow. While she had become fond of the tall, dark man who was now so much like a child, she began to feel uneasy about this, particularly as he sometimes called her *mistress*. Was he confusing her with someone else, perhaps his mistress on the slave plantation, who might have had white hair? He often sang to himself in a strange language, as if he were back in Guyana, and Harriet felt uncomfortable about that, too. She tried asking him questions about his past, but of course he was unable to answer. Davy's story, she thought sadly, would never be told. Like Davy himself, his past was an enigma.

Then she did find out that he was fond of horses, and was a fine horseman — had he been an ostler, maybe? A uniformed groom, perhaps? Had he escorted his mistress on horseback, as Ah Wong had escorted Harriet herself, during her wild gallops about the vast Vidrie holdings? It was impossible to tell. All she knew was that Davy liked to linger at the horse market, which was sited at the bottom of K Street.

Harriet didn't mind, as the horse market ground was the most picturesque spot in the burgeoning city, sheltered by an immense oak tree, and surrounded by tents of blue and white canvas. The livery stable was an open frame that was roofed with thatch, and which had a single rear wall made up of piled bales of oat straw and hay. Saddles, bridles, horse blankets and spurs were sold there, as well as the straw and hay, at prices as high as the market would bear.

There was a round track in front of the stable, where the stock were led or ridden, to show off their qualities for prospective buyers, who leaned on the fence to watch, and Harriet found it amusing to watch the judicious expressions on the customers' faces. Despite what Captain Mervine had told her, all these newcomers were keen to get to the mines before the rains set in properly, but though they needed both mounts and pack animals, they were very choosy about what mules or horses they bought, because the prices were so high.

One day, on impulse, she struck up a conversation with an Irish horse-trader by the name of Murphy, pretending to be interested in one of the steeds, a lean sorrel mare with an asking price of fifty-five dollars. The animal had a wicked gleam in her eye, which didn't bode well, but Harriet urged Davy up into the saddle. To her surprise — or was she really surprised? — Davy sat up straight, his bearing absolutely confident as he controlled the spirited mare with just a touch of his knees and his hands.

Encouraged to try her out, he galloped out the end of K Street to the paddocks beyond, did a few dashing circuits, then wheeled about and returned with a flourish, making such a brave show that watchers in the street and in the market clapped and cheered.

Mr. Murphy lifted an eyebrow at Harriet as Davy slid down from the saddle. Harriet shook her head, but another customer shouldered up and bought the horse on the spot, complete with equipage, without jibbing at the total price of one hundred and forty dollars.

"Sell him to me?" said the horse trader in an undertone. He didn't mean any kind of horse or mule. Instead, Murphy jerked his chin in Davy's direction.

Harriet shook her head again, and then stalked away angrily. Davy was a shipmate, not a man to be sold like a horse or a mule.

FOURTEEN

THE weather continued to be very uncertain, with the occasional downpour, and though there were plenty of sunny days, the level of the river was rising. Sacramento City was becoming as muddy as the Embarcadero had been the previous autumn, and men were beginning to talk about the necessity for levees, while Jake remarked in his sardonic way that the waterfront buildings would have to be moored, being only one step better than riverboats.

Others, even more ironically, speculated about turning the whole damn city into rice fields. But, despite the rain and mud, the work on the theater continued, as the framework and cladding were complete, and the carpentering was all under shelter. Then, so suddenly it took Harriet by surprise, Chips announced that the theater was finished.

It was time to plan the staging of Mrs. Marchant's great drama. Mr. King gave a party to celebrate, and did it in his usual openhanded fashion. The counter in the theater foyer, where tickets for seats were destined to be sold, was turned into a serving counter for the free distribution of pies, while a bar was set up at the other end, complete with little barrels of brandy. Naturally, everyone who happened to be in Sacramento City at the time attended, so that there was a long queue at the double door to the wooden sidewalk in the street. Then, as each miner or businessman arrived inside, he took a tumbler in one hand, and a pie in the other, and then strolled through more double doors, which were set between the bar and the ticket counter, and led into the auditorium, where they gathered in groups to gossip and nibble and drink and admire.

"Oh-h-h," yodeled Valentine Fish from the open stage —

The axes all go clack, and the hammers bang like hell
To build a wooden frame for a canvas drilling shell
There's only one door for the folks to come in
But she's a damn fine theater — for the shape she's in!

"A damn fine theater!" boomed Mr. King, from his station behind the ticket counter. He was wearing a top hat for the occasion, because not only was he the host of this party, but he was an important figure. *He* was the man who had hired the theater, and was paying for the production, even if the theater itself belonged to the *Gosling* Company.

"How much be she worth to you?" he hollered, as Jake Dexter arrived.

Jake grinned at Harriet, who was behind the counter with Mr. King. "Malvina?" he queried with a wink. And before she could stop herself, Harriet twinkled back.

Her mood was ebullient — because she, as the legal owner, had been the one to sign the papers renting the theater to Mr. King. It had been intoxicating to find that her signature was valid again — because she was a widow, and not the property of a man. And the price she had reached after a bout of lively bargaining was a most favorable one — forty ounces of gold per performance, eighteen carat pure, plus ten per cent of the takings.

The money, of course, belonged to the *Gosling* Company, but it was wonderfully intoxicating to have a lawful presence again. And so she smiled at Jake, whose lean, brown face creased mischievously in return.

"The theater, sir!" boomed Mr. King, failing to see Jake's joke. "How much do you reckon she is worth?"

"Why do you ask?" Jake countered. "Does an eye for the balance sheet, cost and profit come naturally in Calafia's Kingdom?

"Of course it do, sir."

"Then I wonder why I asked," said Jake, and began to figure out loud as he looked around the crowded foyer, and through the doors that led into the theater auditorium, to the many people who were gathered there.

"Calico ... h'm, that is surely a significant item," he meditated, "because we used such a great deal of it. Calico costs more than fifty dollars a bale in San Francisco, or so I am told, and at fifty-five yards to the bale... And then the lumber, reckoned at six hundred dollars per thousand feet ... and the roofing iron cost six dollars per square foot! And we have to think about the panorama my sailmaker has sewn — fifty yards of sail canvas. It's old canvas, I admit, but when you think of what old canvas will fetch if sewn into tents — the worth of ten tents at fifty dollars each, shall we reckon? And then there is the paint that our artists have lavished so freely on the panorama and drop curtain ... and the rollers for winding the panorama back and forth. Then, the labor, at an ounce per day per man..."

Jake silenced, while they all waited. Then he said decisively, "Seventy-five thousand dollars."

Men all round whistled and shook their heads in wonder. They surveyed the theater with new respect, and looked at Captain Dexter more respectfully, too. The value placed on possessions here, thought Harriet, certainly marked regard for a man.

"Is that so?" said Mr. King, looking thoughtful.

"A monument to American energy and initiative," boomed Captain Mervine, arriving with a glass of brandy in his hand. He was wearing regimentals and braid, as this, Harriet gathered, was his last call before he headed downriver for 'Frisco and a return to his proper post on the frigate *Savannah*.

"American energy and initiative," Royal muttered, in his usual mood about the immoderation of Yankees, and said, meaning to be sarcastic, "So why don't we put a gold American eagle on it?"

And the *Goslings* heard him, and took him quite seriously. They pried off the great gold American eagle that flourished on the sternboard of Colonel Sefton's abandoned schooner, and nailed it above the fancy double doors of the outside entrance.

As Harriet noted with great amusement, it was a huge success. Everybody cheered, and sang *Yankee Doodle*, and drank more brandy to celebrate.

Then there was a distraction, as Bodfish arrived with what appeared to be an ancient scroll in his bony hands.

This, when he whipped it out to its full length, proved to be the page proof of the program for the production, fresh from the press. Bill, who had carried it from Mr. Giles's press tent to the newly finished theater, hovered importantly, a notebook in his hand and a pencil behind his ear, ready to take down an order.

"What do you think?" Bodfish said proudly.

He, as he then bashfully revealed, had been the copywriter, while Bill had been the editor.

Accordingly, Harriet read it with some caution, while Royal breathed heavily from behind her shoulder.

GOSLING THEATER
FRONT STREET
SACRAMENTO CITY
GRAND OPENING THURSDAY
AND, THEREAFTER, EVERY WEEKDAY EVENING AT
EIGHT
The First Production in California of the Great Sensation,
the Poetic and Musical Drama of the...
CALIFORNIA MINER
OR,
The Journey of A Miner and his Beautiful Bride Malvina to
the Mines of California by Way of the Isthmus of Darien
and their Fortunes in the Diggins

WITH THE FOLLOWING POWERFUL CAST

Bert, Hopeful Miner ... Mr. Royal Gray, late of Covent Garden,
London
Malvina, his Faithful Bride ... Miss Harriet Gray, late of the
Royal Theatre, New Zealand
Bert's Mother (the Grieving Parent) ... Mrs. Abiah Marchant,
painter on velvet
Two Cheerful Young Gamblers ... Mr. Valentine Fish and
M'sieu André Crozet
With an Orchestra of Five Musicians and a Bevy of Supporting
Players

SYNOPSIS

ACT ONE: THE FATEFUL DECISION – Bert's Courtship
— "the holy wedding vows they spake" — Decision to
Tempt the Mines — Malvina's Brave Decision to go with
him — His Grieving Mother pleads — Malvina's obduracy
— "all earnestly he strove to paint the hardships of the
sea" — the departure.

ACT TWO: THE AWFUL JOURNEY — "the tossing deck
with slender feet she trod" — storms and thunder —
arrival at the Coast of Darien — "the appalling wilds of
Panama, that Place of Skulls" — at sea again — "And then

111

upon the shore of 'Frisco, with a motley throng from ev'ry clime she stood" — the Sacramento.

ACT THREE: THE DIGGINS — Disappointment — the Awful Demise of Malvina — "Death met her there, And with Cold Grasp his Fatal Welcome Seal'd" — the Sympathizing Surgeon — "With her he would have solac'd all his Care, but 'neath his Feet now fill'd a Stranger's Grave" — the motherless child.

ACT FOUR: THE HOMECOMING — Bonanza at last — packing up the Dust — "the raging main again he dared" — the Rejoicing Grand Mother — "Come, my boy, to my Loving Arms" — Malvina's Smiling Specter — LOVE CONQUERS ALL.

PRODUCER: JED KING
TICKETS at the theater door.
Early doors 7 until 7:30, Booking $1 EXTRA
PRICES — Five $$$$$ — Three $$$ — One $ and FIFTY
CENTS

Having shaken her head in wonder, Harriet handed it on to Captain Dexter, who read it as solemnly as she did, and said, "Jehovah," at the end, his tone properly amazed.

"A wonderful production," said Harriet, while Bodfish blushed.

"You approve, Miss Gray?"

"I most certainly do."

"Then that is what we will print!" he beamed. "Mr. Giles has promised that once I obtained your approval his apprentice will print off this poster by the hundred, to seize the attention of the multitudes. Hundreds of them! We will do it this very night! And Bill will paste them up on every possible wall and tree."

"Twenty dollars per thousand," said Bill, firmly taking his pencil out from behind his ear. "In advance."

"Jehovah!" said Jake again, and laughed.

FIFTEEN

"IT'S not wonderful at all," muttered Royal. He and Harriet were walking the well-worn path to the fort, on the way to rehearsal.

"But we are being paid," Harriet pointed out. That was another part of her arrangement with Mr. King. She and Royal were each being paid the magnificent sum of one hundred dollars, or eight ounces of gold, for each and every performance.

"But Valentine and Crotchet are getting almost as much as we are, just for warbling some songs!"

"I know," she said. While Valentine and Crotchet had no spoken lines at all, they were being paid ninety-five dollars each. "And the musicians are getting the same — but you know how much in demand singers and musicians are here. They could probably get more if they were hired by the gambling saloons."

That, as Royal knew, was perfectly true. A walk down K Street at any time of day or night was hurtful to the ears, as musicians vied with each other to drag in custom, creating a cacophony of twanging guitars and scraping violins, and the clashing of cymbals and banging of drums.

"Mrs. Marchant is not just hogging a place on the program," he grumbled with a change of tack, "but she's being paid one hundred dollars, too — the same as we are!"

"She's a woman," Harriet pointed out. "Which means that she has scarcity value."

"But it's ridiculous for an amateur to be paid the same as a professional actor!"

"I know, I know, but what could I do, when Mr. King made it a condition? It's what happens when ingénues have what one could call a *special relationship* with the producer, you know."

"Ingénue?" snorted Royal. "*Her?*"

"What else can you call a woman who was stepping onto the boards for the very first time? Though she has had some acting experience," Harriet added.

"You're jesting."

"I'm not. She told me that back East she was hired by preachers to perform at camp meetings. She played the part of a simple countrywoman with a dubious past, and apparently fooled the multitudes when she broke down and repented, leading the way for hundreds of others."

"Good lord above! She would drown the stage with tears?" Royal demanded with a sardonic snort. "And cleave the general ear with horrid speech, make mad the guilty, appall the free, and confound the ignorant?"

"I suppose you could put it like that," she admitted, laughing. "If, that is, you happened to be Shakespeare."

"What the devil have we let ourselves in for? We know already that she's apt to improvise!"

"I hope it's only because she's still learning her lines," said Harriet fervently. While she had never had the experience of treading the boards with an actor who threw his fellow actors off-balance by making up as he went along, she vividly remembered her parents' horror stories.

"But surely she should know them already. She wrote them, remember."

They were walking past the mule corral, and Harriet saw that there were horses in there, as well as many mules. The corral at the barracks must still be the domain of the bear, she thought.

To change the subject, she said, "What did you think of the program?"

Royal laughed, abruptly cheering up. "Now, that truly is wonderful. If Bill does what he has been paid to do, and gets it pasted all over town, it'll drag 'em in by the hundreds."

"Do you think Mr. Giles submit a review of the play to the San Francisco papers?"

"God, what an awful thought. Don't mention it to Jed King, or he'll give Giles a free ticket."

Harriet sighed. "He's probably thought of that already, his commercial sense being so infallible. I think we can expect Mr. Giles to be sitting in the front row of the box tier."

Royal silenced a moment, frowning down at his feet as he walked, and then he abruptly said, "Giles has been quizzing me."

"What?" Harriet turned her face to him, frowning.

"He reckons there is a story in us. The famous Gray family in the diggings — what's left of 'em."

"So what questions did he ask?"

114

"Giles wanted to know how Father died."

Harriet stopped short, and stared at him with her eyes narrowed. "Why?"

Royal shrugged. "I couldn't tell. But he behaved as if he thought there was something suspicious about it, as if he scented a mystery. He checked that you were a minor when you married, and then commented that Father's sudden death was bloody convenient for Sefton."

Harriet silenced, remembering the long, painful walk to her father's hotel, and how her mind had reeled when she found he was out, because she needed him so badly. She remembered hearing the screams, and the shouting, and how the street had been packed with people who had been drawn by the commotion. She remembered people around her saying that a man was dead, had been killed, had been knocked down by a horseman, had fallen under carriage wheels ... And then her mind was blank. There was no memory of what followed. All she remembered after that was how she had waited, waited for Sefton, who had never come...

She said evenly, "All you could tell Mr. Giles was that Father's death was an accident."

"And Sefton wasn't even on shore when the accident happened."

"That is what his lawyer said."

Royal waited, as if he expected to say more, and then prompted, "You were told he was sailing out of the harbor at the time?"

"Not right then, but later — by the lawyer who came and repossessed the house. He said Frank left the same morning that Father was killed, and was on the way to Canton."

"Without a word?"

"I had no warning at all. One minute he was in Auckland, and the next he was not."

Royal grimaced, and then said, "Jake was asking about it, too."

Harriet pressed her lips together, and said, "Yes?"

"Have you told him something that you haven't told me, Hat?" Then, when she was silent, he said, "What is it, Hat? Don't I have a right to know?"

She shook her head. It was impossible to tell her brother exactly why she was so certain that Sefton had killed their father. It was a private matter between her and Jake Dexter.

"Is that why Jake thinks are you are in danger?"

"What?" Her pulse jumped. "How did he guess that I was in danger?"

Royal stared. Men shoved all about and a horseman thundered past, riding breakneck in the infamous Californian fashion. Mud spurted up from the horse's hooves, spattering his trousers, but he paid no attention, staring at her narrowly instead.

Then he said flatly, "So you *were* in danger."

"Yes!" Harriet wavered. She looked about wildly, and then back at her brother and muttered, "I might have been in danger — well, I'm sure that I was. Ah Wong made me run away the night that Sefton's house burned down. He came to my bedroom and told me get up and get dressed. I put on two sets of clothes, because he said it was too dangerous for me to take my baskets. I suppose that was because there was so little time, or maybe..."

Her breath caught, and then she went on, "And he helped me escape. He had the horses ready saddled — in the barn, and we had a most nervewracking time getting to them, because the Murietas were there."

"The *Murietas?* At Sefton's hacienda?"

Harriet mutely nodded.

"But what did Sefton have to do with those goddamned desperadoes?"

"I don't know what they were doing there, but..." Again she had to pause to steady her voice. "Ah Wong and I rode to the hill that overlooked Don Roberto's fort, and then Ah Wong made me get off the horse and start walking. He said he had to take the horses back to the ranch — had to get them there before anyone realized I had gone. He turned and rode off, and left me to get the rest of the way on my own, so ... so I went to Bedstead Gully..." Despite all her efforts tears were running down her cheeks. "Oh Royal, I feel so bad about Ah Wong."

"So that's why you were at Bedstead Gully." Royal broke off, and snapped, "Have you told Jake all this? How you escaped the night the ranch burned down?" She looked away, but did not have time to prevaricate, for he snapped, "For God's sake, stupid wench, I don't believe you have."

"I don't see why I should..."

"Of course you should! He has a right to know. He worries about you. The man adores you, Hat."

Her heart jerked. She said stiffly, "You don't know what you are talking about."

116

"Don't be ridiculous. He loves you, and you know it."

"How can he love me, when he... When he..." She couldn't say it — that Jake had *taken* her, possessed her without a word of love. As if she was his property, to do with as he liked.

Just the way Frank Sefton had used her, the night of their wedding. The night Frank Sefton had destroyed her innocence.

Royal snapped, "Jake did ... what?"

Harriet turned away. "I can't tell you."

Royal's hand came out and pulled her face around, and he squinted down into her eyes. "Hat, something happened at Bedstead Gully — something happened the same day that I arrived there with Abner and Tib and Dan. I remember it well, because you seemed so strange — so shocked. You said you had been chased by a bear — was that true?"

"I was certainly chased by a bear," she said, looking down so he couldn't see the tears welling in her eyes. "And Jake saved me."

"How? Did he shoot it?"

"No — his rifle was back at the cabin. When he found me, I was frozen with panic, and he pushed me into a run, and we both ran ... ran..." She took a deep shaky breath, remembering the smell and sound of the bear in close pursuit. "And then I fell — down a hole. I suppose it was a mine that hadn't worked out, or had been worked out ... quite some time before, because there were ferns growing at the bottom, which cushioned..."

She couldn't go on. The ferns had done more than cushion her fall. They had become a bed, where Jake had ... had taken his reward for saving her life. Had just *done* it, she thought bitterly. She remembered how he had trembled with passion, and the demanding heat of his kisses, while his hands... She remembered the possessive weight of his body.

Royal was frowning deeply. "And that's why you pretend to hate him — because he saved you from the bear?"

"Don't be ridiculous. And I am not pretending."

"You're the one who is being ridiculous, sis. And I damn well believe that you love him too. Ain't that the truth? Of course it is! I see it in your eyes every time you look at him, Hat!"

Harriet looked around, at the Embarcadero, at all the men pushing by, the riders and the touts, and none of them were paying her a single bit of attention. She looked back at Royal, and then looked down, and muttered, "I don't want to talk about it."

"You love him."

"Royal, leave me alone."

"You love Jake Dexter."

She said angrily, "Even if I did, it wouldn't make any difference."

"Why the bloody hell not?"

"Because he doesn't love me. He wants me, but doesn't love me. Men d-don't love me, Royal, not really. They want me, but they don't love me. I'm property... I'm..."

"What utter poppycock!" he snapped. "Just because Sefton treated you so shabbily, there's no need to make the same judgment of Jake."

"So you admit that Sefton did treat me badly?'

Royal grimaced. "I know now that he cheated you, and that he sent me off to Peru to get me out of the way, and that he tricked Father into signing documents that somehow made him rich and left you penniless. It was Jake, though, who made me see how we had all fallen for a confidence trick. All the time we were dug in over winter, he worried that you were in danger — and he worries that you're in danger, even now."

Harriet stared at him. "That's ridiculous."

"Why so?"

"Frank Sefton died in that fire, Royal. Yes, I do think I was in danger in the past, but Sefton died — he died! What danger could I possibly be in now?"

"Then why did Ah Wong tell you to run away?"

"I don't know!" she cried, and turned on her heel, forcing Royal to follow.

SIXTEEN

NEXT morning, Davy was not waiting for her in his usual place at the foot of the outside stairs.

Harriet waited, looking around, but when she searched the compound he was nowhere to be seen. She felt puzzled, almost panicked, because though he might be strong in body now, he was so vulnerable, with the mind of a small child. Then, when she arrived at the brig, she couldn't find him anywhere, and no one answered when she called.

Abruptly, she was gripped by panic. Running into the mess cabin, she cried out Jake's name. He came quickly through the door to his transom, but when she stammered out her worry, he seemed merely amused.

"Come," he said, and beckoned. Then he led the way up to deck. The sun was shining, warm on the planks. Slowly, she followed Jake to the rail, and put her hands on the warm wood, and looked at Sacramento City.

The broad Embarcadero stretched before her, as busy as ever with horses, men, and drays. Mr. King's hotel stretched up into the sky, dwarfing the theater. A man was standing on a trestle at the side of the road to the fort, haranguing a crowd — to sell something, she supposed, or maybe he was a preacher, exhorting them against the sins of the city. The crowd was there because this was a new excitement, no doubt.

Right across the other side of the waterfront street the *Goslings* were working on the theater, mostly inside, because she could hear Chips and Charlie Martin shouting orders, and a lot of happy hammering. And Davy was there, too, standing on a trestle and painting the clapboard front of the theater. As she watched, the brown boards turned white in the wake of his brush.

She laughed rather weakly, and said, "What a fool I am. It's just that I'm so used to seeing him every morning ... and I still feel protective of him, I suppose."

When she looked up at Jake he was studying her pensively. She

119

had called out his name without thinking, she realized. His eyes were crinkled at the corners, as if he understood something at last, and she wondered uneasily if Royal had been talking to him.

Then she was sure of it, because he said, "Harriet, you need to tell me more about the time you came to Bedstead Gully."

"That's just past history," she said evasively. A little wind gusted, and she brushed loose hair away from her face.

"I was sick and feverish. I couldn't believe that you were really and truly there, and I was delirious about it, and I wasn't in a fit state for anything, really ... certainly not to ask questions, not then. Now I need to know why you came to Bedstead Gully."

She pushed irritably at her errant hair, and snapped, "I've already told you, and it makes me ashamed, so why make me repeat it?"

"But I don't remember what you said."

"Very well then! But I warn you that you will like it as little as I do. Sefton told me that if I took you as my lover — openly, flaunting it — he would do me a favor and sue me for divorce — for committing adultery, and bringing a scandal on his name."

"He told you to *use* me, to give him a reason to divorce you?"

"I found it as insulting as you do," she said sharply. "Frank thought we were lovers already, and when I denied it he laughed — and said he was amazed I hadn't found a protector in New Zealand. He said that he fully expected I would have done so when I found myself alone, and that he was very surprised that I hadn't."

Jake winced again, but then, suddenly, his eyes sharpened, and he said, "When you found yourself alone? He said that? Are you sure?"

"I remember it vividly, believe me."

"You remember his exact words?"

She recited them. *"You should have found yourself a protector after you found yourself alone in New Zealand — I had every expectation that you would."*

"So he knew you would be alone, that your father would be — "

She nodded, meeting his eyes defiantly. "Yes. Frank knew that my father had died — and yet he was on the China-bound ship that left the harbor that very same day that my father was killed. Unless he had something to do with my father's death, he couldn't possibly have known that I would find myself alone."

Jake pursed his lips in a soundless whistle. "So that's how you know he killed your father."

"There was little time for him to do it, as the ship was leaving that same morning, but somehow he must have managed it. He might have bribed the captain to wait — or he might have bribed someone to do the job for him. Either way," she said flatly, "he was a murderer. He killed my father so I would have no one to support me after he had gone — that I would find myself alone." In a foreign land, she thought bleakly, remembering. Actresses were dubious enough, and deserted wives even more so.

Jake paused, scowling in thought, and then said, "Tell me again how your father was killed."

Harriet didn't think she had ever told him, but shrugged instead of arguing. "A horseman knocked him under the wheels of a passing carriage. It was in the street right outside his hotel. I was there — in the hotel, asking for him, when I heard the thud, and the screams, and the sound of galloping hooves."

"And the horseman didn't stop?"

"Of course not."

"So it could have been Sefton, hurrying on to catch his ship after he had done what he'd stayed to do."

"He was an expert horseman," she said.

That was how Frank had first caught her eye, because he had looked so elegant on horseback. When he had paid court to her at the theater, he had been just one of the throng, different only because he was older than the others, and obviously much richer, and she had paid him little attention. But then, when her father and Royal had taken her to the horse races...

There was another long silence, and when she looked at Jake, he had his thumbs hooked in his belt and his hat tipped back. The wind whisked, and she pushed her hair away from her face yet again. Then, suddenly, Jake let go his belt and dipped into his pocket. Then he held out his hand, and she saw dozens of hairpins on his palm.

He said, "Running short of these, Harriet?"

She shook her head in amazement, and more hair fell down. "I'm short of everything," she confessed. "Only two gowns, two petticoats, two shifts, and hardly any pins. Where did you find them?"

"Everywhere."

The breeze flicked again, and to her discomfort, Jake stepped close, and pushed his other hand into her loose hair. Drawing it out into a thick, long tress, he twirled it with his fingers, and held it on

121

the top of her head while she took a hairpin from his other palm, and secured it.

The touch of his rough seaman's fingers was warm, but made her shiver. It was a shiver of awareness that reached deep inside. Jake had collected her pins and saved them, she thought. Why? She was scared to blink, in case the stinging tears dropped from her eyes.

Blindly, she took the rest of the pins, and started poking them into her topknot. He was still standing close to her, and she was acutely conscious of his arm brushing against hers as she moved.

His low voice brushed her ear, too, as he said, "Only two of everything?"

"Yes," she mumbled. Her mouth was full of pins as she worked at getting the rest of her errant hair into some sort of order.

"You were wearing all your wardrobe?"

She took out the remaining pins, and said, "As much as I could gather together in a very short time ... there wasn't time to pack, or put on more clothes. Ah Wong seemed to think there was too little time — or perhaps there was some other reason he wanted me to leave most of my wardrobe behind. So it would look as if — look as if I had never left."

When she looked defensively up at him, his eyes had sharpened even more, but instead of commenting, he smiled. He said, "That reminds of the time you first came on board the brig. I thought you were fat, but it turned out that you were wearing half your wardrobe."

"Well," she said, and smiled weakly. "It was an old family tradition."

"Why?"

"Sometimes we had to leave boarding houses in a hurry. Actors are not very respectable, you know."

"Rather more respectable than pirates," he said dryly.

She didn't answer that, working with the last of the hair pins, instead. Then, once her hair was finished, she said, "I've been thinking."

"That sounds dangerous."

"About Sefton's schooner. I suppose it's mine, now, so I want to give it to the Company."

"Ouch," he said.

"What's wrong?" she said, surprised. "I know that no one can sell a large ship here, for I saw one offered for eight thousand dollars without finding a buyer — but the schooner was built for the river trade. You should get as much as two thousand dollars, or even three, if the Company decides to sell."

With his eyebrows slanted, he said, "You know that means another meeting."

"Oh dear." She had realized at last that he was teasing.

Then he said more seriously, "And it could be a little inconvenient for me if they accepted your kind offer."

"Why? How so?"

"I would have to find a crew — and seamen looking for seafaring work are scarce on the ground around here."

"They will be coming down from the diggings again, soon. And there are bound to be some who will be pleased to give up and get back to sea."

"But I'd have to find shipkeepers in the meantime."

Harriet frowned. "Does the schooner really need a shipkeeper?"

"Lodgings are scarce," he pointed out. "Especially free ones."

"Yes," she said slowly.

But there was a ruffle of uneasiness lifting the short hairs on the back of her neck. The schooner had been unattended all the time they'd been here, and yet it was always deserted. While it would be hard to steal, because of the lack of seamen, it seemed strange that no one had tried to take up lodgings on board...

Then Jake said, "Let's get back to the topic."

"What topic?"

"The time you joined me at Bedstead Gully." He ducked his head, so that he could look straight into her eyes. "I don't believe you've told me everything, Harriet."

She avoided the bright hazel-green stare. Royal had definitely repeated their conversation, she thought, and wondered uneasily if he had left anything out.

Prevaricating, she said, "It's not a nice story."

"When he met up with us at Bedstead Gully, Royal asked if you had left your husband, and you said, a better word would be *escaped*."

"Yes," she admitted. "I ran away from him the same night the house burned down."

"So it sounds to me as if you're not quite telling the truth when you say that you came because Sefton suggested that you should be my mistress."

"Jake! I told you exactly what he said! And I certainly had no way of knowing that the ranch was going to be burned down."

"I still don't think it was the real reason you trekked to Bedstead Gully with nothing but the drafts on Sefton's bank, the deed for the land here, old Schouten's journal of gold jottings — and just the clothes you stood up in."

"I had what I thought was a good reason for carrying the drafts," she said, avoiding the real question again. "When Mr. Giles and I arrived at Don Roberto's fort, the day I left the Vidrie hacienda, Don Roberto told me about Royal's claim being jumped — and that the gold that had been confiscated was estimated to be worth twenty thousand dollars. And I know it seems a strange coincidence, but the drafts were worth exactly twenty thousand. So," she said, and sighed. "I fell for the trick. Sefton had asked me to sign for those drafts, but I had refused to do it. But while Don Roberto was talking I changed my mind — and so I went back to the hacienda and agreed to sign for them, so that I could give them to the *Gosling* Company. Which," she said bitterly, "turned out to be just another one of my mistakes, because it gave Frank the legal right to steal the Company's gold."

"Tell me about Ah Wong."

"Ah Wong?" Again, tears stung her eyes. Every day, she watched for him, but had never glimpsed him again.

She took a deep, shaky breath, and said, "He was my servant, but he was also my friend. My only friend. Such a small, harmless man, and so frightened. His ambitions were innocent enough, just to learn good English, and ... and I often wondered what kind of person he had been in his homeland, because he was so well educated. Perhaps he was a teacher, certainly a scholar. He liked to hear me recite, so he translated ancient Chinese poetry for me."

And then, before she knew she was going to do it, she was quoting softly, with more tears in her eyes —

> *Yellow clouds beside the walls; crows roosting in the sky.*
> *Flying back, they caw, caw, calling in the vines.*
> *In the loom she weaves brocade, the Feather River girl,*
> *Made of emerald yarn like mist, the window hides her words.*
> *She stops the shuttle, and thinks of the distant man.*
> *She stays alone in the lonely room, her tears just like the rain.*

"Poetry like that," she finished lamely. She wondered why she had chosen that poem, and wished that she hadn't.

When she looked at Jake, he looked startled. Then his eyebrows came down and he said, "Was Sefton the distant man in the poem?"

"My God, no! How can you think that?"

Then she went on quickly, to distract him, saying, "Ah Wong had sacrificed something ... I don't know what, but it was something valuable, and in exchange for that ... something, Sefton had brought him to California — paid for his passage, and brought him to the ranch. He was indentured to be Sefton's servant, for five years, I think. All I really know is that Ah Wong was terrified of him, of Frank. And I think Frank beat him, treated him cruelly..."

She broke off, swallowing, then said, "I thought he was dead, but then I saw him on the Embarcadero. But he ran away, and told me to run away — and I haven't seen him again."

"And he helped you to run away from Sefton's ranch."

She sighed at his persistence, but said, "Yes, though it wasn't really *helped*, because it was his idea entirely. He came to my bedroom in the middle of the night, and woke me up. He said we had to leave very quickly, so I pulled on those few clothes, and put my face creams and powders in a wallet, and the papers and the book in a bag, and ... he had two horses already saddled. He seemed panicked, Jake — and yet he was so well organized for us — me — to run away. And I do wonder if he somehow knew what was going to happen, and saved my life, because if he hadn't made me run away I could so easily have been in that bed when..."

She bit her lip as she ran to a stop, and then blurted out, "You've been talking to Royal."

"He did tell me that Ah Wong helped you run away, yes."

"And what else?"

She held her breath, waiting, but Jake merely said, "He didn't say anything about Sefton killing your father."

"No, he couldn't, because I've never told him."

"Why not, Harriet?"

"Because ... because..." Then she burst out angrily, "Because I would have had to tell him what Sefton said about what I should have done when I found myself alone in New Zealand, Jake — and it's so mortifying!"

"His suggestion was insulting, I agree," he said steadily. Then he looked at her, and said, "You still haven't told me why you came to Bedstead Gully, Harriet."

"Can't you understand?" she exclaimed, suddenly at the end of her tether, desperate not to tell him the truth. "It was because there was nowhere else to go!"

To her huge relief, when she ran down the gangplank he didn't follow.

SEVENTEEN

DESPITE the fact that there had been a drenching downpour all day, when Harriet arrived at the theater at seven on the opening night, there was a long line of men waiting at the double doors to pass through the foyer.

To her alarm, there was a brisk trade in liquor as well as tickets, which reminded her rather too much of the Fitzroy theatrical establishment in Auckland, New Zealand. However, there was nothing she could do about it, not even have a word with Mr. King. When she went backstage, Chips was swearing as he tried to unlock the rollers of the panorama, which somehow had become stuck, and Tib and Dan were rolling the wooden cannon back and forth to ease the wheels, while Mr. King was prompting and encouraging Mrs. Marchant, who was practicing her lines in a deafening soprano.

By seven-thirty the theater was packed, box tier and pit both filled to capacity with miners dressed in heavy overcoats, felt hats, and knee-high boots. The rain had stopped, but the canvas walls were saturated, and so it was stiflingly hot inside, but instead of shucking their overcoats, the miners were making a tremendous racket. The drop curtain had been painted tastefully with a Californian scene depicting dark-brown trees in the foreground, and lilac-colored mountains against a yellow sky, but such vistas were too familiar to the diggers to hold their attention very long. As the clock ticked past the hour, the impatient roar became deafening, augmented by much stamping of boots.

Backstage, Mr. King made an imperious gesture. A bell rang, the commotion in the amphitheater hesitated, and the five musicians Mr. King had hired launched themselves into a tune. Another fraught pause, then Valentine and Crotchet, dressed as Italian troubadours, pranced out in front of the curtain.

There was an instant roar as the audience recognized the two dashing young men who had already made themselves famous by caroling outside the entrance of The Plains gambling emporium in

K Street — applause that was so uproarious that for some moments even the orchestra could not be heard. Finally, however, after a few hollers from the back of the pit, the audience settled down — for the moment.

"I'm old Mister Brown from the South," sang Crotchet —

I left Lynchburg in the time of the drouth
The times they got so bad in the place
That we poor folks dared not show our face

"And everybody!" shouted Valentine, and the entire theater rocked to the chorus.

It will never do to give it up so
It will never do to give it up so
It will never do to give it up so, Mr. Brown
It will never do to give it up so

Dear lord, thought Harriet, had ever an audience been worked up to such a pitch? When the curtain creaked open with her standing center stage in the role of the angelic Malvina, the crowd was enraptured already. A roar of delight went up, so loudly enthusiastic that the opening lines were hardly heard.

"Malvina!" she cried, in the voice that was trained to hit the back wall of any theater. "Malvina was fair, and of a tender heart!" — but all they did was cheer, and Royal, when he bounded onto the stage, was greeted with equal affection.

"Fain would I marry and place you in a home, Lofty, such as you deserve," he cried, to cries of acclaim —

The land of gold
That wondrous coast, that place of dreams
Will make us rich, if I but go!

"Will make us rich if we but go!" roared the audience, and the theater fairly shuddered with the stamping and cheers. Outside, the heavens opened again, but the thunder of the rain on the tin roof was outdone by the thunder inside, while the five-man orchestra scraped away manfully, quite unheard.

Royal, equally manfully, did his best to carry on with the script. "That mysterious California," he cried —

That kingdom of Calafia
That shrine of gold, where weary exile pilgrims toil
To fill their hats with the shining gold
Where great multitudes have left their bones
Felled by the Californian ague —

But the audience didn't like the reminder of the rough side of their California adventure, and loudly demanded a return of the Italian troubadours. As responsive as ever to their audience, Valentine and Crotchet scampered onto the stage before anyone could stop them.

With a grand flourish, Valentine announced, "This here be Crotchet, who hails from lower Carolina, and I be Valentine, who comes from ole Virginny," and then launched into his song, while the orchestra valiantly tried to follow —

On the floating scow of ole Virginny
I've worked from day to day,
Raking among de oyster beds,
To me it was but play;
But now I'm old and feeble,
An' my bones are getting sore,
Den carry me back to ole Virginny
To ole Virginny shore.

"And everybody," hollered Crotchet —

Den carry me back to ole Virginny
To ole Virginny shore,
Oh, carry me back to ole Virginny,
To ole Virginny shore.

"Are we ever going to get on with this goddamned play?" hissed Royal in Harriet's ear, but Harriet, holding her pose as a girl of fixed purpose, didn't have a chance to answer, because Mrs. Marchant bounded onto the stage, sending Crotchet and Valentine off with an imperious wave of her hand.

And the roared chorus abruptly stopped.

She was wearing a country-red cloak with a hood, and her black hair was down and disheveled. "No, no, woe, woe, my only child!"

she cried, her words ringing out in the rapt silence —

Must you, must you, my only child?
To California for to go, to seek your fortune weal or
woe
To the diggin's must you be bound

"Yes! Yes!" shouted a dozen miners in the pit. "To California for to go!"

"Aye, my boys, to the land of gold!" cried Mrs. Marchant, completely unshaken. "California, once the land of the bear —

With only the Indian to dispute possession
Now clothed with the tented home of the miner
Where hillsides echo to ten thousand eager cries
The din of innumerable picks and crows
And ten thousand cradles incessantly rocked,
California, the land of gold!

She stopped, and spread out her arms in a grand gesture, and the air was split and split again, with stamping, cheering, whistling, and shouts of, "*California, the land of gold!*" and, "Mrs. Marchant! Mrs. Marchant!"

The audience adored her!

"I'll be damned," said Royal.

It was love at first sight. Here, without a doubt, Harriet incredulously realized as the rafters rattled with the applause, was the Darling of her Admirers, the certain Rage of the Season. Her parents had spoken with awe of actors who were idolized by their audience from the very first moment they stepped onto the planks, ingénues who were instant Stars of the Stage, but Harriet had never really believed it. But it was happening right before her stunned eyes.

Mrs. Marchant took the wild acclaim in her stride, accepting the miners' adulation as if it were her natural right. Visibly palpitating, she swept back her cloak and curtsied like a cork in a rugged sea, while every man in the pit stamped and roared, and the boards of the box tier rattled with cheers. She kissed her hands, threw them out, and for quite five minutes it was impossible for the show to go on.

Then, when she struck her Grieving Mother pose again, hands

130

clasped to her breast, the theater silenced as if by magic.

> *His mournful mother spake*
> *Dissuasively of perils and pains,*
> *A scene of danger was her theme*
> *As all earnestly she strove to paint the hardships of the*
> *   sea!*
> *But did he listen — no, he did not!*

And, with that, she walked off the stage, loudly weeping, and the orchestra, sounding very shaken, was able to start scraping again. The tune finished, and Royal opened his mouth, obviously apprehensive about what would happen when he spoke his lines, but the miners were blessedly quiet.

It was only a short respite, however. The panorama ground on, to show the grassy hollow where the nuptials were to be held, which brought the Grieving Mother back on stage, and the audience erupted into cheers again, while men in the pit roared out admiring comments, which Mrs. Marchant didn't hesitate to counter. It was more like pantomime than drama, Harriet thought rather hysterically, and what was even worse was that Mrs. Marchant, encouraged by her banter with the audience, was improvising as she went along.

Harriet, as Malvina, and Royal, as Bert, were married, as per script, while Mrs. Marchant rushed about, threw herself into attitudes of alarm, wept noisily, and had hysterics, a melodramatic performance that had never been rehearsed, but which was received with ecstatic applause. It seemed an eternity before Malvina and Bert were able to set foot poetically on the deck of the ship that would bear them both to Eldorado, but at last the panorama creaked by, to display a scene of storm at sea, and the awesome journey began.

The stage effects were everything that Royal had desired. Thunder crashed, lightning flashed, sea splashed and waterspouts gushed, while Chips worked manfully at winding the rollers, so that it looked as if it was the ship, not the scenery, that was moving. The vessel arrived at Portobello, Tib's cannon was rolled out with a satisfying crash and lots of smoke, and Bert and Malvina stepped on shore to yet another roar of applause — which was more riotous than expected, because Mrs. Marchant was back on the stage.

"What the hell is she doing here?" hissed Royal.

"Ignore her," Harriet advised. The panorama creaked by, to show a lot of jungle as they trudged, which was exactly according to the program — but when Harriet opened her mouth for her next lines, Mrs. Marchant beat her to it.

"Once more upon the land," the Grieving Mother cried —

> *O'er the appalling wilds of Panama*
> *That place of skulls, they took their pilgrim way!*
> *Strange hardships came upon them*
> *Strong men fell down and died!*

At the word *fell* she collapsed to the floor, and then set to shuffling along on her knees, clasping Harriet about the skirts, weeping, imploring her to repent and come home, "a-fore 'tis too late, too late!" It was like some strange feverish dream. Harriet lifted her trained voice to recite her next lines —

> *Yet still her course she held!*
> *Her strength was in her heart!*

— but they went unheard in the din of applause, as another bout of curtseying and kiss-blowing commenced.

It was with great reluctance that Mrs. Marchant left the stage, but leave it she finally did, leaving Bert and Malvina to step on board another ship. The panorama moved on to another scene of stormy sea, but Harriet had only a brief moment to exclaim, "The raging main, again they dared," before Mrs. Marchant raced out of the wings, and was back on stage.

"And then, upon the shore of San Francisco, with a motley throng from ev'ry clime she stood!" shouted the Grieving Mother, and then stood center stage while the audience applauded deliriously —

> *Out, out, thou strumpet, Fortune! All ye gods*
> *Who cast your vile spell, take away your power*
> *Break all the spokes and return this child's innocent*
> *   hopes*
> *Return her home, afore she dies!*
> *Expires in California!*

"Have you heard that before?" hissed Harriet to Royal.

"Never," he groaned — but the cheers rattled the rafters.

After what felt to Harriet like a thousand curtseys later, Mrs. Marchant finally wafted back into the wings, allowing the drama to proceed. As Malvina, Harriet succumbed to mountain fever, while the scene on the panorama behind her depicted the lofty hills and mountains of Calafia's kingdom. It was all dramatic and moving, as the applause from the miners testified, but never had she felt so wracked with suspense, not in a lifetime of playing on the stage. It was peculiarly nervewracking, as she was discovering, to have no idea what your fellow actor might get up to next.

Hopefully, she thought, she would have the stage to herself when she expired. Harriet lay gracefully stretched out on a bower in her Titania pose, her draperies cast around her, ready to move the audience to tears. And there was indeed a reverent hush, as she lifted an arm, raised her head, and intoned, "Death met her there —

And with cold grasp his fatal welcome seal'd
Faintly, her pale lip sigh'd,
The vale is dark, but my husband is beside me

She was speaking too slowly, she realized with a lurch, because Mrs. Marchant seized her chance to get back on the boards.

"There she lay," the Grieving Mother cried —

Breathless, and wasted to a skeleton
Yet on her brow a smile…

"Don't say a word," said Harriet in Royal's ear as he leaned over her prone body.

And, to her great relief, the curtain came down to mark the end of the act, accompanied by a cry of woe from Mrs. Marchant.

Backstage, Mr. King was delirious with the success of his lady love. They embraced and exchanged feverish congratulations, all of which were washed down with a lot of champagne, while the crowd beyond the curtain roared for the final scene. After Harriet held a hurried conference with Royal, a reasonably professional conclusion to the drama was devised, and Crotchet, hurriedly recruited, walked out in front of the curtain.

Turning his eyes to the ceiling, he clasped his hands together, and recited as that curtain slowly rose, "Amid the grief with which the stricken husband bowed him down —

With remorseful sorrow o'er the haste to be rich
He remembered the sweet cottage 'mid New England's
*   hills*
With her, to solace all his woes
Who now, beneath his feet, filled a foreign grave.

And the curtain was up, the stage revealed. Harriet, holding a spermaceti candle under her chin, glided onto the boards within a wire frame with a calico cover, which was Chips' version of a phantasmagorium. Peering through the material, she saw to her disbelief that half the audience was openly weeping. Unfortunately, as she quickly deduced, her role as a ghost could not be credited for the mass demonstration of emotion. The panorama had turned all the way back to the original scene of a woodland clearing in New England, and this reminder of home, it seemed, had inspired the miners' sentimental tears.

Royal, as Bert, strode out from the wings, a bundle in his arms — and out from the opposite wings rushed Mrs. Marchant, to greet him with her arms flung wide. "My only child," she grandly declaimed. "My only hope, returned to me at last!"

"Mother," he cried. "After this fateful quest for gold —

I dreamed a return to my cottage 'mid my native hills
Where sweet Malvina's favorite flowers would grow
And dwell content, forever at her side
But —

"I have been propositioned, my lad," Mrs. Marchant interrupted. Her hands were clasped before her agitated breasts, a pose that Harriet had come to recognize as a signal that the Grieving Mother was about to abandon the script again.

Royal blinked. "You've been *what?*"

"While you was gone, and I a lone, defenseless woman, I was propositioned by that monster, the tax-collector!"

"The tax collector?" Royal's voice had gone high.

"He propositioned me, my son! Just as you warned —

Afore you ventured on seas afar
Mother, beware the hidden serpent near

That poisons the air and hopes do mar
In vain, I vow'd
That my life is devoted to my absent son and heir!
In vain, I cried — I am a defenseless woman
Who'd rather a basilisk wrap its cold fangs around me,
Than be clasped in the embraces of a heartless robber!

Royal opened his mouth, but whatever he had thought to say went quite unheard. The applause rocked the theater, as men stamped and clapped and Mrs. Marchant dropped her quivering pose to dip a dozen curtsies.

The din was deafening, battering Harriet's head inside the phantasmagorium. Mrs. Marchant threw kisses, the clapping became rhythmic, and the stamping took on a repetitive beat, too. Mrs. Marchant was bobbing and bowing, the miners stamp-stamp-stamped and cheered, Harriet glimpsed Chips alarmed expression where he stood in the wings ... and there came a series of ominous creakings from the theatrical building, and ... *thump!*

With an abrupt jolt the theater settled. The stage was suddenly four inches higher than it had been before — or perhaps, thought Harriet as she took rapid little steps to keep her balance, the pit was four inches lower. Whatever, the audience didn't seem to care a whit, and Mrs. Marchant paid no attention to it at all. Instead, she threw another dozen curtsies — and with another *thump* something flew out of the pit and plopped down at the poetess's feet. Incredibly, it was a wallet, presumably holding gold, followed by a hail of nuggets.

"Bloody hell," said Royal, arriving beside Harriet.

"I know," she said, and began to laugh.

EIGHTEEN

AN hour later, Harriet was on the way to Sutter's fort. It was late, and dark, and it was the first time that she had walked this long street by herself at night.

Everyone else was at the party — the party Mr. King had thrown to celebrate the new Star of the Stage, the huge Success of the Season. Everyone, that is, except Chips and his gang, who were in a state of consternation, wondering how the devil they were going to stabilize the theater. When she had left, Chips and his gang were crawling through the mud among the foundations, bracing the piles to make sure the building didn't float away in the night.

When she had stepped out into Front Street, there had been pandemonium there, too, as all the gambling hells on J and K Streets were battering the night. Innumerable musical instruments were splitting the fog and the darkness. French horns, flutes, squeaking violins and rowdy trumpets wailed outside the smaller establishments, while the bigger establishments employed full bands, which played different tunes discordantly, competing with each other to make the biggest racket.

There were singers, as well, and to her amusement the songs were the same ones that Valentine and Crotchet had sung, swiftly adopted by men who had heard about their huge success at the theater. The night rang, as shouted encouragements to never give it up so battled with roared entreaties to be carried back to Ole Virginny. They were all entrepreneurs, she thought. As Royal had said, those who lived to please, must please to live.

Then the ruckus of J and K Streets faded as she walked on towards the fort. The restaurants and cafés were still open for business, so that she could see humble Chinese cooks working at the open braziers, and smell roasting meat, but the tables were mostly empty. She passed many tents, and wherever a lamp was set up inside a tent, that tent was transparent, so that she could watch the inhabitants in silhouette.

She could hear the men in those calico houses talking , and

136

thought that everyone spoke so loudly in California, as if they were on some stage. Or was it because there was something about this land that made everything bigger, more blatant, louder?

Then, all at once, it was very quiet. There were still many tents, but they were dark and silent, evidently because the occupants needed their exhausted sleep. It was beginning to mist with rain again, a dank mist that smelled colder than it felt, and clouds hid the moon. There were few lanterns to speck the dark, and the road she trod was full of shadows.

The town she thought she knew so well had become a bewildering labyrinth of half-light and deep darkness, and she stepped very carefully, holding up her skirts. Once she stepped into a puddle of mud, and probably something worse, and stepped back with a muttered curse, and after that she walked with even greater caution.

Then she smelled manure and horse sweat, and realized she was walking past the mule corral, and that the shadows had become square. The shapes were the hanging hides, she realized. She could hear the snuffling and whickering of animals, and mules shifting at their hobbles, and smell the rank stench of the hides ...

She heard a step. The hairs on the nape of her neck rose up. She stopped and called out, "Davy? Davy, are you there?"

Nothing. She tried again, but there was no reply from the darkness.

Clouds silently flickered across the moon, and in the intermittent moonlight she could see the shape of the fort in the distance, and beyond that, the barracks. There were no lights. Everyone outside the Embarcadero was asleep, it seemed, except for the restless horses and mules.

When Harriet moved again she guided herself by brushing the damp hides with the back of one hand. Because of the rain, the path had become even more treacherous, slippery with mud. Then all at once she heard the thunder of hooves, and froze.

And the clouds scudded past the moon, letting out a slant of light — and in the shaft of moonlight she could see the silhouettes of men galloping — galloping towards her. From beyond the fort. They were galloping fast, racing toward her in the headlong Californian style. The shadows of the riders became clearer in the moonlight as they approached — silhouettes of men with serapes flying from their shoulders.

Then she saw the shapes of raised guns.

Harriet was too terrified to run. Instead, she cowered against the side of the mule corral, though the hides gave poor protection. She heard the agitated calling of mules and the wild yelling of the horsemen as they pelted down the road. Then — a shot. It blasted the night, and sang past her ear.

She lurched back, shocked out of paralysis, crying out, and there was another shot, which slapped viciously into the hide by her head. Then, a horribly human-like scream echoed from inside the mule corral as a mule went down in a terrified threshing of hooves.

Harriet screamed, men shouted — shrieked. A man galloped right up to her, his horse reared, and hooves struck the air by her face. She saw a hatchet swing, and she saw the billow of a flying serape — and then Davy. Davy came out of the darkness, running.

Davy. He was *howling*, and he was whirling something — a cudgel? — around his head, and behind Harriet the terrified mules were lending a chaotic chorus as they bucked and tried to break free of their ropes.

Davy ran — not for the rearing horse, and not for the man, but for her. With his free arm, he hit her. Harriet felt his arm like a flail. She was knocked down, shrieking with fear, plunging through the fence as wires bent and snapped. Loose wires scratched towards her, reaching with singing claws for her eyes. She rolled over and over in the mud, among the plunging hooves of the panicked mules.

A shot — another shot. Another mule fell with a crash, screaming like a man as it fell, dragging other mules with it. Harriet blindly plunged to her feet and fell again instantly, tripped by whipping picket ropes.

Shouts in the distance, and shouts nearby, the horsemen shouting to each other in superstitious terror — in Spanish. Then the galloping of hooves as the horsemen fled, Davy howling as he sprang onto another horse, one he had grabbed from the corral, and then more galloping as he pursued them.

Then all the horsemen were gone. Something hot and wet was pumping over Harriet as she lay sprawled in the mud, and she realized that she had rolled up against one of the dying mules. Sick with disgust as well as fright, she struggled to her feet.

She heard steps running towards her, a familiar voice shouting. She put out her hands, touched the trembling sides of mules, stumbled over ropes, and at last found him. Jake, Jahaziel, his voice hoarse with fear, saying nothing but her name. He scooped her up against him, his hands moving over her, his body shuddering with fear for her, trembling with protective passion ... and this had happened before, she thought confusedly. Jake had held her like this after he had saved her from the bear.

Understanding at last, she clung to him, and he hauled her up into his rough arms, and carried her away.

NINETEEN

AS Jake carried her up the swaying gangplank of the *Gosling* Harriet thought she was going to be sick, but to her relief the nausea passed. Then she realized where she was. Her teeth were chattering, but she managed to say, "Where the devil are you taking me?"

"Home," he said briefly, and headed down the companionway, ducking so they wouldn't hit their heads, and then right along the passage to the door of his transom cabin.

Shouldering it open, he dumped her on the sofa. Then, after turning his head to yell for Bodfish, he went down on his knees by the settee and cupped her face in one broad palm, pushing back her hair with the other, searching her face for wounds. Then his fingers parted her hair, while he inspected her head and the back of her neck, again obviously looking for gashes. After having satisfied himself that there was no hurt there, he helped her to her feet, and turned her round. Then, with hands that shook but were nevertheless were quick and certain, he started pulling at the buttons that fastened the back of her dress.

She squirmed away, and said, "What the hell are you doing?"

"Stop swearing at me. You're covered with blood — you're bleeding. Oh dear God, your head seems fine, so hopefully there is no concussion, just awful shock — but you must be badly hurt to have lost so much blood, and I have to find out where you've been cut, and stop the bleeding."

Jake was beginning to sound panicked. "We have to see how badly you're hurt before you faint … or … or… Hot water!" he snapped as Bodfish arrived. "Lots of hot water!"

Then, as the door shut again, he helped her to her feet, reached down and grabbed the hem of her gown, and then straightened to haul her gown up and over her head.

She grabbed at the fabric that covered her breasts. "Jake!"

"Sweetheart, this is absolutely no moment for false modesty." There was blood on his shirt, she saw. Then she saw that he was right — there was blood ... blood everywhere.

Her dress was sodden, clinging to her, so that he had to tug hard. Underneath, her petticoat was soaked with it, and her hands were red with blood. Trembling, terrified that she was bleeding to death, Harriet helped him as he pulled off the rest of her clothes.

Then, she was naked. He checked her front and then turned her round, while she waited apprehensively for the horrified exclamation.

Instead, he said incredulously, "You're not hurt. I can't believe it, you're not hurt!"

Harriet slumped to the sofa and thought about it, remembering the plunging mules and singing wires, and the ax swung by the murderer on horseback. It was a miracle, and Jake was right — so why did she feel so bruised and sick and dazed?

And naked, she remembered. Reaching round to grab a cushion and hold it in front of her, she said huskily, "Poor Davy...?"

Jake sat down on the chart table chair, and shut his eyes while he thought. "He went after those men who attacked you — he was following you, I think. He was ready for them, as if he knew they were coming, and he had a gun — he was like a maniac, screaming revenge, swinging the gun around his head like a cudgel. I think he believed they were the men who killed his people."

She said as steadily as she could, "They *were* the men who killed his Indian friends, Jake."

"Sweetheart, how could you possibly know that?"

"They were the Murietas."

"The Murietas!" he exclaimed, and abruptly stood up.

The door opened, to reveal the steward and two buckets of hot water. She shrieked, "Bodfish!"

"I have my back turned, Miss Gray."

"Well, thank God there is one gentleman around here." And the steward certainly did have his back to her. She saw his hand come round, and grope on the floor for her pile of blood-sodden clothes, and she said sharply, "Cold water, Bodfish. Don't you dare put them in hot water, or I'll have only one gown to my name."

"Yes, Miss Gray." And, with his back emanating every appearance of relief, Bodfish fled. No sooner was the door shut behind him, though, than someone tapped, and she heard Charlie Martin's anxious voice asking for the captain.

Jake shifted. He had been gazing at her naked form, scowling deeply and lost in thought, and now he roused himself to complain,

"Am I never to have any peace?"

"There's a deputation from on shore," Charlie's voice said. "And they want to talk."

"Damn it," said Jake, and then to Harriet, "Do you think you could manage to wash yourself?"

"Gladly," she said, and she did manage to clean herself thoroughly, getting off all the mule blood and mud even though her hands insisted on trembling so violently. By time Jake returned she was decent again, too, having stolen a quilt from his stateroom and wrapped it around herself like a shroud.

When he came in he was carrying two more buckets of hot water. He said, "There's general outrage in the city that their favorite actress was attacked."

"Second favorite," she wryly corrected.

"As you will. Anyway, it's too late to do anything now, but they're forming a posse tomorrow, early."

Then Jake said, "Your hair."

"I beg your pardon?"

"It's stiff with blood. If you kneel on the floor in front of that bucket..."

She thought about it, then decided he was right, and dropped down from the sofa to the floor by the bucket, holding the quilt around her.

She felt him press against her, hunkered down behind her, and then his hands pushed her head down into the water. She crouched obediently, with her hands braced on either side of the bucket. Then he lifted her head, clear of the water. With her eyes tight shut, listening to her hair drip water, she felt him massage shampoo into her scalp. He rubbed briskly, dipped her head again, brought it up, and soaped again, yelling for Bodfish for more water as he did it.

Her scalp was throbbing with the firm probing of his fingertips, a throbbing that seemed to echo through her whole body. His chest was pressed hard against her back, warm and hard and reliable. Then he rinsed her hair, first in the first bucket, and then, turning her, in the second.

She said dimly, trying to get her errant thoughts into order, "Posse?"

"The one to find and capture the men who attacked you. One of Sutter's Indian workers will be the tracker, they say. They're determined to find Davy and decorate him as a hero."

Too late, but too late, she thought. She was certain that Davy

142

was dead. She remembered the way the horsemen had cried out with superstitious fear when he'd come howling out of the darkness, and how they had fled. But they would have gathered their courage and turned on him by now.

"But it's too late, too dark," Jake said. "We'll go in the morning."

"We? You're going too?"

"Of course."

She exclaimed, "Why do you have to go with them?"

"I'm Davy's captain. Of course I have to go."

There was a tap on the door, and when it opened Bodfish brought in another bucket of water. Then, briskly, he went out again, leaving the bucket. Apparently, there was a mug, too, because Jake poured water over her hair, gradually rinsing it clean.

When he finally allowed her to come up for air, she said, "But they're the Murietas, Jake."

His hands paused as he wrapped a towel about her hair. "So you said. You're sure it was them?"

"Yes, I am very sure. They — they chose me deliberately as their target. They knew I was coming up the road from the theater, Jake — how did they know that?"

"Those bloody posters," he said, and then she found that she was being urged back onto the sofa. As she sat up, holding the towel in place, she saw that he was coming toward her, and that he had a glass of amber liquid in his hand.

He sat down beside her and held the glass out to her.

She said, "What's that?"

"Don't ask."

"I don't drink brandy."

"Nevertheless."

Harriet had thought that being washed and shampooed and dried had been soothing enough, despite that disturbing throbbing, but to her surprise her teeth chattered on the edge of the glass, and he had to hold it for her.

The first mouthful tasted dreadful, and she drew back with a grimace. "Don't you have any port?"

"Good God, no. Is that all your family drank? Come on, another sip."

She managed another mouthful, but though it wasn't quite so bad, her mouth having gone numb, she pushed the glass away. "You have it," she said, so he settled back beside her with the tumbler in his hand.

She watched him drink, and then said again, "They were definitely the Murietas. I recognized them at once."

"So you said."

"They knew I was going to be there, and they would certainly have killed me if Davy hadn't come. But why? What kind of threat am I to six Ecuadorean bandits?"

"I wish I knew," he said somberly, and drank more brandy.

"Unless they knew that I had seen Joaquín Murieta, the night I escaped from Sefton's hacienda, and that I had heard them all talking. Ah Wong and I were so scared, especially when Joaquín came out of the house, and walked to his horse. It was tethered under an oak tree right up close to where we were hiding. But he didn't see us, because he went back inside. If he had seen us, he certainly would have dragged us back into the house."

"Oh, God," he said, and when he held out the glass, his expression imperative, she reluctantly sipped a little more.

"And it was Joaquín who galloped right at me, swinging a hatchet — but then Davy came screaming out of the night. He *materialized*, and the Murietas — they were terrified, Jake, as if they thought Davy was an apparition from beyond the grave. I'm sure they thought he was a ghost, that he was dead — that they had killed him when they slaughtered those Indians. They killed Pablo and Joseph Fayal too, you know."

"You've told me that, too."

"And scalped them, just as they scalped those poor Indians. But why me? My hair isn't black."

Jake winced, and put his free arm around her, and she crept into the curve of his side, knowing at last that he was no threat, feeling his arm tighten, smelling the brandy they had both been drinking, feeling the fumes in her head.

"Oh Jake," she said. "I was so glad to see you."

"And I was glad to see you, too — you have no idea how glad. You should have told me a long time ago that you came to Bedstead Gully because you needed me. I knew all along that you were in danger, and if you had said..."

"You were sick," she pointed out.

"And I've had this terrible nagging feeling ever since that you are still in danger."

"The Murietas," she said, and shuddered.

His arm tightened still further around her, and then she heard him finish the brandy and put the glass on the floor. Then both his arms held her, while he rested his cheek on the top of her head, and she huddled tight against him while her shivering gradually eased.

Then he shifted, kissed her forehead, and said, "It's time we went to bed."

"*What?*"

"What else were you going to do?"

"Go back to my bedroom in the fort, of course."

"Dressed like that? As Malvina's ghost?" he asked, and she felt him laughing. Then he said quite casually, "You're safe. I promise." Then he stood up and lifted her up and carried her into his stateroom and dumped her on his bed.

His bed was an extended berth, with a wooden lip to held the mattress in place. It was wide enough for two, and she thought that Captain Schouten, the builder of the brig, must have been a dirty old dog who entertained women in his stateroom.

However, it seemed quite natural and homelike when Jake turned the lamp down low after stripping off his clothes, and clambered in beside her, and she felt perfectly relaxed as he pulled her into his arms.

She was still swathed in the quilt, but he didn't seem to mind. It was as if all he wanted was to hold her, and nothing else. He was studying her face, she saw, and then he touched her cheek gently, tracing it with the tip of a finger.

He murmured, "I've been waiting."

So had she, Harriet thought. She said, "For what?"

"To find someone respectable enough to marry us. There are camp preachers enough on the Embarcadero, but they're all half mad."

"Marry?" she exclaimed, and her eyes opened wide.

"Yes. Why not?"

She thought about it — and thought, too, about how good it was to have a signature of her own. She prevaricated with a grimace, saying, "Marrying has never been high on the Gray family's list of priorities."

"So I gathered."

She waited, but he didn't explain, so she finally said, "As a matter of fact, I have spent the last two years strongly regretting that I ever broke that family tradition."

"I gathered that, too." Then he said with quiet savagery, "I would kill that bastard Sefton, if he wasn't dead already."

She was quiet, because her eyelids were heavy, and then she

said, "Why is the lamp still lit?"

"Because I want to be able to see you. Just as at Bedstead Gully, I can't believe you are here."

She remembered him saying something like that, and remembered what she had answered, too. "Well, 'tis I, me, Harriet, complete with bumps and bruises."

She felt the quiver as he laughed, and then he said wonderingly, "But you survived the attack. I couldn't believe it. You looked so... Dear God, Harriet, I was never so scared in all my life."

"And I was never so pleased to see anyone as I was pleased to see you." She lifted her face, and kissed him. Her eyelids were still very heavy, so she kissed him with her eyes shut.

She told herself that she merely wanted to kiss him in gratitude, but it was like the first time she had kissed him, in Valparaiso, because the kiss immediately became passionate. The world narrowed ... to the deep kiss, his touch, his heavy breathing, the quilt pushed roughly aside.

Jake seemed dazed, just as he had at Bedstead Gully, and she could feel him tremble, just as he had back then. But now it was different, because she understood what was driving him — that it was not just mindless lust, but love, as well. She felt cherished, protected ... and then he gasped, and drew back.

"Oh dear God, Harriet, I've done it again. *Goddamnit.*"

She whispered, "No, Jake — no, please."

He said huskily, "I'm sorry, so sorry. I should get out of your life, Harriet, because I can't — I can't seem to help... And I promised you'd be safe..."

But she *was* safe, she thought confusedly. He began to draw away from her, and she exclaimed, "No!"

"For God's sake, Harriet!"

"I mean no, just shut up and kiss me again."

For a suspenseful moment he was absolutely still. He hovered over her. She saw him slowly grin.

He buried his face in her neck, and whispered, "You want me to make love to you?"

"Jake, all I ever wanted was to be your mistress!"

"Sweetheart, you have to do me a favor before I succumb and obey."

"Jake!"

"Tell me you love me."

"You know it well enough already."

"Harriet!"

"Damn you, Jake, I love you."

"Thank God," he said, and all at once his laughter stopped, in a groan of, "Dear lord, and how I love you, Harriet."

And at last, thank God, he moved, and the night became a blur of mutual passion.

TWENTY

WHILE Harriet and Jake were sitting on the sofa sharing breakfast from a tray, Charlie Martin called down the skylight to say that Captain Dexter was needed on deck. The posse was collecting on the Embarcadero.

Harriet could hear the shouts quite clearly, and sense the anticipation and sense of mission. It was like the mood of Don Manuel's guests around the bear-baiting arena, just before the bull came out.

Jake's eyebrows were slanted wryly as he came back into the transom cabin. "The posse's after more than ordinary justice," he said. "They're packing shovels, as well as pistols and rifles."

"Dear lord," said Harriet, beset with conflicting feelings.

Remembering her terror as she had fallen into the corral with the terrified and dying mules, she thought that she wouldn't care if he came back to report that the Murietas were caught, hanged, and buried. In the night, she had woken from a nightmare with a stifled scream. It had taken Jake a long time to soothe and reassure her, before she stopped trembling and they could make love again. But if it hadn't been the Murietas who attacked her, how would she have felt about it? She found the prospect of lynch justice in California disturbing.

"Giles is one of the party," Jake said.

"On his mule?"

"Of course."

"There must be a story in it," she said, and supposed that Bill would be left to look after the printery and the other mule and the llama.

Jake wasn't listening. Instead, he was wondering aloud who he could spare from the theater and the brig. Chips needed a gang to help finish off the job of bracing the foundations, and there were benches that had slumped with the enthusiastic jumping about, too. And, of course, Valentine and Crotchet could not be spared from the show...

148

"I'll take Tib and Dan," he decided at length.

"I do wish you didn't have to go with the posse," said Harriet. "Can't they manage without you?"

"I must go, for all kinds of reasons. You were the one who was attacked, so the mission is personal. And I'm Davy's captain. And I'm the one who knows what the Murietas look like."

"Then I'll come, too," she declared, and he laughed.

"Like Malvina's ghost?"

She had to smile. The clothes that had been soaked in mule blood were hanging in the rigging to dry, now that the cold water had done its work, along with some soaping and rinsing. After hanging it out, Bodfish had gone to the fort with a message inviting Mrs. Marchant to come for morning tea, and asking whether she would be so kind as to bring the rest of Miss Gray's wardrobe with her. So, until the Star of the Stage arrived, Harriet was trapped in the captain's quarters.

"Do try to behave yourself while I'm away," Jake said, getting up. "No adventures. And don't forget your lines."

"I never forget my lines," said she haughtily. "We Grays are famous for being fast studies and never missing a cue." Though coping with fellow actors who insisted on abandoning the script without warning was something new, in her experience.

Jake kissed her thoroughly as she clung to him. Then he headed out into the passage, and she heard his steps retreat as he headed up the companionway to deck. For what seemed a long time, she listened to the shouting as the posse got themselves into order, but finally she heard the sound of hooves fading away into the distance. Then, after a long time more, she got up, holding the quilt around her, and rummaged through Jake's shelves until she found Captain Schouten's scrapbook of golden tales.

Back on the sofa, she leafed through it, thinking about the strange man who had once owned the *Gosling*, and his obsession with gold. When Jake had first shown her the book, at Judas Island, he had told her how he had found it in a secret drawer, when he had taken down the bookcases that had once lined the mess cabin. What a lot had happened since that conversation, Harriet mused now. It had been over a year ago — back in June 1848, when the rumors about gold in California were only just starting to spread along the Pacific coast of South America.

California was Captain Schouten's Calafia's Kingdom, she thought, and pictured how animated the old pirate would have been if he was alive to see the excitement in this modern Eldorado. Had Captain Schouten ever found any of the treasure he had written so much about? Jake had also told her that his predecessor had died a poor man, his only possession this brig, so maybe all the old pirate had gained was dreams.

The book fell open naturally at the page with the map of Judas Island, where the *Goslings* had dug in vain for the gold of Panama. Captain Schouten had disguised it as the chart of a lake, surrounded by fanciful foliage, and drawings of many animals — bears, llamas, tigers, dragons — but the longitude and latitude had not been hidden, so that a seafarer like Jake Dexter could easily find the island. According to Schouten, the Panamanian treasure that had escaped the buccaneer Henry Morgan had been hidden there ... but all Jake's men had uncovered was a memorial to long-ago violence and terror, a pit full of ancient sprawled skeletons.

Then, with a jerk, Harriet realized that someone had traced the map. The light that fell over her shoulder from the gallery of windows showed up the grooves the tip of the pencil had made. But who had done it? It must have been Frank Sefton, after he had stolen the book from her bedroom at the Vidrie mansion, she thought. She remembered making its return a condition for signing for the shares in his bank — and she remembered the contempt in Frank's eyes as he had pushed it across his desk to her. Now, she knew that he had copied it. Why?

A tap on the door brought her out of deep thought. It was Bodfish, to announce Mrs. Marchant's arrival with her clothes. Hastily, Harriet hid the book behind a cushion and stood up, the quilt held tightly around her.

Mrs. Marchant's eyes widened. "Miss Gray!"

Harriet said wryly, "You are carrying the only dry garments I own."

"But how ... why..."

"Just a moment," Harriet said, and excused herself to take the clothes into Jake's stateroom. Mrs. Marchant had brought her toilet things too, so after she had dressed she was able to brush her hair, and pin it up with some of the many hairpins she found in the desk at the head of Jake's bed. It took more than a moment — time enough for Bodfish to deliver a tray of coffee and cake, and when she returned to the transom Mrs. Marchant was sitting on the sofa, and pouring two cups.

Her erstwhile roommate looked up roguishly. "Would I be right in my guess, Miss Gray?" asked she in a piercing whisper. "That your heart has finally held its sway?"

Harriet sat on the chair opposite her. "I'm not sure what you mean, Mrs. Marchant."

"You insinuated to me, once — in the strictest confidence, of course! — that you had an ... affection for a man who was not your husband, that your heart lay with another. Could that man have possibly been Captain Dexter — the gallant one, the hero who rescued you from certain death, last night?"

Harriet merely smiled mysteriously. She thought it was plain and obvious enough for a child to guess that the man was Jake, but Mrs. Marchant was enjoying herself too much for her to spoil her fun.

"Aha!" said Mrs. Marchant. She winked — actually winked! — and her grin became salacious. "Tell me more, Miss Gray! Tell me how your dreams came true!"

"Mrs. Marchant," Harriet said firmly. "I really would prefer to talk about the play."

"A raging success! Ain't it wonderful? Mr. King is beside himself with delight. He is greatly gratified at the sureness of his commercial acumen in making the decision to invest in our dramatic production, and I say that without a word of a lie, Miss Gray."

Harriet said curiously, "Has he told you what the takings were?" The *Gosling* company was due to get ten per cent of that, so she hoped Mr. King kept very straight accounts.

"But that's man's business," Mrs. Marchant said severely. "And not a woman's sphere. It is not the realm of women at all."

"Oh," said Harriet, foiled. She drank coffee and then tried again, saying, "Mrs. Marchant, if we could talk about the script..."

"My poetic drama."

"Your poetic drama," Harriet agreed. "The words are effective, dramatic, and definitely poetic, and so, Mrs. Marchant, I really do think that if we could keep to the..."

"Tell me, Miss Gray," said the lady, leaning forward and dropping her voice to a conspiratorial whisper, "how did you first meet Captain Dexter? Was it at Judas Island?"

Harriet looked at her very suspiciously, wondering if the inquisitive lady had found Captain Schouten's book while she had been getting dressed.

Then she remembered that the name of the island wasn't

written on the map — that there were just the enigmatic letters L A S at the very top of the page. It was not even certain that the letters really read L A S, because the page was frayed, and there was a particularly detailed drawing of a bear just beneath the symbols, which overlapped them in parts.

Greatly puzzled, she said, "How did you guess it was Judas Island?"

"You mentioned Judas Island once, when you were endeavoring to escape from your husband, Colonel Sefton, God save his soul. You were planning to fly somewhere with the man who had seized your heart, the captain of your affections, and you said the name *Judas Island.*"

Mrs. Marchant's voice sank to a melodramatic whisper, and a reminiscent chill lifted the short hairs on Harriet's neck, bringing echoes of skeletons and past terror with it. And suddenly she realized why the miners loved Mrs. Marchant, why they adored her — why, unlikely as it seemed, this overblown woman should be the Rage of the Season. Despite her awful histrionics, Mrs. Marchant had the rare ability to evoke a emotional response in her audience — to speak to something primitive in the mind and heart. It was little wonder, Harriet meditated, that Mrs. Marchant's dramatic talents had been much in demand by camp preachers.

"So how did you meet your love, at this place with the awful name?"

Harriet shrugged, and said, "I had taken passage in a whaleship from Auckland to Valparaiso, and paid for it, too — but the captain of the whaler made up his mind that he wanted to go straight home to New Bedford instead of calling at Peru on the way. So he hauled aback when he saw the *Gosling* laying off Judas Island, and tricked me into going on board. The moment I set my foot on the deck of this brig, he made all sail and headed for the horizon — and so Captain Dexter was stuck with a passenger. Me."

"So that was the first time Captain Dexter raced to your rescue, Miss Gray!"

"Well..." said Harriet, and remembered how angry Jake had been.

"He's your knight in shining armor, Miss Gray!"

"Mrs. Marchant," said Harriet, very firmly. "I really would like to discuss..." But again she was interrupted, this time by by a tap at the door.

It was Bodfish again, come to announce a visitor. Harriet said,

"Have you told him that Captain Dexter is away?"

"He asked for Mrs. Sefton, Miss Gray."

"Mrs. Sefton?" she echoed with a grimace, but told Bodfish to bring the man in.

The visitor was a complete stranger, a tall, thin, dry-boned fellow with a peevish high-nosed face. He was wearing a blue swallow-tailed coat with a stand-up collar and a great many dark-blue buttons over narrow white trousers and a tight white vest, and he was carrying a fancy cocked hat.

As Harriet rather cautiously shook his hand, he introduced himself as Dr. Stirling, naval surgeon. "From the frigate *Savannah*," he said.

Harriet introduced Mrs. Marchant, poured coffee, offered cake, and then said, "Captain Mervine sent you?"

"Yes, indeed," he said. Then, after clearing his throat, and glancing uneasily at Mrs. Marchant, who was gazing at him with blatant curiosity, he said to Harriet, "I hail from Philadelphia, ma'am."

"So you were acquainted with my late husband?"

"I was indeed, ma'am."

Harriet was silent, not sure whether she should offer condolences. Dr. Stirling had neglected to express any sympathy of his own, she noticed.

He said in reproving tones, "Colonel Sefton belonged to a most highly regarded family, Mrs. Sefton."

"So I believe, Dr. Stirling."

"And he was a member of the United States militia, ma'am!"

"I understood that was why he called himself a colonel," she agreed.

"On both counts, the means of his entombment is quite unacceptable!"

"I beg your pardon?"

"That he should lie without a properly crafted tombstone in unconsecrated ground is bad enough for any American, but that his mortal remains should be treated so cavalierly in a foreign land is unworthy of the man Colonel Sefton was, ma'am!"

Harriet gazed at the surgeon, remembering the grave that had been dug beneath the oak tree near the ruins of Sefton's hacienda, and the rough board that had been set at its end. "I had nothing to do with it, Dr. Stirling," she said at length.

"But how could that be so, when you are his relict, his widow?"

"He was buried by the time I got there." She hesitated again, and then said, "The only graveyard at Pueblo San Marco is Roman Catholic. Would you have preferred him to be buried there?"

"Good heavens, no, ma'am!" He looked more scandalized than ever.

"So isn't it right that he should be buried on his property? It seemed perfectly in order to me."

But, in truth, she hadn't even thought about it. And was the ranch his property? She simply didn't know.

"It was not appropriate at all, ma'am!"

"So what do you want of me, Dr. Stirling?"

"Why, ma'am, I need to know the exact whereabouts of his grave."

"Oh," she said, "that's easy. You sail up to Pueblo San Marco, cross the river by the ferryboat, and then ask your way to the ruins of the hacienda. You did know it was burned down? That Colonel Sefton died in the fire?"

Dr. Stirling nodded on both counts, so she smiled, and said, "Just look for the oak tree that grows close to the ruins, and the grave is underneath its branches." Then, after she had watched him note all this down, she said, "What are you going to do? Put a headstone there, or something?"

"Certainly not, Mrs. Sefton! The remains of officers of the United States militia merit much better treatment than that, particularly men of the — h'm! — high social standing of Colonel Francis Sefton. No, Mrs. Sefton, I have come to collect the corpse."

"But ... how? And what are you going to do with it?" she said, astonished.

"I have a metal coffin in my baggage and I intend to proceed directly to the grave, disinter the body, and send it in decent order to the grieving brothers and sisters in Philadelphia."

And, that said, he produced official-looking papers. "So, Mrs. Sefton, if you would just sign here — and here, giving permission..."

Harriet saw him to the rail. A pinnace from the frigate was waiting at the Embarcadero, and Dr. Stirling did indeed have a coffin with him. It was propped in the amidship thwarts, and its metal sides sparkled brightly in the sun.

"Well, what do you think!" exclaimed Mrs. Marchant.

"Amazing," said Harriet. Her tone was absent, because she was lost in deep thought.

"Such propriety, Miss Gray, for a man who be dead and beyond

154

caring."

"Indeed it is strange," agreed Harriet.

As she watched, the oarsmen propelled the boat into the middle of the stream. And then the pinnace disappeared upriver, while she was still wondering what the high-nosed Philadelphia surgeon would think when he saw that the grave was a double one.

TWENTY-ONE

THE Indian tracker was at the head of the posse, riding a rawboned pony. He wore the usual Californian costume of buck-skin cloth pants, checkered shirt, and knee-high boots, but his fierce ancestry spoke in his bronzed high cheekbones and the snaky disorder of his long black hair. He said little, concentrating instead on setting a fast pace — so fast that as the day wore on the less fit men dropped back.

At first the trail was easy to follow. Even Jake could see it. The tracks headed east along the river valley with almost no deviation, as if the Murietas had known exactly where they were going. It was as if they were heading at breakneck speed for some hideout. Then, as evening descended, bringing the long shadows of late summer, it was harder to see the scuffles in the dust.

In contrast to the downpours of the previous day, the weather had been fine all the time, and now the foothills were blue and mauve. Jake could see the distant creases of gullies and terraces, sharply delineated by the low sun, and he thought about the twenty-four-hour lead the Murietas had, and how the night would fall soon. The Indian's pace slowed, and he leaned far out from his horse to scan the ground. Slower and slower he went, with many pauses, and then he stopped altogether. With no more than a grunt, he let them all know that it was time to make camp.

He lit a tree for their campfire, California style. He chose the right-sized tree for the number of hours they needed a fire, about three feet through at the base and growing in the right direction, so that it would fall away from the camp when it finally burned through. Lighting it was easy. He frayed the bark with his tomahawk, and applied a spark. Within moments the tree was glowing like a candle, sending out heat like a hearth. When the men woke in the morning there was just enough left of the tree to make coffee safely. As they galloped away, the pine fell with a crash.

The Indian found the trail again, but not as surely as the day before. It wound north, following the winding of the Feather River.

He rode slowly, dismounting now and then to sniff and peer. Jake sat easy in his saddle, watching him. Not much further, he thought, and they would be in Pueblo San Marco. The trail scratched past rocks and thickets, only faintly discernible, and then only in the dusty patches. It was late morning, hot, silent. The air smelled of dust and pines. The posse had long since quietened, so that the only sounds were the hesitant clop of hooves and the thin rattle of harness. Once they put up a wood fowl, and one of the men swore with fright as it flapped and cawed off.

Then the Indian became very cautious, his movements stealthy. He was on foot now, leading his pony, and he halted at each bend in the path, looking at the ground, then straightening to sniff the air. Then he stopped altogether, holding up his hand, palm forward.

The posse came to a halt. There was an indefinable sense of ambush. Horses snuffled and stamped uneasily. Jake was to one side of the group of men, near the front. His hat was tipped forward, so that the hard shadow guarded his eyes. When he looked up, birds were wheeling miles high in the sky, tiny commas against the blue. It was as if the birds were lying in wait, too.

Suddenly the Indian ran forward, his body crouched low. Men shifted in their saddles, some easing pistols in their belts, and lifting rifles in their saddle holsters. There was nervous muttering from some, hushed by others. Jake felt braced for the first shot, the first shout.

And with a decisive movement the Indian stood up straight, and openly walked forward. Jake tapped his heel on his horse's side. He was the first to follow the Indian. At the next bend in the path the view abruptly opened out, so he could see down a steep slope to the gully below. In the valley floor a heap of ashes remained where a camp fire had burned, and unmoving bodies lay like the numbers of a clock around it.

Five bodies. Jake stopped while he counted them. Then he set his horse moving again. The animal slid and scrabbled slantways down the slope, breathing noisily. He heard the others following, and Dan Kemp swearing as he struggled to keep in his saddle. When Jake arrived on the valley floor and looked back, the men were straggling in a line down the hillside, with Giles in the rear, his mule descending sideways, like a crab. Then Jake dismounted, leading his horse by the rein as he followed the Indian to the camp fire ashes and the bodies. The corpses were lying face down, because they had been shot in the back of the head. As men arrived, swearing and muttering to each other, one or two went forward to tip them over with the toe of a boot. And they were the Murietas ... all five were Murietas. Not Joaquín, but his five brothers, their faces stiff in death. Jake identified them. Four of the faces held shock and surprise, while the fifth was blank. Obviously, he had been the one who was shot first.

But though Jake looked all round, there was no sign of Davy.

The Indian took Jake to the place from where the rifle had been fired, which was a flat patch on the slope of the opposite hill, which was hidden by bushes. It had been a long shot, fifty yards downhill, but all Murietas had been shot only once. Had the marksman been Davy? Jake had never seen the ex-slave fire a gun, but whoever had done it had been a crack shot.

Whoever the marksman had been, he had been lying in wait for the Murietas. Even after they had lit their fire and settled down, he had taken his time to start killing, it seemed. There were little piles of ash and twisted paper where he had waited in ambush, evidence of how leisurely he had been. Jake could imagine him watching them as they lit their fire, made their supper, and then sat around it. All the time, he would have been calculating the distance, testing the breeze, and selecting his first victim. And then he had shot them, one after another, very quickly, so quickly that it seemed evident he had had more than one rifle.

The Indian showed Jake where the marksman had stood as he fired his gun, the scuffling where he had planted his boots. Jake looked down at the gully floor, thinking that the Murietas had chosen unwisely when they had made their camp in this spot that was so easily overlooked. Perhaps they had been driven past the edge of alertness by their superstitious panic. Davy, driven by thirst for revenge, must have been a fearsome sight as he came screaming down upon them to defend Harriet. It had been an apparition that had set them into flight and kept them running — to this roulette of death around a fire.

It wasn't until the Indian turned to zigzag back down the slope to the gully that Jake realized that Giles had climbed to this spot, too, and had been watching and listening. He almost expected to see the reporter jotting notes on a pad. Instead Giles was staring around thoughtfully, with a particularly long look at the sky, where the birds wheeled far up, in the distance.

Buzzards, Jake thought, and grimaced.

TWENTY-TWO

THE Indian showed Jake the faint trail where Joaquín Murieta had fled, and the marks that Davy had made as he pursued him. And again, Giles was there, intent on getting his story.

When Jake looked at him, Giles was staring around, frowning. Jake tipped back his hat to follow his stare, noting the outline of the hills, the trees and the mountain tops, the familiar edge to the sky. They were past Pueblo San Marco, he estimated, and in the foothills beyond the town. Down there, by the river, ran the road to Don Roberto's fort.

The men who had brought along shovels took turns to dig holes and put the bodies out of sight, and after that was done, the posse held a conference. Most of the men were for turning back. They didn't want to catch the black man, as they considered he had saved them the trouble of executing the desperadoes themselves. One loose desperado was not much of a menace, surely — and if Joaquín Murieta surfaced again, he would be easily taken care of.

So, in pairs and groups, they took their departure, saying that the further they got before they had to make camp, the closer they were to Sutter's Fort. When the Indian followed them, the gully was suddenly very empty.

Jake was left alone with Tib and Dan. After the sounds of the posse's retreat faded, the gully was almost silent, without even birdsong to give the afternoon normality. It was hot. The sun bounced off the pale rocks that stood out on the slopes, but Jake shivered. The sense of ambush was with him again, as if someone watched and waited.

Watched down the barrel of rifle, he thought, and worked tense muscles under his shirt as he stared around. He thought of Joaquín Murieta — and Davy, avenging Davy, Davy who had certainly gone mad.

Tib's uneasy voice said, "Cap'n?"

Jake roused himself and turned. Both Tib and Dan were seated on their horses, ready to return to Sacramento City.

Jake pointed up the trail that showed the way Joaquín Murieta had fled, and said, "That joins up with the track to Don Roberto's fort."

They stared at him. Tib said, "You reckon that Joaquín Murieta and Davy went that way?"

"I think — no, I'm sure — that the Murietas were heading there. They knew exactly where they were going, and exactly where they were going to camp on the way, and the fort is the logical place. And we must find Davy."

Tib said, "We must, Captain?" He sounded very reluctant.

Dan Kemp was staring around, looking at the slopes above the gully as if checking them for something, and Jake looked too. One of the buzzards was floating lower and lower in its huge, invisible circle, cheated of its feast.

Jake's neck crept again. He mounted his horse without a word, and led the way along the faint trail. Within fifty yards the scene of the massacre was left behind, out of sight. The track was easily followed, but the terrace it ran along was so narrow that they had to ride in Indian file, hemmed in with rock slopes and thickets of pine.

Then Dan's voice said from the rear, "Cap'n, do you get the feeling we are bein' followed?"

Jake reined in. He heard the rattle of stones. He looked at the slopes and skyline — out of habit, he told himself — and then back at the trail they had ridden. And a mule came plodding round the bend. Giles was sitting in the saddle, as elegant as a quarter-full sack of potatoes.

Oddly, he was looking warily around, too. Then he saw Jake, Tib, and Dan. He half-bowed in the saddle, and lifted his hat.

"I thought you'd gone back to town," Jake said.

"I decided that you know what you are doing, Captain Dexter."

"I'm glad someone is sure of that," Jake said.

He turned in his saddle, ready to set his horse into a walk again, and the journalist said, "Do you know what I heard about the Murietas, Captain?"

Jake turned again, sighed, and said, "Tell me."

"I heard that they'd been seen in San Francisco."

Jake tipped back his hat, surprised. "What? When?"

"Not long after the fire that burned down Colonel Sefton's house. The Murietas went on board one of the stranded ships, and Joaquín offered the captain a thousand dollars to land them back at the Tombez River. All six would help work the ship, he said."

160

"But the captain didn't take him up on the offer?"

"He did not. One can only assume that he didn't like the look of the Murietas."

"Wise fellow," Jake commented. "So what did the Murietas do then, according to the gossip?"

"That's the mystery. The captain, being very suspicious, raised the alarm. He mounted a posse, which galloped to the house of the San Francisco alcalde to get official orders. The alcalde, however, wasn't there, having headed for the mines, and so the posse looked for a second alcalde, the captain being convinced the bandits were still on the coast. But the second alcalde wasn't there, either, he having headed off to the diggings, too."

Jake said incredulously, "Is there no agent of law and order in San Francisco at all?"

"Apparently vigilante justice rules."

"So did the posse take the law into their own hands, and go in pursuit?"

"Nope. Instead, they had a conference, and on the captain's advice all the ships in the harbor were boarded, to convey a warning to watch out for anyone trying to bargain large sums of money for a passage to the Tombez River. However, none of the other captains in port had anything to report. A squad from the frigate *Savannah* was going around the fleet at the same time, inquiring for deserters from the frigate who might have been trying to quit the territory on neutral vessels, which would have been a problem for Joaquín. So, for all kinds of possible reasons, the Murietas gave up trying to flee to Ecuador."

"So they came back to Sutter's Fort ... to attack Miss Gray. But why come back? And why attack her?"

Giles shrugged. Then he turned in his saddle, and set his mule into a walk.

Jake touched his horse with his heel, and followed, his hat pulled well down as he thought about the bodies about the dead camp fire, and the fact that Joaquín had escaped. He was convinced now that the Murietas had been heading for Don Roberto's fort ... but why? And was Joaquín still heading there now?

Heat, and silence, except for the clatter and rattle of their progress. Time passed ... passed, while Jake turned the issue round and round in his mind. Then suddenly his horse was descending a short slope. He leaned back in the saddle to keep his balance.

Looking back, he saw the other men following. Then he and the others were at the bottom of the slant, on the broad trail to the fort.

The track was more bold than Jake remembered, widened by the trampling of many boots and hooves, its dusty width marked with the ruts of many cartwheels, and piles of drying manure. However, it was not until they were near the fort, and it was late evening, almost night, that they encountered other people.

Jake heard the rattle of the mule train bells before he saw the mule train itself. The line of animals was coming down the trail that led out of the hills, the same trail that he himself had followed to Bedstead Gully and back. His little party met the mule train at the fork, and they all crossed the bridge to the fort together. The mules were heavily laden, and the men who trudged beside them were in a celebratory mood. They had made their pile, and would be heading into Pueblo San Marco in the morning.

Jake congratulated them, and then was silent. He had expected the fort to be empty, but now realized how illogical he had been. There was no chance at all that Joaquín and Davy would be here, or that the Murietas had been making for the fort. They must have had some other destination in mind before they were ambushed. When he clattered through the entrance into the cobbled courtyard he reined in his horse and looked wearily about, feeling defeated.

Dan and Tib and Giles joined him. "Well, Cap'n?" said Tib.

"We head back to town in the morning," said Jake, and dismounted and led his horse to the stables. For the first time, he noticed that there was a flag flying from one of the bastions. It was too dark to see what kind of flag it was. Then he saw the animal in the stables.

"Jehovah," he said, and began to laugh.

It was a llama, the lost llama. Bill's llama, back at Sacramento City, would be glad to have its company, he thought. Perhaps saving the llama made this pointless ride worthwhile.

Then all at once his laughter faded away, as he realized the significance of the flag.

He turned, to see Don Roberto coming across the courtyard.

TWENTY-THREE

THE alcalde's trotting footsteps had been muffled by the general din, because the compound had become very noisy with men arguing with each other.

The mule-skinners were heading off for the night, leaving their clients to find their own lodging. Jake realized then that they had been dickering with Don Roberto, but hadn't been able to bargain for a reasonable price for stabling. Now, they had gone to the river to make their own camp, and would collect the miners in the morning.

Don Roberto came to a stop, holding a lantern high as he peered to see who they were. Jake pushed his hat back, and said, "Well, well, and what are you doing in these parts, Mr. Ross?"

"I could ask the same of you, Captain Dexter." The alcalde's tone was peevish in the extreme. Then, as he looked from one man to another, his voice rose to an offended squeal. "You!" he shouted. "You, you lying bastard, 'ow dare you come here!"

Jake blinked. Then he saw that Don Roberto's trembling finger was thrust squarely at Mr. Giles's chest. "Muck-raking reporters!" he bawled. "Lying scoundrels! You've been printing lies about me, you 'ave! My reputation has been savaged as far as Mexico, it has, and all on account of your lies!"

"Lies?" Mr. Giles echoed. He smirked, as if this kind of confrontation was an everyday experience for roving printers like himself. "May I take it that you are persona non grata in Mexico now?" he queried. "That the authorities slung you out? May I quote you, sir, for the next dramatic revelation of the true state of law and order here?"

Don Roberto let out an enraged bellow, but though Mr. Giles waited, nothing intelligible came out, so the printer went on, "Tell me, sir, have the folks in these parts all given up pestering you for their confiscated gold? The last I heard, they wanted to see the color of your guts, sir. Is it really safe for you to come back?"

"Git out, git out!" Don Roberto screamed. "Git your nasty face and your nasty insinuations out of my sight!"

The miners who had come with the mule train were gathering close, Jake noticed, their faces alight with curiosity. Some of them looked seasoned enough to have gained and lost gold the previous year, he reckoned.

He turned to Don Roberto with a tight grin and said, "Have you hidden all that confiscated gold here? Is it stowed somewhere in this fort? Did you and your deputies burn down Sefton's ranch with him inside it, and then steal the gold from his vaults and bring it to this fort?"

"Lies!" bawled Don Roberto. "Lies!"

"Then why don't I suggest to all these gentlemen here that they dig up the cobbles and the floor of the stables and do a little prospecting? And if they find nothing in the courtyard, they could pry up the floorboards in the fort, perhaps, and hunt for hollows in the walls."

Jake waited, hat pushed back and his hands on his belt. He watched the alcalde's mouth slowly close and the little eyes flick about, as the implications got through to him. Then Don Roberto jerked his head and set off inside.

Jake followed him through the first, vast room. As remembered, it was empty of furniture. Don Roberto trotted on into the second room, which, also as remembered, held nothing more than a billiard table and a side-table. Then the alcalde stopped, and so Jake stopped too, looking around. A fire had been lit in both lower rooms, despite the warmth of the weather, and the shadows danced weirdly. In the far corner of this second room, stairs rose to the upper floor, where Don Roberto stored all the rest of his furniture. A draft corkscrewed down those stairs, setting the fire to twisting.

The place didn't look any different from when he had been here last, but Jake felt very tense, as if he was about to learn something awful. That feeling of someone spying on them chilled the back of his neck again.

He took off his hat and put it on the billiard table, and when Tib and Dan came in he told them to check the room upstairs. They went up quickly, in a nervous rattle of boots, while Jake watched Don Roberto. The alcalde was very nervous, he thought. He had his head tipped back as he listened to the two men treading back and forth, pushing heavy furniture around.

Giles came in, and shut the door firmly in the faces of all the curious miners, who were now crowded into the front room. The journalist looked about casually, as if he had been here before and was just checking for differences, and then he sat on the edge of the billiard table with his legs dangling, just as they had when he sat on his mule.

Tib and Dan came back down the stairs. When Jake looked at them, they simply shook their heads. He turned to Don Roberto, and snapped, "So where is Joaquín Murieta?"

"*What?*"

The alcalde seemed genuinely stunned by the question. Jake frowned, and said, "How about my seaman, Davy Jones Locker?"

"Nivver 'eard of him, whoever he might be."

"But it was you who sent the Murietas to Sacramento City."

Don Roberto frowned, patently puzzled. "I don't know what you're talking about, Captain Dexter. What is this Sacramento City?"

Jake was silent. If the alcalde didn't know about the change of name for the settlement, then it was plain that he had only just come in from Mexico.

He said slowly, "Sutter's Fort — the Embarcadero — is now called Sacramento City. It was there that the Murietas attacked Harriet."

"Harriet?" Don Roberto echoed, his voice impatient. "Who is this Harriet?"

Jake said, "Miss Gray."

"Mrs. Sefton, you mean?"

Jake had sworn never to call her that again, but he nodded. Then he thought that it was very strange that Don Roberto wasn't surprised that Harriet was alive — that she hadn't died when Sefton's hacienda burned down. Had the alcalde been the coroner, as well as everything else?

It was all too likely, he thought grimly, and said, "Two nights ago, your deputies attacked Miss Gray, and because they were your deputies, sir, I find it very hard to credit that you had nothing to do with it."

"Well, you just have to credit it, Captain Dexter," the alcalde snapped. "For I ain't got any deputies now, not having need of 'em."

"That's true," Jake agreed dryly. "Or, if any, you have but one. What I want to know is why the Murietas were heading here when five of them were shot dead."

He saw Don Roberto's eyes widen. The red face was going white, he thought, or perhaps it was the dancing reflection of the

165

yellow fire. But then he was sure of it, because the alcalde's voice was hoarse with fear as he said, "The Murietas was coming here?"

Giles flicked back his moustaches, and drawled, "I reckon they were coming here to retrieve that gold you all hid."

"No! That ain't true, and don't you dare print it! There ain't no gold 'ere, I swear it! I had nothing to do wiv its disappearance, nothing! I sent it to Sefton's bank while I adjudicated, but I had no hand in the stealing of it!"

"Then why were the Murietas headed here?" Jake demanded. "Did they have some kind of issue with you? Were they after revenge, perhaps? Did you cheat them of their share?"

"No! No!" Don Roberto's fear was blatant. The little eyes were sliding everywhere, hunting the dark corners of the cavernous room. Then he whispered, "Dead? Shot dead?"

"Yes," said Jake, watching him intently. "You have only one to contend with now — but Joaquín Murieta is the worst of the lot."

"Unless he's been shot, too," said Giles. "By the posse," he added.

"Posse?" cried Don Roberto.

"The citizens of Sacramento City were mighty riled up about the attack on Miss Gray, so a posse was assembled. That's how we found the bodies," Giles added. "And also found Joaquín's tracks, which were heading in this direction, sure as the birds do fly. Though he might have turned back," he said meditatively. "To put the rifleman off the scent, as it were."

"But why would the Murietas attack Miss Gray?" exclaimed Don Roberto, disregarding all this. "Why?"

The Cockney's terror was more apparent with every word. Jake stared at him, feeling very puzzled, and said, "That's exactly what we want to know."

Giles said in the same contemplative tone, "It might have been a spur of the moment thing, when they saw her in the street."

Jake was silent, remembering Harriet saying that she had been their target — that they had come galloping straight towards her, screaming and flailing their weapons, that they had behaved as if they had known she would be there. Giles was wrong, he thought, which made it even stranger that Don Roberto knew nothing.

"Though it's hard to think of any other reason they would come to town, considering how people feel about them," Giles went on.

"Perhaps they came to collect the schooner, sir," said Tib to Jake, while Dan nodded in agreement. "We've thought of it often, how it lies there moored at the Embarcadero as if its lying ready for someone to come and claim it, and sail it away. The six of them Murietas could have done it, for sure."

Don Roberto screamed, "The *what?*"

"Sefton's schooner," Jake said, more puzzled than ever. "We found the schooner moored there when we arrived at the start of April, and it has been there ever since."

"Oh, my Gawd." The little eyes shut, as if to shut out a nightmare, and Jake could hear the alcalde's teeth chattering. "April, you say? And Mrs. Sefton is there, too? Oh, my Gawd," the shaking voice muttered. "Oh, my Gawd, I'm dead."

Jake's stomach muscles clamped. The combination of Harriet's name and the schooner made no sense, because surely there was no link between them, but he felt an overwhelming urge to run outside and jump into the saddle, and gallop all night to get back to Harriet.

Don Roberto's face was as white as cheese. Then all at once, before anyone could stop him, the alcalde fled up the stairs. The sob of his panicked breath was audible as he ran, and then the door slammed at the top. As Jake pursued him the bolt shot loudly, with rusty emphasis.

Slowly, he came back into the room. "We keep watch, turn about," he said. "And in the meantime we may as well have supper."

It was like the time the *Gosling* prospecting party had paused here on the way to Bedstead Gully, he thought, because the same meal of bacon and beans was cooked, and the men slept on the floor like spokes in a wheel, their feet pointed to the fire.

The difference was the acute sense of danger.

Some hours later Jake was wakened by the yapping of dogs. They sounded frantic, as if there was a disturbance in the stables. Tib was supposed to be on watch, but when Jake opened one eye it was to see him slumped asleep. Don Roberto was stealing down the stairs. Jake lay very still, watching him with that one eye.

What was the alcalde up to? Was he about to make his escape — or was it the racket in the stables that drew him? Perhaps Don Roberto was meeting someone there. When the stealthy silhouette slipped through the door, Jake took up his rifle and quietly followed.

In the front room, the miners were all obliviously snoring, while Jake picked his way through the comatose forms. At the outer doorway, he paused until the alcalde had reached the courtyard, and then went silently down the stone steps. The moon was shining, and the air was cool.

There was a scent of ... something. Horse sweat? Manure? The dogs were still frantically yapping in the stables, and the horses were snorting and plunging. Nevertheless, Don Roberto headed inside. Suddenly, with a sick lurch, Jake realized that the smell was blood — and then he heard Don Roberto scream.

Jake ran. He was holding his rifle at the ready. Then he was in the stables, and was forced to pause to adjust his sight, after the bright light of the moon. Then he saw the alcalde, crouched by a cask, the kind used for pork. Don Roberto was terrified — was trying to hide, he thought. Then the alcalde saw him, and bolted out from his hiding place, running towards... Jake whirled, as he sensed swift movement behind him.

Too late. A crack on his head, and then his sight clouded, as he dimly heard a shot.

TWENTY-FOUR

IT was Sunday when the miners who had arrested Jake at Don Roberto's fort brought him to the Embarcadero.

Harriet heard the shouting and commotion, and ran up on deck with her heart pounding. It was like the day her father had been killed. The shouts were the same, and there was the same air of calamity. The cavalcade was coming up Front Street. Jake was sitting on his horse with his hands tied behind his back, and Joaquín Murieta was leading the horse by the bridle. The Ecuadorean bandit was filthy, stubbled and stained. His black, thick moustache writhed around his smirk.

Harriet stood at the rail, frozen, distraught, utterly incredulous. When she ran down the gangplank and grabbed the horse's halter, Jake didn't seem to see her. His face was stubbled, too, but he was not as dirty as Joaquín. Then, as Joaquín jerked at the bridle to get the horse moving again, Jake's hat fell off, and Harriet could see the bandage around his head.

She cried, "Oh my God, Jake, what has happened?" He did not seem to hear. Dimly, she heard a man in the group answering her instead.

Jake Dexter had been arrested for the murder of Don Roberto Ross. Joaquín Murieta was the witness who had accused him of the shooting. The miners who had been at the fort had wanted instant justice, and had brought Jake to Sacramento City only because Tib and Dan had insisted on it. They had refused to allow lynch law to happen, demanding a civilized trial. And Sacramento City, they had argued, was where Captain Dexter belonged, and so Sacramento City was the only place where a civilized trial could be held.

The trial was held that very afternoon. Because of the great public interest it was held in the compound of Sutter's Fort. A rough deal table was dragged out of the dining room and into the sun. A bench was put at the back of it for the jurymen, and more benches were hauled out and put in rows for the growing audience.

169

Jake sat on a stool under a tree, where a noose hung from a stout branch, in readiness for a verdict of guilt. Joaquín Murieta stood guard over him. Harriet and the *Gosling*s were not allowed to approach him, or talk to him, but he seemed too dazed to talk, anyway. His head was slumped, but his eyes were turned up, so that Harriet could see the whites as his stare flickered over the gathering in the courtyard, moving from face to face.

Tib, Dan, and Mr. Giles stood over to one side as witnesses, and Harriet saw that Mr. Giles was scanning the crowd closely, too. He even checked all the windows in the fort that overlooked the compound. Why? What threat were he and Jake anticipating?

Then she forgot it, watching Jake tensely from her place by Royal on the front bench. It was all unreal, like a feverish, horrible dream. The smells were too sharp, the light too bright, the colors too brilliant, the shouting and laughter too loud.

How could the men treat this as a festive occasion? Royal muttered about Americans in Harriet's ear, but she felt intensely alone, completely foreign. Where was the decorum of English courts? Where was the etiquette of the justice? Certainly not here.

There was a jury of eight men, headed by an old man in a yellow scratch wig, who was wearing a blue coat with tarnished brass buttons. He was a perfect stranger. None of the jury was familiar at all. They either came from the upper river forks or were old Californian frontiersmen. Two, she was told, were once shipmasters, but they looked no more respectable than the others.

There were barrels of brandy on the table and members of the audience as well as the jurymen helped themselves freely. Other men chewed tobacco as they chatted and joked, and tobacco juice was freely spattered about. The beaten earth of the compound was becoming slimed with yellow and brown, and the din of talk was tremendous. Then the commotion stopped abruptly as the old man in the wig slammed a hammer on the table, and the jurymen, who had been wandering around, took their places on the jury bench.

He said, all in one breath, "Wa'al, Captain Dexter, you be in this here place to answer to the charge of murder, how do you plead, guilty or not guilty?"

For a long moment, Jake said nothing. It was as if he had to force himself to return his attention from his secret study of the crowd. Harriet waited tensely, terrified that he hadn't understood the question.

Then at last Jake shook his head and said, "Not guilty."

Joaquín Murieta laughed.

"Not guilty?" cried a voice from the back of the audience. "Yer be a fool, Captain Dexter! A blimey idiot! Why not jest say you shot the alcalde because you found him a-rustlin' yer llama beast? That'll git you off, sure as eggs!"

"Because it wasn't Don Roberto who slaughtered my llama!" Jake retorted. Harriet jumped with shock to hear him speak so loudly and firmly, and the men in the crowd were quiet with surprise, too.

"The llama was mine, it belonged to the brig *Gosling*," he went on. "It had run away, and we had forgotten about it. I was as amazed as anyone to see it in the stables at Don Roberto's fort, and God alone knows how long it had been there. But it was *not* Don Roberto who killed and butchered the animal! It couldn't be. He arrived at the stables only a moment before I did."

"And what were you doing there?" someone shouted.

"The dogs were yapping as if the gates of hell had opened, which woke me. When I saw Don Roberto going there, I followed him. Once I got to the stables, it was obvious what was upsetting the dogs — the smell of blood, and the noise as the llama was slaughtered."

"Fool!" cried the first voice. "Why tell 'em all that? It don't do you a mite of good. You've jest gone and wrecked yer best excuse for shootin' the alcalde!"

"But I didn't shoot him!" Jake shouted.

The head juryman banged his hammer on the table again. "We ain't established that yet," he said severely, and turned his head to eject a gob of tobacco juice.

Jake said evenly, "Nevertheless, I do insist that I did not shoot the alcalde. And Don Roberto did not slaughter my llama. It was Joaquín Murieta who killed and butchered the beast."

Immediate uproar. Everyone stared at Joaquín Murieta, and discussed the probabilities in a babel of commotion. The head juryman had to hammer for quite a minute before he got silence again.

Then he turned to Joaquín and said, "Wa'al, señor, do he speak the truth?"

Joaquín shrugged.

"Be that yep or nay?"

"I needed the meat. I had every right to it. The llama belonged to the alcalde and I was his deputy."

More commotion. Incredulously, Harriet heard men wondering aloud what llama meat tasted like. Mutton, she supposed, but then was distracted by the expression on the face of the head juryman, who seemed highly diverted by this revelation.

"Captain Dexter," he said to Jake, when he could make himself heard again. "Why didn't you kill Joaquín, then, instead of the alcalde?"

Harriet saw Jake's mouth open, but he didn't have a chance to answer, as the jury and most of the crowd thought this was a huge joke. The uproarious laughter echoed about the adobe walls for a long moment. One of the jurymen was pounding the table with his fist in time to his roars of merriment.

Then at last there was a semblance of formality, as witnesses were called. Members of the posse that had gone out after Davy and the Murietas stood forward one after another, to testify that Captain Dexter had ridden with them. They described the twenty-four-hour chase, and then the gruesome discovery of the gully where the Murietas had camped. Everyone stared with fascination at Joaquín as the five bodies were described, but instead of screaming vengeance at the heavens, he merely strutted and smirked.

Throughout, men in the audience called out corroborative details, and the jurymen seemed to pay as much attention to this evidence as the rest. "Then we all come back," shouted one, who evidently had been one of the posse. "But Cap'n Dexter and his men, they carried on."

"And Giles," said another, but Mr. Giles scarcely looked at him. Instead, he was busily scribbling on a pad.

"That's right," said Jake. "The rest all gave up the chase, reckoning that Joaquín Murieta was not so much of a threat on his own, but I was determined to see the job through. So I pressed on, and followed the trail to the fort."

"After your man Davy Jones Locker?"

"I certainly hoped to find him, yes."

"Because he was the murderer of them Murietas?"

"Because he was in pursuit of Joaquín Murieta."

"And your two crewmen went too."

"And Giles followed us," said Jake.

Like everyone else, the head juryman looked at the printer. "And why, sir, did you follow them, sir?"

Mr. Giles audibly sighed, put down his pad of paper and pencil, and stood up. "Perhaps I was interested," he said casually. "Call me intrigued, if you like."

"And why should I call you that, huh? I don't even want to call you Giles."

This was the signal for another round of uproarious mirth. Mr. Giles merely looked world-weary. Then, when he could make himself heard, he said in his off-hand way, "You can say that I wanted to have a good look at this Davy, that I wished to admire the man who'd dispatched five desperate bandits so uncommonly neat. All single shots, in the head. A fine marksman, don't you agree?"

"Do I have to?" queried a juryman of no one.

More merriment. Mr. Giles looked more sardonic than ever. Then he said, "You can say, too, if you like, that I wanted to learn more of the fort's owner. Don Roberto Ross was the cause of much heartrending in this here province, on account of jumped claims and remarkably long drawn-out adjudication, sir, while he held the gold that was in contention in the vaults of Sefton's Bank for Miners. Then, when that gold disappeared in a very mysterious manner, men didn't just want to complain about it, sir, they wanted to see the color of his guts. In fact, Don Roberto was forced to run off to the hills, on account of there being so many who felt that strong desire. I'd heard, you see, that he had run all the way to Mexico. So imagine my astonishment, sir, when we found that man at home!"

"From what I heared he was plumb thunderstruck, too," someone in the audience shouted. "And from what I also heared, he flew at you like a hog at his dinner. You're certain you ain't the man what shot him?"

"That's a point," said the head juryman thoughtfully. He picked his teeth with the point of a jackknife, staring at the reporter all the time. "Did you shoot Don Roberto?"

"I did not, sir. I'm not any kind of marksman, I assure you."

Harriet frowned. The statement carried an odd emphasis, as if it was important. She saw Jake lift an eyebrow, and nod to himself.

"It don't take no marksman to shoot a man from the length of a rifle barrel," one of the jurymen objected.

"That, indeed, is true — if Don Roberto was shot from close quarters."

"You reckon he wasn't?" the juryman said incredulously.

The head juryman, Harriet saw, was scowling at Mr. Giles, and the others were frowning, as they worked this out.

Then one said, "You're tryin' to say that the man what shot all the Murietas in the back of the head from a distance as they ate their grub around their fire was the same feller who shot the alcalde?"

"Seems logical," said Mr. Giles in his insouciant way. He looked up at the windows of Sutter's Fort again, before returning his attention to the jury.

"And this Davy Jones Locker, he be a great marksman?"

Silence. Jake was sitting very still. Harriet waited tensely. She didn't want to remember how Davy walked into obstacles as if he didn't see them, but she did. Had he been a fine shot before his illness and his accident? She doubted it strongly. Slaves had very little opportunity to practice with guns, she was sure.

Then Tib Greene said heartily, "Why, good lord, sir, but Davy was famous for his shooting."

"You can vouch for that?"

"Aye, indeed." And the *Goslings* all called out affirmations of Davy's famous skill with a gun, their grins ingenuous. Even Bill, who was no longer with the Company, testified to his famous prowess with a rifle.

Harriet saw Jake shift uneasily. She had her arms folded tightly, gripping her elbows with her hands as she willed Jake not to speak. She saw him open his mouth ... and Mr. Giles forestalled him, saying thoughtfully, "Maybe good marksmanship don't come into it. Perhaps it isn't a factor."

Jake closed his mouth. Then Harriet saw that everyone was staring blankly at the printer, including the whole of the jury.

The old man in the wig snapped irritably, "What plagues your mind now, sir?"

"Why, naught but the thought of all the men who lost their gold on account of Don Roberto's trick with the legal confiscation while he considered long and hard about the rightful ownership. The same men who wanted to see the color of his guts after all that gold vanished, sir. The way I see it, half the miners in the diggings wanted to see Don Roberto dead — and some of them were right there at the fort, sir, I warrant you that."

"And how much gold did he steal from you, Giles?"

"Why, none, sir, none, on account of the fact that I've never had any. Nor was I one of his fellow conspirators."

"*Conspirators?*" echoed one of the jurors blankly.

When Giles nodded, there was a babble of comment all over the compound.

When it quietened again, the head juryman said, "What in tarnation do you mean?"

Mr. Giles paused before answering. Then he lowered his voice as if he was sharing a confidence, though his words were still perfectly clear.

He said, "This has been a most interesting affair, sir. I have written much about it, and expect to publish a great deal more. It has intrigued me greatly, and intrigues me still. The way I see it, there was a gang of seven, headed by an eighth, all with a fine trick to worm men out of their gold. First, there was the alcalde who couldn't make up his mind about who rightfully owned the gold that came from a claim that had been reported to him as being jumped, and was therefore in contention. And then there were his six deputies, who dug up all the gold in that contested claim, and carried it off to the bank. And then there was the banker himself, who by yet another trick claimed that gold as collateral on failed debts owed to his bank. And then, somehow, all that gold vanished into thin air. And what is most interesting of all, sir, is that only one man of that gang of eight is still alive."

Silence, blank silence. Then Joaquín screamed, "It was not me, the alcalde, no, not me. I was there, yes, in the stables, yes, making the llama into meat, yes. I was there, and I saw it, I saw the alcalde shot dead. I was the one who catched the captain, yes, me, I hit him senseless, arrested him, he did it!"

Jake roared, "But I had no bloody motive! Why would I kill Don Roberto?"

"Because of the cask!" Joaquín shrieked. "Because he discovered what was in the cask, your cask, he broke it open, and you saw him find what was inside."

The cask? What did he mean? Harriet was shivering with foreboding, and the crowd was muttering in equal mystification.

Joaquín Murieta whirled about and grabbed a canvas sack from the ground behind him. He gripped it, heaved, and hauled the dripping sack to the jurymen's table. Then he stood in front of the row of old men, holding out the bag, jerking with his hands so the contents rolled about inside.

"This," he screamed. "This is what the alcalde discovered when he opened the cask, and Capitán Dexter saw him do it!"

Silence. The jurymen all looked at each other. The headman stood slowly, and leaned across the table to peer into the open mouth of the bag. Then he said, "Oh holy Jesus," and sat down again

175

with a bump. He took a fast gulp of brandy.

As Harriet watched, the other jurymen did the same — they leaned over the table, they looked into the bag, and they sat down again very abruptly. Men in the crowd were shouting, "What is it? Show us, we wanter to see too," but the jurymen ignored them.

The old man in the wig said to Jake, "Do you know what is in that there bag?"

"I do," Jake said grimly. "But I swear I didn't see what was inside that cask until after Joaquín Murieta knocked me out. And that was after Don Roberto had been shot."

"Did you know that cask was there?"

"Yes. It came from the brig, and had been left at the fort."

"It was part of your own cargo?" one of the shipmasters asked.

"Aye, but I thought it held salt pork. At Tombez we took on provisions to bring to California, and that cask was one of many. We bought so many casks of salt pork and beef from the local people at Tombez that not all of them were inspected, because it was impossible to check every single one. We did find one in a spot check that proved to hold pigs' heads and trotters and no meat at all, and turned it down, of course, but this particular cask slipped by the inspection. The men who sold it to us had gotten away with their ghastly jest."

The crowd was growing rowdy and restive, scenting drama and feeling cheated. The cries of, "Show us! Show us!" were turning into a chant. The head juryman looked at them, nodded at Jake, and said, "Tell 'em what was in it."

Jake paused as the expectant silence fell. Then he said grimly, "Heads and feet. The heads and feet of men. Pickled."

A blank pause and then a roar of disgust and outrage. Never had a crowd tasted such sensation. One voice called out, "What yer reckon happened to the bodies?"

The head juryman hammered on the table for silence, and then said to Jake, "Did you recognize any of the heads?"

"Only one. He was an American deserter who had settled on one of the plantations. His name was Honest Mill Mason — or that is what he called himself. He was the one who told us about the discovery of gold in this territory. The last I saw of him, he was at work at his plantation, slaughtering pigs and cattle, ready to salt them down and buy his passage with the casks of meat. But he never turned up at the brig. I never saw him again."

Another uproar. Without bothering with his hammer, the head

juryman shouted, "Captain Dexter, why don't I ask you why you shot Don Roberto?"

Jake paused. The shadow of the hanging noose was lying on his forehead. Then he snapped, "Why don't you ask who sold me that particular cask of so-called salt pork?"

The old man in the wig looked at his fellow jurymen, and then shrugged. "Wa'al then, sir, what would be your answer to that question?"

"It was sold to me by Joaquín Murieta and his brothers."

Joaquín screamed, "He lies, yes, he lies! The desperate man, he lies to save his skin!"

"Then why, señor," drawled Mr. Giles, "did you have to butcher the llama for meat?"

"Exactly," said Jake with grim satisfaction. "Why did you need to kill the llama, when there was a cask of good salt pork for the taking? Was it because you knew exactly what that cask held?"

Dead silence. Then an outcry as men saw the logic of the argument. It was obvious, Harriet thought with a surge of relief, that this American crowd preferred a Spanish-American scapegoat to an American, if they could get one. Joaquín Murieta stared about wildly, his arms spread, his mouth wide. Men began to throw stones and dirt and bits of rubbish at him. One piece hit the noose and set it swinging, and the scent of lynch-justice was strong in the air.

Joaquín whined with fear and fury. Then he was running, bounding into the saddle of his horse. The animal reared and screamed, and bolted for the great open gate of the fort. The crowd scattered, and then regathered in his wake. Some men were calling for a posse to be formed, but the fascination of the trial brought them all back inside the compound.

The jury conferred for quite two hours while the shadows grew longer, but still the crowd waited. Men were placing bets on the outcome.

Jake sat on his stool and watched them all expressionlessly. The shape of the noose was lost in the shadows above his head.

When the old man who was the headman of the jury at last stood up, Harriet's arms were stiff from being folded so tightly for so long. Then, as she watched, the old man took off his wig, and replaced it with his hat. He waited until the shouting for a verdict had stopped and then he said casually, "The jury be a hung one."

Hung. Harriet's heart lurched at the word. Then she realized that the opinion of the jury was divided equally. Men in the crowd were as incredulous as she was, judging by the shouting, so the old man sat down again, hammered for silence, and then deigned to explain.

"It were theorized that the murder of the alcalde and the shooting of the five Murietas was done by the one fine marksman, and if that theory be a good one, then the shooter can't be Joaquín, for even a bandit don't shoot his own kin. And if that black man Davy was the one what shot them all, then Captain Dexter in part be culpable, on account of the black man Davy bein' one of his men, and his responsibility.

"Four of us think that, and four of us think that it were Captain Dexter who shot the alcalde. So," the old man said, "we've made up our minds California fashion. Captain Dexter, you have twenty-four hours to pack up your affairs and get quit of this place.

"If you're still 'ere this time tomorrer, then we'll stretch your neck and no debating about it. That's what you've got, twenty-four hours. Understand?"

TWENTY-FIVE

TWENTY-FOUR hours. Harriet couldn't believe the injustice of the verdict. The men in the crowd, however, had seemed happy with the outcome. Or perhaps, she thought, they had dispersed so fast simply because night was falling and their bellies were empty. It was Sunday, and maybe there were a few half-mad camp-preachers around, but there certainly was no church.

It was dark by the time they got back to the brig. Jake strode along as normally as usual, but though Harriet kept on insisting, "It isn't fair," he made no answer. When they arrived at the top of the gangplank the men vanished forward, all of them, even Charlie and Bodfish, following Tib and Dan to the galley under the forecastle deck. Undoubtedly, Harriet meditated, they were as keen to get the full details from Tib and Dan as they were to get their supper.

Then the decks were empty — except for Jake, who stayed, so Harriet stayed with him. As she watched, he stared for a long moment at the Embarcadero, but everything was quiet, the town lit only by lamps in tents and little campfires. The theater was dark and silent — as dark, silent, and deserted as the deck of the brig.

Then, to her utter disbelief, still without uttering a single word, Jake went to the other side of the deck, stripped off all his clothes, and dived over the rail into the river.

After only the slightest hesitation, she did exactly the same, surfacing alongside him with a splash and a gasp for air.

He said, "Harriet!"

"Have you gone mad?" she demanded.

Instead of answering, he said, "Can you swim?"

"Of course I can swim! Can you?"

He began to laugh, and then said, "I've been dreaming of swimming in this river for the past four days. I've never felt so dusty and ... *dirty*, in all my life."

"I didn't think seamen could swim."

"I thought the same of actresses."

The current was beginning to seize them. She ducked down

beside the brig, came up holding the end of one of the ropes that dangled down the side, and he grabbed the rope, too.

Then she said, "When we were not living with my great-aunt Diana — who had a mansion in London, you know, with long baths, and maids to bring hot water — the nearest pond was usually the only way we could get clean. The boarding houses that come as part of the acting contract aren't the kind that have bathing facilities, believe me. And water costs a penny a bucket, in England!"

"I thought English people liked being dirty."

"Jake!" She splashed him with her free hand. Then she said, "Do you really think you should be swimming?"

"My head is not as bad as it looks. I was turning at the time, so it was a glancing blow. And," he said with a wicked grin, "I've got you here to rescue me."

"Well, that is why I jumped in," she allowed. Then she said, "Oh Jake," and let go the rope and threw her arms around his neck and kissed him. They both went under and came up gasping, while the current threatened to float them downriver.

Jake struck out and grabbed the dangling rope again, and reached out an arm and grasped her arm. Then, when they were back alongside the *Gosling* she said, "I thought I would die during that farce of a trial."

"I had bad moments myself," he confessed, and pulled her close with his free arm, and kissed her, managing to do it so they didn't go under, this time.

Then he thoughtfully observed, "You have no clothes on."

"Neither have you."

"It's not a problem for me, but how do *you* expect to get back on board the brig? Abner should be in charge of the watch," he added.

But Abner had not been on deck when she'd jumped over, she remembered. Nevertheless, she said very firmly, "You are going to go up first, and hand down something for me to wrap myself in. My gown will do," she added. "It's on the deck by the rail, right by your dirty clothes."

She watched him swarm up the side of the brig, and then she had to hold onto the rope for some moments before he reached down an arm to help her up. He had been in the cabin to fetch a blanket — for her, she imagined, but when she stood up he wrapped it around them both.

They stood inside the blanket with their cool, wet bodies

pressed together, and then he said softly, "Dear God, how glad I am to be back with you, Harriet."

"So I notice," she said demurely, and he laughed and stepped back, and let her have the blanket to herself.

There was still no sign of Abner or the watch. The decks were as empty as the rigging, and so was the mess cabin when they arrived down the companionway. There was no one in the pantry, either. So where was everyone? Where was Bodfish? In the foc'sle, hearing the story from Tib and Dan, she supposed — or maybe they were all clustered about the galley under the forecastle deck, eating while they listened.

While she had waited in the river Jake had dropped her gown, shift, and petticoat on his berth, but when she made to get dressed he said, "Don't," so she perched on the sofa in the transom cabin with the blanket wrapped around her, her hair dripping about her shoulders.

Still without a stitch on his body, Jake disappeared, evidently into the pantry, because he came back with two bowls of hot baked beans and hunks of soft bread. After the strain of the day, she wasn't hungry, so he ate most of it himself, seeming to be starved. Then he took the bowls back to the pantry, and returned with coffee in mugs, and a basin of steaming water.

"Shave me," he ordered, and sat on the chart table chair.

"Yes, sir," she said, and went into the washroom to fetch shaving brush, towel, soap and razor. Then, standing behind him, she inspected the crown of his head, to find nothing more than an abrasion. As he had said, it had been a glancing blow. His dazed condition must have been due to shock, she thought, though the trek in the hot sun would not have done him any good. No wonder he had craved a cool swim.

He leaned his head against her as she lathered his cheeks, and she said, "Tell me exactly what happened at Don Robert's fort."

"Have you been there? Do you know what it's like?"

She nodded, and then said, "Yes," realizing that he couldn't see her face.

After wiping her hands on the towel, she dropped it on his thighs, and picked up the razor. Then she said, "I called there with Mr. Giles, when I ran away from the Vidries' ranch. He was going as far as Don Roberto's fort, so I left him there. Don Roberto ... *received us* ... if that is the right word ... on the top floor, and then Ah Wong and I carried on to Sefton's place."

She paused, remembering the horrible moment when Don Roberto had told her that two men had been killed at the *Goslings'* claim. Then, scraping lather and stubble with careful strokes of the razor, she said, "Don Roberto said he had plans to turn the place into a hotel. Did you see the furniture on the top floor? I wondered how he had hauled it all up the stairs."

Jake said, "I wondered if Davy was hiding up there. Tib and Dan looked around, but when they came down they said they found no one."

"Were they sure?" She remembered the great wardrobes, and the way the chairs and tables were piled in dark, massive heaps. Davy was tall, but he was also slender and lithe. She remembered how he would crouch in sunny corners of the deck, crooning to himself.

"Did they call out Davy's name? He would have been very frightened."

"They seemed very sure that no one was there."

Drawing out his left cheek with her fingertips as she scraped with the sharp razor, she wondered if Jake wished he had searched there himself. Davy would have certainly responded to his captain's voice.

Finally, she said, "There are windows in that room overlooking the courtyard and the stables. Or so I remember. A man with a rifle would have a good view from up there, even at night."

"A man with a rifle would have had a good field of fire from the bastion, too — and he could have fled from there with less chance of anyone noticing."

"Bastion?" she said, and then remembered the bastion on the corner of the wall, where Don Roberto flew his flag when he was home. There had been two bastions, she thought, and either one would have a good view of the stables.

"Anyway," Jake went on, "Don Roberto ran up the stairs and locked himself in the top room. We stood guard in the billiard room, but I was the only one awake when he crept down in the night. I took up my rifle and followed him to the stables, and found him crouching behind the cask — as if he was hiding from someone. When he saw me he came running out, and when I turned someone hit me — Joaquín Murieta, obviously. But it was almost as if Don Roberto was running *towards* Joaquín, not away from him. Then — everything went dim, but only for a minute. I remember seeing Joaquín break open the cask, just before he raised the alarm."

She paused, frowning. "So you don't think Joaquín shot Don Roberto."

"I think Giles might be right — that Don Roberto was shot from a distance, the same way the Murietas were shot. He was shot from either the upstairs windows, or one of the bastions."

"By Davy?"

Jake simply said, "What do you think?"

"Poor Davy," Harriet said, instead of answering.

She remembered Davy coming out of the night, how he had screamed, and how he had pushed her into the corral, out of the line of fire. He might be mad, she thought, but he had saved her life.

Then she scraped off the last of the lather. She came round to the front, picked up the towel and wiped Jake's face, knelt down, and said very wryly, "Dare I kiss you?"

He shut his eyes. "Oh, Harriet."

"Yes?" she said. "No?"

His eyes opened, and he shook his head as looked up at her. "I just don't know why I jerked away when you kissed me at Bedstead Gully ... I had dreamed of you, pictured you with Sefton ... and when you kissed me after shaving me it all came back to hit me, and..." He broke off, and stood up and gathered into his arms, and said very softly, "That poem, the Chinese poem you quoted. Was I really the distant man you wept for?"

"Well, let me think," she said, then saw his expression, and said, "Of course you were, dear idiot." And with a swoop she was being carried into his stateroom, and with a thump they were sprawled together on the berth.

He made love with utter concentration, without another word. She could hear his rough gasping, and feel the thud of his heart in his chest. Then with a groan he grasped her hips, hauling her tightly into him, fetching her at the same instant as he spent, throbbing for ever and ever.

After a timeless interval, moist and lax, they lay quiet in each other's arms. It was almost entirely dark. The one low lamp had been left behind in the transom.

Jake said quietly, "I'm not running away."

Harriet lifted herself on one elbow, staring down at him in consternation. "But you can't stop here and let them hang you! There's no question about it, we have to make sail in the morning!"

"If I go, it's a confession of guilt. You heard the verdict. And I have a big enough load on my name already."

He was talking about his reputation as a pirate, she thought. She leaned down and kissed him hard, and then said, "You must go. We all must."

He shifted, and she thought he smiled. "What about the play?"

"Mr. King will find another Malvina. The audience won't care, as long as Mrs. Marchant is there."

"She's still the Rage of the Season?"

"Actually, in this place and at this time, justifiably so."

He chuckled, smoothing her damp and tangled hair, and said, "No, you must stay here. Charlie will look after you and the brig. I'll come back after I've cleared my name — but to do that, I must find Davy. He's the only one who knows what really happened."

She lay with her head on his shoulder, thinking. At least, she thought, if he was in the hills searching for Davy, everyone would think he had obeyed the verdict and left.

Then she said hesitantly, "Jake, was Davy really such a good marksman?"

Jake didn't answer. He was silent so long and lay so still that she wondered if he had gone to sleep. Then he said, "You know, no one thought to ask Joaquín Murieta why he needed the meat."

"The llama meat?"

"Yes. He was emphatic about needing the meat. I think he was on the run. I think he meant to go a long way, where no one — or someone — would find him. He didn't want to steal or hunt food, because that would draw attention. So why was he so desperate? Who was it who could frighten a man like that so much?"

"Perhaps he was frightened of Don Roberto," she said. "Joaquín didn't seem frightened when he brought you to the Embarcadero — not until it looked as if he would get the blame for the murder. So perhaps he stopped being scared after Don Roberto was killed."

"Don Roberto was the scared one," Jake said. "I've never seen a man so scared in all my life."

"Because Joaquín was there?"

"There was no sign of Joaquín when we arrived at the fort, and Don Roberto seemed his usual self. That puzzles me, I must admit, because he wasn't afraid when he saw us, and he didn't seem nervous. Oh, he flew into a fury when he saw Giles, called him a lying muck-raking reporter, or words to that effect. Apparently, the authorities in Mexico had read what Giles had written about him in the papers, and thrown him out. But then, when Don Roberto learned that you were here in Sacramento City, and that Sefton's schooner was here too..."

Harriet frowned, puzzled, because she could see no connection between herself and the schooner — and she was certainly no threat to the little alcalde.

She said, "What did he say?"

"He cried out ... *Oh my God,* and then he said, *I'm dead!* He was terrified, Harriet, suddenly very terrified."

Dead. Harriet shivered, and felt Jake hold her more closely. Don Roberto was dead now, killed by whom? Not Jake, certainly, but perhaps by Joaquín Murieta — or by Davy.

She remembered the Murietas' cries of superstitious terror when Davy had come running down on them. She started to ask again about Davy, but then she realized that Jake had fallen asleep.

He slept like a dead man.

Harriet lay with open eyes a very long time, thinking, holding onto him. Then she, too, went to sleep. And when she woke, Jake was gone.

TWENTY-SIX

CHARLIE Martin told Harriet that Jake had taken a horse and ridden inland, following the same trail that the posse had taken a few days ago. Dan and Tib had gone with him, and Jake had hired the same Indian who had tracked the Murietas as far as the gully where five of them had been shot.

After she had nervously nibbled some breakfast Harriet went on deck, to find the brig deserted again. Chips had a gang at work at the theater, and the rest were on board Sefton's schooner. Harriet could hear hammering and splintering wood from the abandoned vessel. Evidently Jake had left orders for an even more thorough search than had been held before, because of Don Roberto's strange reaction when he had learned that the schooner was moored here.

Front Street was unusually crowded, she noticed then, more packed with restless men than she had ever seen it before. There was a palpable air of excitement. Men clustered in groups, moved on, joined other groups, talked animatedly. They stared at her with open speculation when she pushed her way across the street to the theater, and she could hear the commotion start up again once they were behind her. All the talk was about the murders of the Murietas and Don Roberto.

Men were laying bets on whether Jake Dexter would stay away or come back to defy the jurors' judgment. Apparently few had any idea of where the limits of the district ended, or where Sutter's began. Some called out to others that Captain Dexter would not be safe until he reached Monterey — and Monterey was much more than twelve hours' ride away, no matter how fast the horse or expert the horseman. They were confidently laying money on him being recaptured before he had got that far.

The crowd hanging about the door of the theater was just as riven with sensation. Some of the jostling men recognized Harriet, and tried to stop her, clutching her arm and shouting questions in her face. She ignored them, pulling away and then hammering on the door until Mr. King let her in.

He was red-faced and sweating, and wanted to know where she had been. Royal and Mrs. Marchant were practicing their lines on stage, and Harriet could hear Royal entreating Mrs. Marchant to keep to the script. He was having as little luck as Harriet had, and was as red-faced as the producer, and just as foul-tempered.

And Mrs. Marchant was in a bad mood, too. She tossed off her lines haughtily, with all the temperament of a prima donna, screaming at Royal when she thought he got his cues wrong, though she was always the one in error. Harriet had to brace herself to join them for the rehearsal.

A tray was brought in at noon with coffee and pies, but only Mrs. Marchant and Mr. King ate. Royal was too bad-tempered, and Harriet felt too fraught with suspense. She found herself shivering every now and then, wracked with foreboding. When the head juryman walked through the door in the mid afternoon, looking around with his face grim, it was as if she had been expecting something dreadful all along.

He was wearing the same blue coat with brass buttons, and the same yellow scratch wig. Mr. King had let him in. Harriet walked slowly down the aisle to meet him, thinking that the twenty-four hours was almost up, and wondering tensely if Jake had come back and been caught.

He said, "Miss Gray? Or should I call you Mrs. Dexter?"

Harriet swallowed, and said, "Miss Gray will do — it's my stage name. How can I help you?"

He said crossly, "I'm looking for Mrs. Dexter."

"May I ask why?"

"Wa'al, this theater does belong to Captain Dexter, don't it?"

Harriet frowned, feeling puzzled, not sure what to say. She had the papers for the lot, and the theater was technically hers, but in reality it belonged to the *Gosling* Company.

Prevaricating, she said, "Why do you ask?"

"Wa-al, that there brig out there, the brig *Gosling,* it does belong to him?"

Oh, dear God, she thought, had the news that Jake Dexter was condemned as a pirate reached California, to make his position even worse?

She said curtly, "The brig *Gosling* is his. It is Captain Dexter's legal property."

"But the vessel is still here, in Sacramento City," he said, his voice rising impatiently. "He's gone, but he's left the brig. So who has the papers?"

"Papers? What papers?"

"The ship's papers, ma'am!" He was shouting now, as if she were a child, or an idiot. "Because we need them to complete the legalities when we seize the brig."

"*What?* You can't do that, sir!"

"No? Then you jest watch us, Miss Gray. Captain Dexter heard the verdict, so he knows what he stands to lose. He were told to pack up his affairs within twenty-four hours and make himself scarce. Wa'al, he's gone, but he ain't packed up his affairs, no how, so he'll lose all the affairs he leaves behind. You say the brig is his, so it's clear he'll lose that. Now I want to know about the ownership of the theater."

"The theater is mine, sir!"

His eyes bulged. "But wimmen can't own property, and married wimmen in particular. Everything they reckon they might own belongs by right to their husband."

"I am not married!" she shouted at the full pitch of her acting voice. She was shaking with fury, never so angry in all her life. "I'm a widow, sir, if that's any of your affair, and I signed for this land and the theater that stands on it with a signature that I assure you is legal. Ask Mr. King, if you don't choose to believe me, and then you can offer your apologies, sir, but don't rely on them being accepted!"

The head juryman gobbled, shocked to an incoherent, thunderstruck semblance of his former self. Mr. King, summoned, dithered and looked embarrassed, adding to her fury.

"Tell him I was the one who hired out the theater to you, tell him that!" she shouted, and he winced. "Tell him about our legal arrangement!"

Mr. King was more red-faced than ever. "You hired it out under your stage name," he mumbled. "And I accepted your signature only a-cause Captain Dexter stood as guarantor."

She snapped, "And did he have to countersign, Mr. King?"

He shook his head reluctantly, and he and the juror made despairing gestures at each other. Both men seemed scandalized that she should know anything at all about such legal matters.

It was a long time before the old man took his departure, having reluctantly accepted the situation, still mumbling and shaking his head. The instant he was well away, she flew out of the theater and shoved her way through the crowd to the brig.

Charlie was on board, looking harassed. She didn't have time for preliminaries, so ordered, "Ready the brig for sailing downriver at once."

"*What?*"

"Time is of the absolute necessity, Mr. Martin. If the brig is not well clear of the Embarcadero by the time the deadline is up, the jury will send a posse on board to confiscate the vessel."

"But that ain't possible!" he objected. His eyes were wide and round in horror.

"I assure you it is!" she cried, and stamped her foot in frustration. "The head juryman has just been to see me. The verdict, if you remember, said that Captain Dexter had to pack up his affairs and leave the territory — it's just that they didn't make it clear that he had to take his affairs with him! I know it wasn't clear, and it certainly isn't fair, but the old bastard said that if the brig is still here when the deadline is up, they will come on board, demand the ships' papers, and confiscate the brig! So you have to get the brig downriver before the deadline is up."

"Oh dear Jehovah," cried Charlie. "It can't be done!"

"It can, it can!" she shouted. "He even threatened to take my theater from us!"

"What I mean is, it can't be done, Miss Gray! It takes more than a few minutes to get a ship ready to sail, you know! And in particular a brig what has been lying at a mooring for as long as we've been here. Even if we drop everything else, it'll take more than three hours, maybe four — and how many hours have we got?"

Harriet stared at him, shaken."Three hours?" she whispered, and then repeated it with her voice rising, on the verge of hysteria.

Had the head juryman deliberately delayed his call to make certain that it wouldn't be possible to get the brig away in time? It seemed horridly likely.

"Why?" she cried. "Why so long?"

It didn't make sense to her, for the topmasts hadn't been struck, not the way they were at Pueblo San Marco. Charlie took a frustratingly long time to explain. The hours the men had spent on the theater, Harriet gathered at last, were hours they had not spent keeping the brig shipshape. The sails had to be broken out, and bent on the yards and stays, and the running rigging had to be set up. And as for the standing rigging...

Harriet shut her eyes as her mind raced madly, and then opened them wide as inspiration sprouted.

Quickly, she said, "Get the men together, and do your best. The deadline is at eight, so you've got two hours. I'll make sure that you have at least two more hours after that."

"But how, Miss Gray?"

"Don't ask," she said. "But rely on it. I'll send Chips and his gang back to the brig, but I'll have to keep Valentine and Crotchet. Can you manage without them?"

Charlie seemed to take an age to respond, being lost in calculations. Then, no sooner had she registered his nod, than she was off, pell-mell back to the theater.

Mr. King, thank God, was still there. He was still awkward and inclined to hem and haw and prevaricate, though, and for several precious moments she thought that he would never pay attention. "I took your signature as lawful only to humor you and Captain Dexter," he grumbled, and then declared that if she liked doing men's business so much then he wanted a talk with her on theater business matters.

"I don't have time for that right now, Mr. King," she exclaimed, and threatened to walk off and leave him without a Malvina if he wouldn't pay attention to what she had to propose.

He subsided, and listened to her proposition, but then was more horrified and scandalized than ever. "Give out free tickets to tonight's show?" he cried. "But the house is fully booked! Not only do we have no room whatsoever, but it ain't good business! Why you would want to do something so boneheaded is sure beyond me, Miss Gray, and I don't know what your brother would say about it."

Harriet had yet to speak to Royal, and when she did, she would be sure it would be in private. And she had no intention whatsoever of informing Mr. King exactly why she wanted the jurymen safely installed on a bench in the theater while the *Goslings* got the brig under sail and well away from the Embarcadero.

Instead, she said craftily, "But it is wonderful publicity for Mrs. Marchant. These are important men, men of influence — men who will get word of Mrs. Marchant's stunning success as far as the upper Feather River!"

That clinched it. Mr. King, still humming and hawing, grudgingly allowed her to order two more benches squeezed into the box-tier, and to give complimentary tickets to all eight of the jurymen.

"But we'll have that talk," he threatened.

"Tomorrow," said Harriet, crossing her fingers.

She hurried backstage to send Chips and his gang back to the

Gosling, and to tell Royal and Valentine and Crotchet what was happening. They would have to work the panorama rollers and the stage effects as well as sing like troubadours, she said, and thanked God when they nodded brightly instead of arguing.

Then she set off to give the tickets personally to each and every juryman, as she didn't trust anyone else to do it. They were all in the taproom of Mr. King's partially built hotel, which made it easier than it might have been. The old man in the wig took his ticket with no good grace at all, peevishly declaring that it was a common device to avoid making the apology that she rightfully owed him.

Harriet agreed through clenched teeth, and raced back to the theater. It was time to get ready for the performance.

TWENTY-SEVEN

BY seven-thirty the pit was packed full and the box-tier was filling.

Harriet peeped through the crack at the end of the wooden drop curtain in an agony of suspense. The two extra benches in the box-tier were empty ... were empty. And then, suddenly, the eight men were there. None of them, thank Providence, had turned down the chance of free entertainment.

Mr. King, to her ironic amusement, was seated beneficently in the middle of this row of guests, as affable as if the idea had been all his own. He was smoking a cigar and wearing a top hat. As Harriet watched, the miners behind him knocked the hat off, She withdrew onto the stage before the fight got properly started.

The whole crowd was restive, the atmosphere stifling, sweaty, rowdy and hot. Captain Jake Dexter had stayed away, so they had been cheated of a hanging, and they now wanted a spectacle to make up for the anticlimax. When the five-man orchestra started up their first tune, the miners roared along with the song, but then they got tired of it, and started to clap in slow time.

Backstage, Valentine and Crotchet rolled their eyes at each other, and hurried out in front of the drop curtain. It became evident immediately that many of the men had seen the epic drama before, because the boys didn't have a chance to open their mouths before the audience was bawling out the chorus —

> *It will never do to give it up so*
> *It will never do to give it up so*
> *It will never do to give it up so, Mr. Brown*
> *It will never do to give it up so!*

The audience was still singing as Valentine hauled up the curtain, revealing Harriet, trembling, posed center stage, wrapped in a long blue shawl. Crotchet wound madly at the panorama rollers, to the accompaniment of roars of approval as the view of a New England cottage was revealed.

Was anyone left on the Embarcadero to watch Charlie and the few men he had left work so desperately against time? Harriet breathed slowly to still her racing heart, listening to the cheers. Then at last the miners settled, as Bert, alias Royal, slouched in from the wings.

> *Malvina! Love!*
> *Fain would I place you in a loftier home!*
> *Such as your merits claim —*

— and his voice was drowned out by a roar of adoring acclaim. Mrs. Marchant, as usual, had arrived on stage well ahead of her cue, and the whole audience, it seemed, had gone mad. She threw out her arms, blew kisses, tossed her hair, flourished her cloak like the robe of some fabled queen, and the miners cheered until the rafters rattled.

"Oh, let us be content!" Harriet cried, sending her trained voice to the back wall of the theater, and for a moment the hubbub faltered.

> *She would have said, but saw it was in vain*
> *So a marble pallor o'er her features stole*
> *And when it fled, left the fix'd purpose there*
> *To go with him!*

"He soothed his bride," responded Royal —

> *With promises to tempt the sea no more*
> *Vowing after this one gold-seeking venture*
> *To build a cottage 'mid their native hills*
> *Where all her favorite flowers would grow…*

"Of the house he promised to be builded," cried Mrs. Marchant, to Harriet's stupefaction —

> *He talked with childish delight*
> *No tittle must be forgotten, he vow'd*
> *Nor any flaw allowed!*

Royal hissed, "She's improvising, again!" but before he had a chance to panic, Mrs. Marchant returned to the script.

193

"Mournful kindred spake," she bellowed, while at least fifty miners chanted along with her —

Dissuasively of the perils and the pains
Of dire seasickness, the lack of the company
Of her sympathizing sex, of the rough life
So uncongenial to her soul,
Of the diggins of California!

"But she simply said, My husband will be there!" cried Harriet, and so the drama soared on, through stormy seas with sound effects managed by Crotchet, to the arrival at Portobello, accompanied by the thunder of a cannon, fired by Valentine. And again they trudged through the jungle, to arrive at Panama, and then embark —

"Their bark, a speck beneath the sky!" cried Mrs. Marchant, bounding onto the stage —

His hand conveys along
He makes the winds about her fly
And be gentle, or be strong!

She was stealing Harriet's lines, but the miners roared their approval nonetheless. And Harriet did not mind a jot, because the longer Mrs. Marchant delayed the progress of the play, the longer Charlie had to get the brig under sail.

Even she was disconcerted, though, when the Rage of the Season turned the death scene into rampant farce.

"Death met her there," hollered the drama-struck miner who had been hired by Mr. King to act the bit-part of surgeon —

— and Mrs. Marchant materialized yet again, to point a doom-laden finger at the unfortunate medic. "Afore he was struck with the lust, for Californian dust," she confided to the audience —

He healed the high and the mighty
He steered presidents and princes
Through the vales of many an ill
He treated countesses and princesses, too
... And waited for his bill.

The roar of laughter rocked the benches, and set the whole theater to creaking. Men slapped their thighs in their mirth. Others chanted, "Mrs. Marchant, Mrs. Marchant!"

Harriet, unable to wait an instant longer, rose wraithlike from her couch, hoping that the audience would assume she was now in the guise of a departing spirit, and wafted away through the wings. Then, picking up her skirts, she headed out the stage door and pelted along the alley to Front Street.

It was damp and quiet, dark and still. It was ten o'clock, well past the deadline Jake had been given by the headman of the jury. In the distance dogs yapped, a sad and lonely noise after the rowdy beat indoors. The river made no sound, flowing softly on its long, tortuous route to the sea.

Harriet's heart was thumping as she squinted at the Embarcadero, scared to blink in case she missed what was there.

Or was not there.

The roar from the theater was beginning to be boosted by the dreaded stamp of boots. Harriet whirled and ran back into the theater, where she found the phantasmagorium, crept into it, and lighted a spermaceti candle, set to act the entrancing specter.

"For thee, for thee, vile yellow slave," recited Royal in a bad-tempered bellow, as Harriet drifted onto the boards —

> *I have lost a heart that loved me true*
> *I crossed the tedious ocean wave*
> *To roam in climes unkind*
> *The cold wind of the stranger blows*
> *And chills my wither'd heart*
> *And now this dark and untimely grave*
> *And all for thee, vile yellow slave!*

Unmoved by this pathos, the miners were back to yelling for Mrs. Marchant. But, underneath her calico cover, Harriet was smiling. She had arrived on the Embarcadero just in time to see the brig steal off downriver.

TWENTY-EIGHT

ROYAL and Valentine and Crotchet went to Sefton's abandoned schooner to camp for the night, while Harriet begged Mr. King for the use of one of the rooms in his almost complete hotel.

Despite his grand talk and fine prognostications, the room that Harriet borrowed measured just ten feet by twelve, and was infested with vermin. Though the building looked substantial from the outside, being clad in brick and wood, and adorned with a fancy verandah below and a delicate balcony above, its lining was calico. Rats skittered about in the gap between the cloth and the cladding, and as she listened to the pattering of little feet, Harriet thought she might never get to sleep. But instead she dropped off at once, and spent the rest of the night in the stunned sleep of exhaustion.

She was awakened by a commotion in the street outside. It was very early, not quite dawn, but the noises as some heavy object was heaved off a cart and carried into the foyer were loud. Something was being delivered, she thought.

As she lay still, gathering her thoughts, she recognized Mr. King's voice, and Mrs. Marchant's shrill giggle, which sounded even more hysterical than usual. The other voices were male, and American, one of them very bad-tempered and slightly familiar. She frowned, but was unable to pin it down. Then she heard the visitors leave, and the hotel was quiet again.

It was too late to go back to sleep, so she got up, got dressed, and put up her hair. Then she walked slowly along the calico corridor to the reception lobby.

This lobby was also the billiard room. No one was there. The early light glimmered on the bottles arrayed on the wall behind the bar — and on the *thing* that had been delivered, and which was now sitting on top of the cloth that covered the billiard table.

Harriet stared at it. Then she said aloud, "What the devil?"

Mr. King came in, and beamed widely when he saw her. Mrs. Marchant was with him. They were wearing the same clothes they had worn the night before, and smelled highly of champagne. They looked even more pleased with themselves than usual, Harriet thought, but she scarcely looked at them. Instead, her attention was on the *thing*.

She demanded, "Where did *that* come from?"

"Aha," said Mr. King. "It has only just been delivered. A boat from the frigate *Savannah* brought it."

"Dr. Stirling brought it," said Mrs. Marchant brightly. "He told us to give it to you."

"*Me?*"

"It's a coffin," said Mr. King helpfully.

"I *know* it's a coffin," said Harriet. The last time she had seen it, the coffin had been propped in the pinnace, ready for the containment of Sefton's corpse after it was dug out of the grave under the spreading branches of the oak tree.

"It's yours, he said, all yours," said Mr. King, and guffawed, thinking it a mighty joke.

Then, to Harriet's horror, he took hold of the lid and began to lift it. She gasped, and Mrs. Marchant squealed, but he ignored both females, heaving up instead. The lid was heavy, or maybe screwed down, but then the metal creaked and began to give way.

"That Dr. Stirling," he grunted in a conversational manner, while his muscles strained and the metal creaked, "he told me to inform you it was a scandal — "

And with a screech the lid came up. Harriet squeezed her eyes shut in horror, but when she heard Mrs. Marchant's giggle she opened them again.

And the coffin was empty. The early light bounced around inside its clean metal interior.

Harriet swallowed. Then she heard herself say in a miraculously steady voice, "Scandal?"

"He was enraged, Miss Gray, truly indignant."

"About what, Mr. King?"

"He said it is a scandal to have the bones of a heathen Indian in a grave what is supposed to be the last resting place of a prominent Philadelphia citizen. He said to tell you it was the wrong body, and he was greatly offended to have been tricked."

Wrong ... wrong body. *The wrong body.*

Time froze. Harriet stared at Mr. King, her entire form rigid. The wrong body. Not Sefton. Mei-Mei in that grave but not with Sefton. Ah Wong, shouting, beseeching, pleading with her to run, run away, the day she had arrived in Sacramento City.

Ah Wong. *She had to find Ah Wong.* She had to find Ah Wong and clear Jake's name, because she knew now who had shot the Murietas and Don Roberto. It wasn't possible, and it made no sense, but she knew she was right. All she had to do was find Ah Wong and prove it...

As if from a great distance, she heard Mr. King's voice say, "That business."

"What?"

"You promised to have that talk today. I've drawn up the papers, all I need is a price and your signature."

Then he shoved a document onto the billiard table, alongside the coffin.

Harriet stared at it without seeing the words, and when she didn't speak he picked it up again and rattled it irritably. "Name a price, Miss Gray, name it! Jest name it!"

She blinked, and said the first wild sum that came into her head. Ah Wong, she thought fiercely, Ah Wong had to be at the barracks. His job there would be to translate for the coolies, and persuade them not to do anything that might be regarded as mutinous.

Then, bemusedly, Harriet found the paper under her nose again. Mr. King had written in the figure she had voiced, without any kind of argument. She had to be told several times where to sign her name. She didn't bother to read it — it was like watching some remote drama that had nothing whatsoever to do with Harriet Gray.

Then the document was taken away, folded, and put into Mr. King's inside jacket pocket. He said jovially, "What are you going to do with it?"

"With what?"

"With the coffin, Miss Gray, the coffin. Quite a thing, huh? A coffin, all of your own — to keep in case of an emergency, huh?"

He began to guffaw, slapping his thigh with great enjoyment, while Mrs. Marchant's abundant bosom shook with her own happy laughter.

Harriet said wildly, "Take it, Mr. King."

"What?"

"Take it. Take the coffin, consider it yours."

"But what the tarnation will I do with it?"

"Install it in your best bathroom, sir. It'll be the first long bath in California."

Long enough for a man to stretch his bones in, she thought, and winced.

When Harriet left, Mr. King was staring thoughtfully at his new acquisition. She walked out of the door and down to Front Street. The Embarcadero was almost deserted. She picked up her skirts and began to run.

Most of the coolies would be working at the various kitchen establishments, she thought. This was the best time possible to find Ah Wong, winkle him out, soothe his fears, reassure him, and persuade him to testify to the jurymen. Her breathing was harsh in her throat, her throat sore and dry with her panting, and she had a sharp pain in her side, but nevertheless she kept on running.

The road seemed endless — never had the two miles seemed so long. But finally her steps rattled on the bridge over the stream. Then she saw the horses — the small cavalcade coming down the hill beyond the barracks, coming in from the foothills. Her sight was blurred, but she could count the number ... one, two men on horseback, a man on a mule, an Indian on a third horse, leading a fourth horse by the bridle.

Harriet ran stumblingly, beginning to weave from side to side. The men on horseback were Tib and Dan. The man on the mule was Mr. Giles. And then there was the Indian. Jake Dexter wasn't there ... but the fourth horse was carrying the slung body of a man. She heard her despairing voice cry, "No, oh no." She was blinded with tears, but still she kept running.

She ran past the high fence of the corral and saw the well and the bear in blurred glimpses, through the gaps in the palings and the tears in her eyes. Then her steps rattled on wood again, as she ran into the empty foyer of the barracks.

She screamed, "Ah Wong, please, Ah Wong! Ah Wong, please come out, I know you are here!"

No one answered. The first room of the barracks was empty, except for the long deal tables and the tiers of bunks. As she had guessed, the coolies were all out at work. She ran stumblingly, knocking her hip against a table, crying, "Ah Wong!"

Then at last she saw a man. He was walking towards her from across the second big room.

She said, "Tell me, where is Ah Wong?" And then she blinked hard, and her sight cleared, and she recognized the man.

Joaquín Murieta. *Joaquín Murieta.*

Harriet stopped dead, staring at him. He was holding a knife, a big knife. It had a shiny blade, very sharp, and was probably the same knife that he had used a long time ago, when he had cut her cheek while he was threatening to cut off her hair. Her throat was too frozen to scream.

Then he laughed ... he *laughed*. The contemptuous sound gave her the strength of fury. She whirled, taking him by surprise, and shoved a table hard at his knees. Then, as she heard his curse, she ran into the second of the two ground floor rooms, and slammed the door.

This room was also empty, the blankets on the bunks disheveled, and the tables cluttered with the remains of the coolies' breakfast. Harriet looked wildly around for furniture to wedge against the door handle. She was breathing fast, the sound loud in her ears, panting too raggedly to call for Ah Wong.

And a man walked in through another door — the door on the other side of the room, the one that led to the winding stairway. She recognized him at once.

It was her husband, Frank Sefton.

TWENTY-NINE

Frank Sefton looked the same as always.

Harriet stood staring at him, rigid in every fiber, remembering what a fine horseman he had been, and how he had been admired in New Zealand as a crack shot with a rifle. Colonel Sefton, member of the United States militia, urbane gentleman-sportsman.

Frank Sefton still looked like the nobly born horseman she had first met in Auckland. Even from ten feet away, she could smell the fresh scent of leather and horse sweat. He was wearing a silk shirt and brown riding clothes, and he was carrying a long whip. Though he did not have a rifle, it was obvious that Sefton had been out riding. *Hunting.* Harriet pictured the dead body on the fourth horse, and swallowed on sick misery.

Steadying her voice with a huge effort, she said, "Where is Ah Wong?"

"Dead, my dear Harriet. Dead."

She said, "Oh dear God." Then, viciously, loathing inside her, she cried, "You killed him — poor little harmless Ah Wong, *you murdered him.*"

"No, no, you murdered him yourself, my dear," he corrected in his pedantic way.

Incredibly, Sefton smiled, with the pouting of his little rosebud mouth that she remembered so well. "You murdered him when you came to Sacramento City," he explained, with his usual air of speaking to her as if she were a mere child. "You murdered them all, because when you came I realized that they had all lied to me. I had ordered that you be killed, that your body be put into the bed with the dead Indian — before the house was set on fire, you see. It was a good plan, a plan that would have convinced everyone that the other body, the one beside yours, was mine. It was a clever plan, devised to gammon everyone that I was dead, but even though it was a good plan, they disobeyed me. They failed me, and then they lied. Ah Wong helped you escape, dear Harriet, and so it was you who killed him."

She said with horrified realization, "You're mad. You've gone mad." His eyes had always flushed red with rage, but now she saw that they were eternally red.

"No, no, it was Ah Wong who was insane, my dear. He was insane enough to defy me. He cheated me — me! He lied to me. He killed his own daughter so that I would never know that you still lived, and put her body in your bed. My little Mei-Mei, he killed her and stole her away from me, his own daughter! Because he loved you more."

Mei-Mei — Sefton's mistress — had been Ah Wong's daughter? It was impossible. Ah Wong had been only thirty-two, so how old had she been? Tweve? Thirteen? Sefton had enjoyed despoiling innocence, Harriet remembered, and felt sick. So that, she thought, was the valuable possession Ah Wong had sold to Frank Sefton in exchange for the passage to California — the passage that had proved to be a voyage to hell.

She looked at her husband with contempt and loathing. "So why did you have to pretend to die, Frank?" she demanded. "So you could steal the gold? The gold that Don Roberto deposited in your bank? I think so — so where is it now? Did the Murietas take it, and run off to Mexico with Don Roberto? Or did they have their own poor little share, all spent now, while your share — which I am sure was by far the biggest share — is ... where?"

She stared at him bitterly, but he said nothing. The red eyes were unblinking, as protuberant as a hunting lizard's. Only his hands moved, drawing out the thong of the whip, letting the end drop, drawing it out again.

Harriet's mind was running more and more surely. She said, "Yes, do think that is what happened. And then Don Roberto found he wasn't welcome in Mexico any more — but it didn't really matter, because he thought you and the schooner were well away, with your share of the gold. But then he found he was wrong — because you were here all the time. You stayed here in the barracks with the Chinese coolies you had imported — why? Why did you stay — why didn't you sail away in your schooner, as planned?"

Then she remembered the many times she had listened to Captain Mervine's monologues, and the words she remembered clicked in her mind, making sense, making a pattern. "Captain Mervine was searching every vessel for deserters and their gold — and arrested your crew as soon as the schooner touched the Embarcadero. They were deserters from his own frigate!"

202

But still Sefton said nothing. It was as if her words were just slapping at his ears, making no sense. Instead of speaking, he drew the thong of the lash out, dropped it, drew it out again.

"And what foul luck for you, Frank," she said with contempt. "Because once your seamen were gone, you had lost your only means of escape — unless you rode off, abandoning the gold. What a scare it must have put into you — what evil luck, for an evil man. And then I arrived, and you realized how your fellow conspirators had cheated and lied. Poor little Ah Wong, did you torture him to find out what had really happened the night of the fire? I believe you did, and then you killed him in your rage. For the first time, you realized why your precious little Mei-Mei hadn't come to join you before you sailed from Pueblo San Marco — no wonder your sanity broke."

And he moved. It was as if a pent-up flood of bile had been released. His whip lashed out at her face.

Harriet shrieked, and jumped back. He laughed, and cracked the lash again. The whip was long and thin and plaited, California style. He had no other weapon. His rifle was somewhere else, left behind. But the whip was enough. Harriet was forced to keep on backing away from him while he implacably followed, flicking the lash.

As she stepped away she snapped, "It was *you* who shot the Murietas — because they betrayed you by not obeying your orders. And it was *you* who shot Don Roberto, for exactly the same reason!"

But still he refused to be distracted by words. Instead of answering, he kept on moving, flicking the whip as he came, forcing her to back away, gradually increasing his pace, forcing her to move faster and faster, while a cold smile settled on his pouting little mouth.

Harriet risked a quick glance over her shoulder. She was being forced toward the winding stairs that corkscrewed within the corner bastion of the barracks, and ended up on the narrow balcony with the low rail, the balcony that overlooked the corral and the bear. It was horrifically easy to imagine what would happen after she ran out onto that balcony. There was no escape. The door she had come through was out of reach, because it was behind Sefton ... and it was also the door to the room where Joaquín Murieta could be listening.

She shouted out in her trained actor's voice, projecting her words. "Joaquín Murieta, *escucha!* — listen to me!"

She shouted in Spanish. "Don Joaquín," she cried, "the man

who shot your kin is here, in this room with me, the same man who pretended to be dead! You thought he sent for you because he wanted me killed — properly this time, so he could see it for himself. But he had more plans than that — because he wanted vengeance on you and your brothers for not carrying out his orders, the night you set his hacienda on fire. He went to the place where you planned to camp on the way to Don Roberto's fort, and waited for you, he lay in ambush, and after you had arrived he shot your brothers. From the back, from a distance — he shot them from a distance, with his rifle, from his lair on the hill. Your brothers were killed one by one, each one shot in the back of the head — and this man is a fine marksman, a man who is capable of making such difficult shots. Colonel Sefton is the man who killed your kin — the man who is in this room with me, he put your brothers down like dogs! Listen to me, Joaquín Murieta," she cried in English, "for I speak the truth!"

The whip cracked. Frank Sefton snarled, "Bitch."

The end of the lash touched her shoulder in a fiery strand of pain. Backing off, Harriet shouted again, "Joaquín Murieta, *escucha!* Listen to me, listen, because I will shout this again from the balcony, where you can see my face as I speak!"

Then she whirled and ran up the stairs, round and round in dizzying circles, while Sefton advanced step by step, keeping pace with her frantic flight. Breath sobbed in her ears, and she knew with ghastly clarity exactly what was going to happen, in nightmare progression — her dizzy stumbling burst onto the balcony, tripping, and then the push that sent her over the low rail. And then — the bear, the roar, the gnash of jaws, no mark or shot on her body to tell the world that she had been murdered by Frank Sefton — Sefton, who was innocent, had to be, for Frank Sefton was dead and buried on his ranch on the Feather River.

She lurched out onto the balcony, sobbing, stumbling, sick with dizziness — and Jake Dexter caught her in his arms.

Harriet gasped. It was impossible, the wondrous impossible. She shivered wildly as she touched him all over, Jake, her love, Jake, warm, strong, Jake, alive. *Alive.*

She whispered, "Oh dear God, my sweet love, I thought you were dead." Then, violently, she exclaimed, "Sefton! Sefton is alive!"

"I know," he said gently. "I've known it for quite a while."

And Frank Sefton ran out onto the balcony, moving so fast that Harriet thought for an instant that he would topple to the death he had planned for herself. But he stopped. He caught the sides of the doorway, and stopped. There had been no danger of Frank Sefton toppling. He had simply come to deliver that final push.

He looked at her. His mouth was open a little, like a half-open rosebud. Then he looked at Jake.

"Harriet, my dear, who is this man?" he inquired.

He sounded as formal and polite as if they were at a social gathering, and Harriet stared at him with a horror that was almost pitying, because he sounded so very insane.

Then, incredibly, he tut-tutted. "He will have to die too, you know," he said. "You are too impetuous. Harriet, you should take more care, because you have caused so many deaths already. But it must not be known that I am still alive! There must be no shadow of doubt that I am dead and buried — for how else can I retrieve my gold, in the rainy season, when everyone has gone? I'm dead, and the world must know that, or I shall have to kill ... and kill."

"Dead?" Jake harshly echoed. "If you want the world to know that, you shouldn't drop your cigaretto ends while you lie in wait for the men you are going to shoot."

Cigaretto ends? Harriet stared at him, bewildered. Then she remembered the leisurely way Sefton had scraped tobacco into squares of paper, twisted the ends and then smoked them. Mr. Giles had remarked on it, she recollected. Had he told Jake about Sefton's affectation? When she looked down at the path, Mr. Giles, on his mule, was looking up at her, as if in affirmation.

For once, he wasn't jotting in his pad. Instead, he was staring at the scene on the balcony, fascinated. She could see the shine of his face, and the droop of his damp moustaches. Tib and Dan, on their horses, were further up the track. The Indian was closer, standing beside his horse and the horse that had carried the body. They were all looking up at her — and Jake. And Sefton.

Harriet looked down. The corpse had been dropped onto the ground face up, as if for identification. She took one glance and then had to look away, swallowing. The dead man was Davy, poor Davy, dead and much decayed.

Then she heard Joaquín Murieta scream, "Colonel Sefton!"

Joaquín Murieta came into sight. He walked to Davy's corpse, looked down at it, spat to one side, and then stood straddle-legged while he stared up at the balcony and screamed Sefton's name again.

Harriet felt Jake's hand tighten on her arm, for it was the sound of vendetta, an ancient, vengeful shriek from a barbaric past. It didn't seem to affect Sefton, however. Instead, he walked to the rail, looked down, and said, "Shut up, you fool."

Joaquín Murieta shouted in Spanish, "This man is the black man, the one you told me shot my brothers. But this black man has been dead for days, Sefton. She is right, the gray filly — it was you, you who murdered my brothers!"

Sefton stamped his foot. He snapped in English, "I told you to shut your mouth!"

Then he moved away from the rail. Harriet flinched, and felt Jake shift to shield her, but Sefton merely went to the stairway and ran down. She could hear the furious clatter of his riding boots go round and round and then fade with distance.

Then he came into sight on the path below. He was slapping the air with his whip, and didn't even seem to see Mr. Giles, Tib and Dan, the Indian, or even Davy's body. There were men in the distance, running up the track from the Embarcadero, but Sefton didn't seem to see them, either.

Instead, he said in English, "Joaquín Murieta, you have to get me away from here. We will kill Mrs. Sefton and this other man and bury them, and then we will go away until it is safe to retrieve the gold. I remember well where it is, I hid it myself, the same night that my men were arrested and taken away. All I had was my Chinese servant and a mule, but we had the whole night to get it to its hiding place. When the time comes, when it is safe, all we will have to do is shoot the bear. But you must help me to leave, and hide me until that time comes."

"Yes, I will help you," said Joaquín in Spanish. "I will help you, yes. To leave." He stepped forward. He had the knife in his hand.

Sefton scowled. When Joaquín came another pace he cracked the whip. Harriet heard the crack of leather, but the Ecuadorean merely lifted his free hand, snatched the end, and contemptuously flicked the whip out of Sefton's grasp. Then he threw it away.

He said in Spanish, "And now you die." Taking Sefton by the shoulder, he pushed him down until he knelt in the dirt.

No one moved. Harriet stood rigid, transfixed with horror. She saw the men in the distance run faster, but Tib and Dan and Mr. Giles were as frozen as she was, all three as silent and still as the Indian. Jake stood rigidly, too. It was like watching some kind of ritual, too ancient to be fully understood.

Sefton began to whine with terror. He *groveled*. The sun was rising over the clouds on the horizon, and the shaft of first light hit the blade of the knife as Joaquín Murieta held it high, turning it red.

Sefton whined, "Spare me, and the gold is all yours — all the others who knew about it are dead, I made sure of that, they won't cheat again, or take what is mine ... Kill me, and you will never see that gold, because the answer to its hiding place is one that only I can solve..."

Joaquín Murieta said nothing. Instead, he waited for Sefton's pleading to stop. The men from the fort were running up the path, and when Harriet recognized some of the jurymen she cried, "Stop Joaquín from killing him! We need a confession from the real murderer — Colonel Sefton!"

Instead, the men stopped, mesmerized by the primitive tableau. Sefton silenced, and Harriet saw him take his last look at the hills, the sky, the sun ... and the knife came down.

Jake said, "Oh Christ."

Then he said, "Don't look." Joaquín had set his boot on the slumped body, pressing it as a butcher presses the blood from a slaughtered sheep.

Harriet shut her eyes, fighting sickness. When she opened them again, it was to see Joaquín Murieta mounting the horse that had carried Davy's corpse. Urgency rushed through her, and she shouted in Spanish, "Don Joaquín, tell them that Captain Dexter did not kill the alcalde!"

Joaquín stopped. He looked all around, and then up at Harriet. "He did not," he said loudly, in English. "Colonel Sefton shot the alcalde from the bastion of his own fort, yes. And Colonel Sefton, yes, died a coward."

Then he galloped away. No one tried to stop him, and no one tried to chase him. Instead, they arrested Jake, and held another trial, after which, incredibly, in spite of Joaquín Murieta's shouted statement, the jurymen decided that Joaquín Murieta himself had killed the alcalde.

The verdict didn't make sense.

But it didn't matter, because at the same time they acquitted Captain Jake Dexter.

THIRTY

THE bear was gone.

Everyone had talked for weeks of shooting it, but when they actually looked as if they were going to send someone in with a gun, the two mountain men roused themselves and took the bear away. Now all the gossip was about how those two characters had walked into the corral as casual as you please, put a leash on the bear, and led him out. Without anyone even trying to stop them, they had left Sacramento City, along with their fearsome pet.

Harriet held Jake's arm as they walked over the bridge to the empty corral. Two days had passed, but she still couldn't stop luxuriating in the feel of him, his warmth, his scent of soap and leather, the way he strode so strongly, the fact that he breathed, that both of them still lived. That he had been waiting for her on the balcony.

"Once Giles and I realized that Sefton must be alive," he'd told her, "it was obvious that Davy was dead — and where he'd been killed, too. The poor fellow was following close behind the Murietas, so while Sefton might have been surprised to see him, it would have been easy enough for him to pick him off as he galloped into the gully. So we knew that his body would have to be within range of where Sefton had waited in ambush."

"Where he left all those cigaretto ends," Harriet said, and sighed. It seemed poetic, somehow, that the silly little affectation should have spelled Frank Sefton's downfall.

"And it was obvious where Sefton was hiding. It had to be the barracks. Why else would Ah Wong have begged you to run away?"

"So you lay in wait on the slope behind the barracks, to watch for Sefton?"

"While Tib and Dan and Giles went with the Indian, to find poor Davy's corpse," he affirmed.

They had all arrived at the barracks at once — Tib, Dan, Mr. Giles and the Indian, with Davy's poor dead body, and Harriet, herself. From his hiding place, Jake had watched Harriet run up the track, and at once he had dashed down the hill to meet her. But, by the time he arrived, she had gone into the barracks, and Joaquín Murieta barred the way into the room where she was trapped. Harriet's shouts had warned him what was happening, though, so Jake had run up the second stairway — and had arrived on the balcony just in time to catch her...

Jake stopped. Harriet stopped too, and when she looked around she saw that they had arrived at the corral. The mountain men had left the gate open.

Jake pushed back his hat, and looked at her with his eloquent eyebrows slanted. "You really believe you know where Sefton hid all the confiscated gold?"

"His share of it, anyway — which I bet was a great deal more than half." Harriet paused, thinking it over again, and then said with certainty, "Sefton said the answer was hidden in an old puzzle, and I am sure the puzzle he had in mind was the map of Judas Island in Captain Schouten's old journal. I saw the marks where he had traced it, and it was typically arrogant of him to say that he was the only one who could solve the mystery."

"But you think you've solved it?"

"I *have* solved it, dear Jahaziel. I solved it a long time ago — months ago, while I was at the Vidrie mansion. While you were hunting for gold in Bedstead Gully, I was hunting for gold on Judas Island."

"And?"

Jake was being remarkably patient, she thought, and she smiled at him. "Remember those letters L A S? And how they were printed directly above a picture of a bear?"

"Yes, dear Harriet, I do."

"The well," she said, and pointed at the well in the middle of the corral.

"The well?" She had never seen him so astonished.

"The well," she repeated. "The important animal was the bear. All the other animals Captain Schouten drew on the map were for distraction, to take attention away from the bear. And remember how the old pirate liked to quote French, and make dreadful puns?"

"I do indeed," admitted Jake.

"The French for bear is *ours*, and if you add *ours* to L A S you get l-a-s-o-u-r-s, which is a pun for *la source*, the well."

"Jehovah," said Jake. Then he let out a roar of laughter. "You think Sefton struggled to get his gold up here, threw it down the well for safe-keeping — and then two mountain men wandered along and put the bear into the corral?"

"Not only was it unintentionally poetic, but very ironic, too," she smilingly agreed.

"Or perhaps he paid the two men to put the bear there, to keep other men from getting at his gold," Jake amended, spoiling her fun.

"Oh!" she said.

Whether he was right and she was wrong was impossible to prove — but it was easy to find out if the gold was really down there in the well. Young Bill was summoned, lowered on a rope, and a couple of minutes later a cry of EUREKA-A-A echoed up the funnel.

Bill was hauled up, and so, in due course, up came the gold. The brig arrived back at the Embarcadero just in time for the *Goslings* to claim their twenty thousand dollars' worth, still in parfleshes, and still marked with the names of the owners in dispute, just the way Don Roberto had marked them. The other claimants being the Murietas, who were all either dead or fled, there was no problematical adjudication to be made, and the gold was briskly taken on board.

As for the rest of the gold that was brought up from the well, it was up to the jurymen to decide who rightfully owned it, and Jake Dexter was happy to leave the problem to them.

"Oh-h-h," sang Valentine, "the gold, they say —

Is brighter than the day
And now it's mine, oh how I shine
And sing dull care away, suh!

"Do you reckon the well on Judas Island still holds the Panama treasure, Miss Gray?" asked Bodfish.

The *Gosling* Company was holding a meeting on the deck of the brig, and they were all smiling and complacent, because twenty thousand dollars' worth of gold was a lot better than nothing.

Harriet said, "I doubt it. If Captain Schouten knew where it was, surely he would have taken it away? But the decision isn't up to me. You may well decide to go and have a look."

"But what about the theater?" said Chips.

"Oh," said Harriet, and swallowed. Then she said in a low voice, "I sold it."

"You *what?*" cried Royal.

"I sold it. To Mr. King. I'm very sorry, as I had no right, I should have got permission from the Company first. But he insisted. It was part of the bargain I made when I asked him for free tickets for the jurymen. Mrs. Marchant, you see, is the Rage of the Season, and no doubt about it, and Mr. King's commercial sense is infallible. He is convinced that she'll make a fortune for him, just as long as he owns the theater in which she performs. He doesn't need us, he just needs her. And the theater."

"He could well be right," ruminated Royal.

"So I hope that you're not all very angry," said Harriet.

"Are you angry?" said Jake to Royal.

"God, no," said Royal with passion. "If it means that I never have to share the boards again with the most awful ham I have ever encountered, then I know there really is a divine Providence."

Then Royal said to Harriet, "How much did King pay?" And the men were all looking at her again.

Harriet paused. Then she said ruefully, "I think I could have got more if I had been a tough bargainer." She smiled at Jake, and added, "But I was in a dreadful hurry."

"How *much*?" roared Royal.

"One hundred and fifty thousand dollars."

"*One hundred and fifty thousand?*"

"You rogue, you beautiful rogue!" cried Jake.

"What next?" said Bodfish, after writing down the numbers of the good, round sum.

"Well, as a matter of fact," said Royal thoughtfully, "I've been talking to a man with the latest reports from New Zealand. Did you know," quoth he, "that the colonists from New Zealand and New South Wales are all attention for this gold rush, too? They're baying to get here, and the authorities at San Francisco are all of a dither about it, because these colonists aren't American, you see. So a number of captains are making huge profits out of smuggling these unwanted aliens into the territory."

Chips pulled a face. "You're surely not suggesting we go in for such squalid business?"

"Good God, no!" said Royal, more energetic than ever. "My scheme is much more dashing, adventurous, and profitable!"

"It is?" said Jake suspiciously.

"I've also heard that there is a certain class of wealthy colonist who hankers after the ancient sport of deer hunting. And in New

Zealand they have assembled together to fund a wonderful rich reward to any men who manage to get a herd of deer to the colony, and establish a breeding colony in the forests and the hills..."

"And here we go again," said Jake.

The End

AUTHOR'S NOTE

Many books, newspapers, and journals were read in the quest for background for the *Promise of Gold* trilogy. The following were found to be particularly useful.

Kelly, William, J.P. *An Excursion to California over the Prairie, Rocky Mountains, and Great Sierra Nevada, with a stroll through the Diggings and Ranches of that Country.* London: Chapman & Hall, 1851.

Robinson, Fayette, *California and its Gold Regions,* in, *The Gold Mines of California.* New York: Promontory Press, 1974.

Ryan, William Redmond. *Personal Adventures in Upper and Lower California in 1848-9.* New York: Arno Press, 1973 (first published 1850-1851).

Shaw, William. *Golden Dreams and Waking Realities.* London: Smith, Elder, 1851.

Street, Franklin. *California in 1850,* in, *The Gold Mines of California.* New York: Promontory Press, 1974.

Taylor, Bayard. *Eldorado, or, Adventures in the Path of Empire.* New York: Putnam, 1850.

The Friend, Honolulu, December 1, 1849, pp. 81-83. Account by a Hawaiian missionary (probably Rev. Damon) of a tour in Alta California.

Tyrwhitt-Brooks, J., M.D. (Pseudonym of J. Vizetelly, printer.) *Four Months among the Gold-finders in Alta California.* London: David Bogue, 1849.

Woods, Daniel B. *Sixteen Months at the Gold Diggings.* London: Sampson Low, 1857.

www.oldsaltpress.com

Old Salt Press is an independent press catering to those who love books about ships and the sea. We are an association of writers working together to produce the very best of nautical and maritime fiction and non-fiction. We invite you to join us as we go down to the sea in books.